Newcastle

Monica haunts the quaysid
of a certain a

Then one of them is f

Since nobody knows what she does at night,
she can't be in the frame for the murder.

Can she?

At her lowest point, she meets Bobby
Wilson, an ordinary lad, handsome
in his way.

But is this the right time to fall in love?

As the oily Tyne flows past the wharfs and
under the iconic bridge, middle-aged men are
being targeted by a vicious killer.

Monica Brown, damaged and abused, just
happens to be in the area – just happens to
be excited by the murders.

Dog Leap Stairs is a blend of psychological
realism and crime; dark, claustrophobic and
atmospheric, it is both a portrait of Tyneside
in the 1950s and an account of one woman's
struggle against her true nature.

DOG LEAP STAIRS

Barbara Scott Emmett

PENTALPHA
PUBLISHING
EDINBURGH

Cover design: MadCow at Pentalpha Publishing Edinburgh
Cover Photograph by David A Morrow
All enquiries to pentalphapublishing@live.co.uk
First published by Pentalpha Publishing Edinburgh
2022

ISBN: 9798442066036

This is for the people of Newcastle upon Tyne and for the City itself. I may have made a couple of teeny alterations to the layout of the Toon, and for that I plead poetic licence.

Newcastle upon Tyne
April 1955

Chapter One

Dean Street. Late Saturday night. Early Sunday really. Dark and misty and deserted. I'm waiting for the right one to come along. The right mark. Two have passed in the last hour or so—but neither were right. Too young. Not that I can't reel the young ones in as well. I have no trouble with that. Youth is not my target, though. No. Tonight, I have other interests to pursue.

I've always known I was beautiful. My mother told me so when she dandled me on her knee. She told me again as I grew—every new frock, every photograph, every time I sang to entertain her friends. Men friends, usually, mostly. All Mother's—Manda's—friends delighted in me. Her soirées were where I shone. Of course, I got called Shirley Temple—which I hated. That curly-haired brat was at the height of her fame then and Mother thought I could be the British version—but the east end of Newcastle wasn't Hollywood. Opportunity didn't knock.

Still, Mother knew I was an earner—tips and presents frequently came my way. The half-crowns and two bob bits went straight into Mother's purse but she let me keep the dolls and teddy bears and there were plenty of them. I was the perfect child. Everyone's blue-eyed girl. A silver-haired angel.

That's how I know I can have any man I want. A crook of my finger and they'll come running, eager for my services.

It's a lonely wait, here in the dark, breathing in the dank odour that drifts up from the Tyne, waiting for the perfect match. I walk along the Side, pausing every now and then, standing in the shadowy doorways.

I see him under the Tyne Bridge, appearing out of the fog—long overcoat, felt hat, shoulders hunched. Fuzzy yellow gaslight picks him out as he passes under the street lamp, coming towards me. Middle-aged, soft, a little haunted around the eyes. Looking for something. Something like me, though he'd not expect to get it. Not unless he paid. In the end, they all pay. One way or another.

He startles when he sees me, relaxes when I give him my look—eyelashes lowered for a second, then an upward glance from under them. Shy, coy, but inviting. He accepts the invitation, steps nearer. I bring a Craven 'A' up to my lips. It's corny, but it always works. He rummages for his lighter, steps close, flicks it under the tip of my cigarette and in the brief flare I see his face. I can see the wanting in him, feel the desire radiate from his trembling hand. He's an inch or two taller than me—five eleven maybe—but his hat makes him a good six foot. They don't like it when I tower over them—except the odd one who gets a thrill from it. I let my plastic mac fall open, so he can see my décolletage.

'Are you free?' he says.

I smile. 'Never free, pet, but reasonable.'

He quirks his lip as our eyes meet and we share the joke. Another old one, but it breaks the ice. His glance flickers to the alleyway behind me and I take his arm.

*

When I wake, I'm still fully clothed—rumpled and sweaty like my bed. A weak April sun penetrates the thin curtains. Children's cries pierce the morning. My morning. My sleep. Irritated, I turn over, pulling the covers with me. It's no use though, my peace is shattered. It's Sunday, the back lane is full of kids shrieking. That won't cease until their dinners are ready—hours hence. The sheet has wrapped itself around me and the blankets have gone their separate ways. I can smell my own sweat—metallic with adrenaline, dried now and turning to musk. God knows what time I got in—five? Six? Where did I go—after? Maybe it's best I don't know. I'm tired and uncomfortable and I need a bath.

The geyser roars and the pipes thump and rattle. The water is brown when it spouts into the iron bathtub. At least Aunt Millicent had the decency to have the bathroom put in where the old scullery used to be. No tin baths in front of the fire for me. Pity she didn't have the lavatory brought inside as well. Too much expense for her, maybe. Or too much trouble.

The cold metal chills my skin as I slide down into the water. Steam condenses on the cracked mirror and on the window, and forms clouds above the bath. I relive the memory of him coming out of the mist. He wasn't the first and he won't be the last. It takes so much out of me but it has to be done. I need to take a break now, though. I'm exhausted.

Exhausted, yet tight as an overwound clock. I swipe a clear patch across the shaving mirror beside the bath. Yes, I'm still beautiful but the tiredness is showing beneath my eyes. Maybe a rum would help. To relax me, let me get back to sleep for a while. Charlie got me into that. Tried to get me to drink it with blackcurrant cordial, or that ghastly Coca-Cola stuff. I prefer it as it comes—neat. A tot knocked back, swift and effective. Medicinal really. I don't need alcohol but it serves a purpose.

When I'm out and dry, and wrapped in my robe, I reconsider. The bottle is in my hand but it's only ten thirty in the morning. I don't want to go down that road. I take a couple of aspirins instead and lie on the couch. I need more sleep but can't face the disordered bed. Wrapping Aunt Mill's blanket around me, I settle back. The wool is scratchy and the colours too bright. The old witch spends her time knitting and crocheting these days—not that she needs homespun rubbish. She's not short of a bob or two. Cash, savings, war bonds—and God knows what else she's got squirreled away. Old skinflint. Tried to get me to take up knitting. As if I could be bothered with that. Still got the needles though.

Kept me on a tight leash in my childhood, did Aunt Mill, but she won't do it now. I won't dance to her tune, money or not. She thinks I should be forever grateful. For what? Yes, she took me in after Mother… but so what? She's Manda's sister—family—it was her duty. It may seem strange but I'm all for family. It's important, blood being thicker and all that. Maybe one day I'll have a family of my own. Better get a move on, though. I'm still beautiful but it won't last forever.

*

Around teatime, I wake again. Fourish. As I come to on the couch, I realise I'm famished. When did I last eat? Yesterday sometime. Early. Hours before I went out. I don't work well on a full stomach. I need to feel the hunger. Feel something of what they feel.

There's food in the pantry—sliced ham, a few tomatoes—and a heel of bread in the bread bin. My mother's bread bin—chipped cream enamel—that somehow survived the bomb. I was eight when the war started and still my mother's pet. So pretty. When it ended, I was a 'teenager', as the current term has it, and confined to the ugliness of Aunt Mill's gloomy house in Benton. It's still a creepy place, more so, now there's only her in it, filled with dark furniture and a foreboding atmosphere. I'll inherit it one day and when I do it'll be white paint everywhere and this new Swedish furniture you see in the magazines. Lightness and air to combat the foggy darkness of the nights. I'm hoping that day won't be too far off—that's why I've not done much to my own place—this two-room Tyneside flat given to me by Aunt Millicent—it's not worth the effort.

At least I have the downstairs flat, so I don't have far to go to the outhouse. Stinking place but I have it to myself. Not much privacy if one of the other lot wants to use theirs right next to it, though. The yard itself is shared with the bitch upstairs and her brood. He's not so bad—gives me the eye whenever our paths cross. I smile. I'm polite. They think I'm a divorcée (injured party) and I don't disabuse them of that belief. It's a thrill for him, and something for her to feel superior about. Let them have their gossip behind their hands. Let them discuss me in awed tones. Why should I care?

I eat my sandwich quickly, with a cup of tea. Still too early for the rum. I'm a homebody at heart. Some might say a cheap date—but that's before they know me. I can sparkle when I want to. Put on the airs and graces. Hold my head high with the best of them. I need new clothes though. Time to step out of the dark for a while and into the light. Maybe I should get myself a sugar daddy. Somebody undemanding. Somebody who can't believe his luck. But to find one I need to get out and about—and for that I need clothes to impress. And for that I need—well, you get the idea. Vicious circle.

As I'm rinsing my cup and plate—I'm no slattern— there's a knock at the door. Who calls at five on a Sunday? I don't do tea parties. I hesitate before answering, nerves jangling. Who wants me? It couldn't be… Anyway, I'm still in my dressing gown. The knock comes again, louder, more insistent. I stand well back in the front room, near the kitchen door, as a face appears at the window. Hands either side of the eyes, it peers into the dim room. My breath expels all at once. Janice.

She hasn't seen me but I cross the room anyway and step into the tiny hall. Pulling the front door open, I force a smile—wide and deep. Look how pleased I am to see my best friend. My only friend.

'Jan!' I'm all what-a-lovely-surprise and I-couldn't-be-more-pleased.

She takes in my dressing gown. 'Jesus, Mon, are you just up?'

'Course not. Had a lazy afternoon bath.' I pull the door wider. 'Lazy Sunday all round. Come on in.'

The place is tidy. It always is. Sparse, lacking in luxury, but neat.

'Hope I'm not disturbing anything,' she says with a sly glance towards the bedroom door. She'd be horrified if she discovered I was hiding a man in there but she likes to act worldly-wise.

'No. Just having a cup of tea. I'll put the kettle back on.'

She follows me into the kitchen—a cramped space with a three-ring gas cooker, a deep sink, and an old sideboard housing the dishes. The pantry cuts across the corner—the two outside walls help keep things cool. I add another spoonful of Ringtons to the pot and top it up. If she thinks she's getting fresh, she can think again. Uninvited guests get what they're given. And let's face it—I rarely have any other kind.

'I suppose we're all entitled to be slobs on a Sunday, after our strenuous weekly toil,' she says.

Janice imagines I work on the switchboard at a solicitor's office. Can't remember how she got that idea, but it suits me. She's a secretary at the gas board, so conveniently busy through the day same as me (as she thinks). We meet for lunch occasionally. It's a pain having to put on office clothes and make-up, and rush into the café as if I haven't had all morning to get myself there. I don't have to talk about my 'work' much because, being legal stuff, it's confidential. I did once have a temporary job in a lawyers' office—probably where Jan got the idea from—so I know enough of the terms to get by when necessary. My 'boss' does family law, so I won't get caught out on anything to do with the criminal side of things. Definitely have to avoid that as Jan's husband is a policeman. Makes me smile when I think about it.

'Anyway, the reason I came over,' she says, 'is… well… we haven't heard from you for a while. Wanted to check you were all right. Have you got over that cold?'

That was the excuse I used, week before last or whenever it was, when she wanted me to go to the pictures. Something sloppy, she said—a woman's film that Keith didn't want to see.

'I'm fine now. Thanks for asking. Was the film any good?' Oh, I can make normal conversation when I want to.

'What, Love in the Afternoon? I didn't go in the end. Our Jeannie wasn't around either and, as I said, Keith wouldn't be seen dead going to see something like that.'

Tough man, Keith. 'Shame,' I said. 'Sorry.' I take a sip of tea to hide my smile. I know. I'm not a nice person. Give me credit for acknowledging that much.

'We'll have to meet for lunch again soon. Or you could come over. Keith was asking after you.'

'Mmm. How is he?'

'Fine—but—oh, have you heard? There was another one last night. He's had to go in to work.'

'Another one?'

'Stabbing. Down by the quayside.'

Chapter Two

'Up and under the chin,' Keith says, sucking in a strand of spaghetti. 'Have to be pretty close to do it. Stabbing is such a personal crime.'

Saturday night at their new house. A 'dinner party', as Jan says.

Keith stares across the table at me. 'Same M.O. as the others,' he says. 'Modus Operandi. Same method.'

I simper. Oh Keith, you're so clever. I know what M.O. means—I've read Chandler and the rest.

Janice sighs and puts her fork down. 'Can we not just eat in peace?'

Keith can't stay off the subject of the murders, though. He enjoys being in the know. Makes him feel special, as if he's higher up the chain than he actually is. He's a Detective Sergeant—only a year or two out of uniform. To hear him talk, you'd think he was in charge of the investigation.

'We'll get him, though.' Keith lifts his dark eyebrows. 'Oh aye. He'll make a mistake, you'll see.' He pushes his plate away.

'Did he make a mistake this time,' I ask, eyes wide.

'Nah. He's been clever.'

'Has he ever made a mistake?'

'Doesn't look like it. Not so far, anyway.'

'Then he'll have to do it again,' I say, dabbing my lips, 'so he can leave some clues. So you can catch him. Oh dear, that means some other poor man is going to have to die.'

'Jesus, Mon,' Janice chips in, 'don't be so morbid.'

Keith has the decency to look abashed. 'Well... you know... I mean...' He tries to shrug it off. 'We might find something yet. It's early days. We're still on the case.'

'Let's hope you come up with some evidence before he does it again, then,' I say, toying with my wineglass.

'We will.' Keith's mouth twists.

'Can we talk about something else? Please?' Janice piles the plates up. I stand up to help. 'Sit down, I'll do it. You're the guest,' she says.

If he'd asked me to sit down, I might have taken notice but he just sprawls there—lord of all he surveys. Since he's not going to help, I pick up two serving dishes—the Midwinter range, I note, wedding presents no doubt—and follow Jan into the kitchen. They have a new house—all clean and freshly plastered and painted. Not to my taste. Too boxy and the same as every other one on the estate. Starter homes for young professional couples. Their furniture is a mishmash of old stuff their parents have lumbered them with and new space-age lamps and little tables. The old stuff is heavy and brown and boring, and the new stuff is lightweight and brightly coloured. Plastic—the wonder material of the age.

'I wish he wouldn't go on about it,' Jan says, as she dumps the plates into soapy water. 'Turns my stomach.'

'It's certainly chilling.' I pick up a tea towel—Irish Linen—another wedding present, I expect. 'To know there's someone like that around. You could pass them on the street and not even know it.'

'Stop it, Mon!'

'Keith probably shouldn't be talking about it anyway,' I say.

'No, he shouldn't. Don't say anything to anyone else. It could get him into trouble.'

'Who would I tell tales to?' I give her a nudge. 'You know me—Miss Lonely.'

'Oh really?' Jan is arch. 'I wouldn't know who you see or what you get up to. Miss Secretive.'

Smiling, I pick up the soapy plate she's just put on the dish rack. She doesn't rinse, Jan. 'Nothing to tell.'

'Oh, I believe you. Thousands wouldn't.' Janice isn't really nosy—that's why I tolerate her. She's like me in that respect. Couldn't care less what other people do. She likes to pretend she's all for gossip but she soon loses interest. Too self-centred. I've known her since school—we were both at Heaton High—both a little odd and awkward. Most of the other girls hated me. I was too pretty when they were going through the spots and blackheads stage. Jan wasn't bad looking—dark to my fair. The perfect foil.

When we left school, I tried to shake her off—several times—but for some reason she stuck around. We went through the falling in love with crooners stage together—Frank Sinatra, Perry Como, Dean Martin. Janice's family had a gramophone so I spent a fair bit of time at her house. Aunt Mill didn't run to such frivolities. She'd turn the wireless on for the news or the Third Programme—likes to think of herself as cultured—listening to Beethoven and Brahms and taking an interest in current affairs. That's part of the reason I hung around Janice's house. Her parents were relaxed and friendly and Jan and Jeannie always had the latest records and new clothes. I had to wear the saggy jumpers Aunt Mill knitted, and her cut-down old skirts. Apart from my school uniform, my wardrobe contained only one or two changes of clothes at any one time. I missed my mother. Still do. Manda would have dressed me as I ought to have been dressed—pretty cotton frocks in summer and red velvet in the winter. I dreamt of such clothes. Longed for them. Janice and Jeannie even wore shorts in the summer—Aunt Mill was horrified. Women in trousers scandalize her still.

I glance at Janice. She's wearing slacks now—grey, and a green sweater embroidered with parrots, one on each shoulder. She's sort of stylish, I have to give her that, if a little loud in her taste. My navy and white shirt-waister is understated—I prefer classy clothes, a classic style. If I'm Grace Kelly, Jan's Elizabeth Taylor—shorter and more rounded than I am. She'll run to fat as she ages—probably as soon as she starts having the brats Keith wants.

'You're quiet,' she says.

'Aren't I always?'

'More than usual. Everything okay?'

'Of course. Why wouldn't it be?'

'How's work?'

'Work? Oh, same as usual. How's yours?'

'Fine. Great, in fact. I'm getting promoted. They're making me supervisor.'

I can't help the twinge of envy that shoots through me. Not that I'd want to work in a stupid office, with gormless people, day in day out. Not for me. I prefer a bit of excitement in my life. And my days to myself, reading, thinking. 'That's wonderful. Congratulations.' I almost gush with warmth. 'So, you're not thinking of—you know—just yet?' I cast an eye at her abdomen.

'Oh God no. Not for a year or two.'

'Leaving it a bit late, aren't you?'

'I'm only twenty-four—same as you, madam. Another year won't hurt.' She puts her tongue out at me. 'Anyway, we agreed—Keith and me—that we'd get our careers going first. And have a bit of fun.'

'Fun, eh?' I give her a knowing look.

'Yes, fun. You know how much we've enjoyed going abroad these last couple of years.'

I know how much they've enjoyed inflicting the photographs on everyone.

'Spain and Italy,' Jan goes on. 'Won't be able to do that once the babies come along.' She shrugs the topic off with a smile. 'We're a modern couple.'

I get the feeling she'd put off childbearing indefinitely, but I can't see Cro-Magnon Keith agreeing to that. Modern couple? He'd tie her to the sink by her apron strings if he could. And he will. I'm surprised he's let her get away with it this long. I suppose they must need both wages to pay the mortgage and support the middle-class lifestyle they aspire to. Keith runs a car and they have a television. Up and coming young marrieds. They even have a telephone. Once I get Aunt Mill's place, I'll have all those things too—assuming I want them.

'Amazed you've avoided it so far,' I say. 'How've you managed that?'

'Oh, you know… Marie Stopes.' She casts a glance over her shoulder to the kitchen door. Could it be Keithy doesn't know about her trips to Family Planning? I thought the husband had to be involved.

'How do you manage?' she says. 'I mean… do you… you know… Have you ever?'

'Me?' I moue like a coquette. 'I'm a good girl, I am.' Charlie would be rolling around laughing.

'Well, if you ever need advice… When the right man comes along…'

'I'll know to come to you,' I say. 'O Wise One. Purveyor of all arcane female knowledge.'

She laughs, then says, 'Shh!' She gives her head a quick shake as Keith appears in the hallway.

'What are you two whispering about?' He comes into the kitchen.

'Wouldn't you like to know.' Jan is back to her usual bouncy self.

'Girl talk,' I say. 'It would bore you to tears.'

He leans against the benchtop. They have one of these new kitchens—a long sweep of Formica with cupboards underneath. From the window you can see next door's kitchen and their identical sweep of Formica. Their light is on too and a woman stands at the sink, a mirror image of Janice.

'Nearly finished?' Keith says, without making any effort to help speed the process up.

'Five minutes.' Jan scrubs at a pan. 'Why don't you pour us all a Martini? I've got Amaretti biscuits for afters. I thought a pudding would be too much.'

We had a glass of wine each with the meal. A Spanish red. Rioja it's called with the 'j' pronounced more like a 'k', so Keith says. The Burgess household is so sophisticated. They even have napkins, though Keith calls them 'serviettes'. He likes to show off his knowledge of wine but he's still a working-class lad underneath it all. I can't help my smile and Keith is right on it.

'What's so funny, Monica?'

'Nothing. Just enjoying the evening. You're both such good company.'

'Glad we amuse you.'

He's such a boor. I don't know how Jan stands him. I suppose he's considered handsome, with his dark eyes and

Brylcremed hair and that olive complexion. Very Tony Curtis. Some secret in his family's past, I'd say—stray Italian genes maybe.

We settle down in the 'lounge' and sip our 'cocktails'. I don't need alcohol to have a good time but it would be churlish to refuse. The Martini is a little sweet for my taste and the cherry out of a jar is an added insult. A dry Martini with a twist of lemon, like in the Ian Fleming books, would be preferable.

I notice the *Evening Chronicle* on the coffee table, the front page still taken up with the stabbings. POLICE HUNT QUAYSIDE KILLER. I have to admit, it gives me something of a thrill. Seeing the headline set out in bold type like that and the columns of speculation underneath. Knowing the perpetrator is free and knowing it's likely to happen again, is such a kick.

'Do they have any idea why he does it?' I look from the newspaper to Keith. 'You mentioned M.O. but what about motive? Are they robberies?'

Jan's shoulders sink as she gives me an all-suffering look but Keith is keen to return to the topic. 'Hard to say. The blokes don't usually have much money on them when we find them, so it's likely their wallets have been lightened. But then again, there's always something in their pockets—a few coppers, the odd half crown. The killer doesn't seem to want to clean them out completely. Usually still have their watches and lighters, too—even a signet ring in one case.' He downs his drink. 'Consensus of opinion is that it's not done for gain, he just takes their dosh almost as an afterthought.'

'So it's the actual killing he enjoys? Sticking the knife in. Seeing the blood, maybe?'

Jan objects to this. 'Mon! Please. You're so gruesome.'

'I didn't say it was a knife,' Keith says, with a smirk. 'No information has been released about the weapon.'

'Well what else would it be?' I stare at him over the top of my glass.

He hesitates. 'Can't say. Has to be kept under wraps.'

He's dying to tell me. I shrug. 'My money would be on it being a knife.'

He stares back at me. 'Then you'd lose your bet.'

The phone rings in the hallway—the sudden jangle making us all jump. Keith leaps up to answer it. Jan and I sip our Martinis and fiddle with our cherries, listening while pretending not to.

'Aye. Right. Really?' Keith's voice filters through from the passage. 'Right. Okay. Be right there.'

Jan's head shoots up, the cherry on the stick suspended in front of her mouth. 'What is it? Is that work?'

'I have to go in,' Keith says from the doorway. 'There's been a breakthrough.'

Chapter Three

Tossing and turning all night long. Haven't had a wink of sleep. I don't know why I'm so jittery. My nerves are all on edge. I glance at the clock. Nearly noon. I could easily turn over and go back to sleep, but something stops me. Something niggling at the back of my mind. The sort of feeling you get when you've left something undone but can't remember what it is.

There's nothing else for it, so I get up. Useless to lie here turning it over and over in my mind while my body turns over and over in the tangled bed. I have a quick wash and throw some clothes on—a Sloppy Joe and some stretchy slacks. I look like a beatnik, all in black. The enormous jumper reaches almost to my knees. With my hair left loose and pale face I'd fit right in at a poetry reading.

The Sunday paper is jammed halfway through the letter box and I extract it and sit down to read with a cup of Camp coffee. I'm going to treat myself to a pack of real coffee one of these days and make it milky and frothy like in the Italian cafés. We used to go to Toni's Milk Bar, Jan and me—to play the jukebox and sip coffee from clear Pyrex cups. Thought we were so 'cool' and 'hip'. Jan was always on the lookout for lads to get off with. I was never that bothered. I could have them if I wanted them but mostly I didn't. I smile to myself. I am a good girl really. Not that I believe in the sanctity of marriage or anything as bourgeois as that, but I didn't believe in giving myself away for nothing to some spotty greaser—motorbike or no motorbike. I still don't.

I scan the papers. The stabbings have moved to page three, being all speculation and nothing new. Nothing about the breakthrough Keith mentioned. If something significant had happened it would be headline news, surely? I read through the latest article on the murders; the latest outline of the known facts. Four victims, all late at night, all men of a certain age, all killed the same way—though details are kept to a minimum. It does excite me. All men. Usually, it's women who are on the receiving end of violence. Most of the pulp fiction I read for relaxation features female victims. And in real life too. It's always the so-called weaker sex that come off worse in crimes like this. Yes, men do get killed but usually it's personal in some way—husbands poisoned by wives, or gang related, a fight or robbery gone wrong. This steady elimination of middle-aged men is something different. I'm a traditionalist at heart but I like uniqueness, things that step out from the commonplace. There's originality in not targeting the obvious victims, the easy ones. That shows style.

The rest of the paper doesn't interest me so I drop it to the floor and stretch out on the couch. It's getting a bit saggy, this old brown mock-leather settee—Rexine is the material, according to the label. It came with the flat, like everything else—the dropleaf table in the corner, the pair of upright chairs, and the single armchair in uncut moquette that's almost unusable as the webbing is so slack. Aunt Mill has a lot to answer for. Parquet patterned lino on the floor and faded wallpaper add to the all-pervading brownness of my surroundings. If I took much notice, I'd see how sordid it is but mostly I'm above such things. I live in the mind. Concentrate on higher things.

Though I try to doze off, I know I'll not manage it. There's still that nagging something at the back of my mind. Maybe I'll go and see Janice. I could ring her from the telephone box on the corner but I'd rather go straight over. That way she can't put me off.

I offered to stay with her last night until Keith got back but, no, she wouldn't hear of it. 'I'm used to him being out till all hours,' she said. 'I'll be fine.'

I could hop on the 19 bus and be there in half an hour. There's no denying I'm curious about the alleged breakthrough. Strange there's no mention of anything in the paper. I can't sit here doing nothing, I'm far too on edge. My hands are trembling for some reason. I make a decision. Up off the couch, into the bedroom and on with a change of clothes. Sunday best. Crisp cotton dress—the green stripe with the full skirt, I think. Even if Keith's not there, he'll have told Jan all he knows and I'll get that out of her. She pretends she finds the whole thing sickening but she's as enthralled as everyone else.

*

Janice opens the door with a smile but it drops off when she sees me. 'Mon! Wasn't expecting you.'

'Who were you expecting?'

'Oh, we've got some friends coming over. We're going out for a game of tennis.'

'Who?' I say, still waiting to be asked in.

'Peggy and Al Hughes,' she says. 'I don't think you know them. Come in a minute.' She steps back and ushers me into the hallway.

Keith lopes down the stairs in white shorts. 'Monica,' he says. 'How nice to see you again. So soon.'

I ignore him and follow Jan into the front room. 'Have a seat,' she says. 'They'll be here shortly so I'd better go and get changed.' She lingers as Keith comes in with the tennis racquet he's extracted from the hall cupboard.

'To what do we owe this pleasure,' he says. 'Normally don't see you for months on end and now two visits in as many days.'

'It's always lovely to see you,' Janice says, frowning at him. 'You could come along but we're playing doubles…' She hesitates as if she expects me to let her off the hook.

'I could watch. Where are you playing?'

'Heaton Park,' she says. 'I suppose you could tag along.'

The doorbell rings and she dashes away to answer it. Keith stands watching me, tapping the racquet on his palm.

'How'd it go last night?' I ask. 'Found some clues, did you?'

'Can't really discuss it,' he says. He means he shouldn't but probably will. He's practically bursting with it, whatever it is.

Jan comes back with the friends in tow—Peggy and Al. She does a brief introduction. Turns out Al is a colleague of Keith. Another policeman. I'm not sure if this is a good thing or not. Will they be eager to talk shop, or will the presence of another copper shut Keith up?

Janice heads upstairs to get changed and Keith and Al discuss the football scores. Peggy gives me a smile. 'Isn't it awful about these murders,' she says. 'I'm terrified to walk the streets.'

'It's only been men killed so far,' I say.

'Ye-es,' she says, 'but you never know…'

Oh, I think I do. A perp doesn't change his M.O. in the middle of a killing spree.

'Surely, it's unlikely he'll start on women?' I direct my question at Keith. Naturally, he can't resist getting involved.

'Unlikely, yes,' he says, 'though not impossible of course. But the way he's acted so far suggests not.' He leers at Peggy. 'Always takes place late at night, anyhow. The wee small hours. Now what would you be doing out that late, Peg?'

She giggles. Shakes her little mousey curls. 'I'd be safely tucked up in bed,' she says, 'wouldn't I, Al?'

The husband nods. 'Aye. Nae chance wor Peg'd be out that late.' He shuffles from one tennis-shoed foot to the other.

'Still,' she says, 'you just never know. He might start up in the daytime.' She shudders. It's as if she wants to be a victim. Clearly, the prospect gives her a sexual thrill. Her plump cheeks are pink and her eyes glitter. Somebody should make her dreams come true.

Jan bounces into the room in her whites, swinging her racquet like she's in a drawing-room comedy. 'Anyone for tennis?' she says, predictably.

Peggy giggles again. 'You're so funny, Jan,' she says.

I'm sure the right person would get great pleasure from silencing that ridiculous squeak.

I have to decide. Do I go with them and put up with their banter? Waste a couple of hours watching them bat a ball back and forward? Or do I give up and go home? If I do that, I'll have to come up with an excuse to see them again soon—or at least see Janice. And as Keith has so politely pointed out, twice in a couple of days is remarkable. Three times would be unprecedented.

'I'll walk over with you,' I say. 'I need some fresh air. I can have a stroll in the park while you have a game.'

Keith raises the corner of his lip. He's never liked me. It's mutual, though. I stand up and follow them out. Jan will expect me to come back here afterwards for tea and biscuits. She can't very well get out of that.

*

Later, when we're all walking home, I latch onto Peggy. Keith and Al are holding a post mortem on the last couple of sets they've just played and Jan is chatting to a neighbour heading home the same way.

'What do you think this new information is?' I ask Peg. 'About the killer?' If Al's said anything, she's bound to spill the details. Won't be able to help herself.

'No idea,' she says, looking up at me. 'Al's very tightlipped when it comes to cases he's working on. Very hush-hush.' She simpers. 'He knows if he tells me, it'll be all over town in no time.'

'But maybe the public has a right to know.' I shrug. 'Still, I expect the police know best.'

'Oh, I expect so,' she says. 'It's such an important job— and dangerous. I do admire them.' Her eyes soften as she gazes at Al and Keith a few feet ahead.

'Why don't you join the force, then?' I say, just to wind her up.

'Who, me?' Her eyes widen in horror. 'I could never do anything like that.' She slides a speculative glance up me. 'You could though. You're so tall.'

'Mm.' I give a non-committal side nod.

'Have you ever considered it?'

What is she, a recruitment officer for the City police?

'Not my sort of thing.'

'I'm sure you'd look wonderful in the uniform.'

I'm sure I would too but it's not likely to happen.

The conversation ends as we reach the Burgess house. We huddle on the narrow front path waiting for Keith to unlock the door. When we all troop in, Jan goes immediately to the kitchen to put the kettle on. Peg follows her. 'I'll give you a hand.'

I did my bit last night so I go into the front room with Keith and Al.

'Do you play tennis, Monica?' Al is a gangly man, pale, freckled, with sandy hair, but he seems willing to be friendly.

'Now and again,' I say, 'but my favourite form of exercise is swimming.'

'Aye, you look like a swimmer,' he says. 'Powerful shoulders.'

I accept it as a compliment though I'm not sure I like the implications. He makes me sound like an all-in wrestler.

'Oh, our Monica's a big lass,' says Keith.

I give him a twisted smile. That definitely wasn't a compliment. Some men just can't take tall women. They have to look down on their females—makes them feel strong and protective.

Keith breaks into song: 'She's a big lass and a bonny lass, and she likes hor beeor…'

Al joins in. 'And they caal hor Cushie Butterfield, and Ah wish she was heeor.'

Jan comes in the with the teapot. 'What's all this racket?' She sees my face. 'Have you been tormenting Monica?' She puts the pot down. 'Take no notice, pet, they're just jealous.'

Peggy enters to an awkward silence. The cups and saucers rattle on the tray in her hands. 'Al?' she says.

'Ah, we're just joking, man,' he says. 'You've a lovely figure, Monica. You could have been a model.'

Could have been? I grit my teeth to hold back the vitriol I could cheerfully spit at spindly Al. He might be friendly, but he's a fool.

Keith's eyes are on me, dark and brooding. 'She could indeed,' he says.

What does he know? What can he know? I want to leave now but I also want to stay. I need to stay. I slump into an armchair. Surely, if there was anything to know, Al would know it as well, and he gives no sign of that.

'Here's a cup of tea, Mon,' Jan says. 'Ignore them. You're very rude, the pair of you.' This last is mainly directed at Keith.

'Ah, I'm sure Monica can take a joke,' he says, flinging himself into the chair opposite. His eyes are still on me, as if he's looking into my mind. There's humour in them too, though. This is certainly all a joke to him.

I sip my tea and look away. Little Peggy perches on an upright chair as if she's afraid to settle. She clutches her cup and saucer with both hands. Al sprawls on the settee, pasty legs wide. Jan squeezes in next to him. 'Biscuit, anyone?' she says, pointing to the plate on the coffee table. Ginger snaps and lemon puffs. Al reaches for a couple and happily munches them, spraying crumbs everywhere.

No one says anything for a while.

'I was just saying to Monica,' ventures Peggy, her tea still untouched, 'that she'd make a good policewoman, with her height.'

'Pahaha!' Keith practically chokes on his tea. 'I'm sure she would. Fine upstanding citizen, our Mon. Model of propriety.'

What is it? What does he know? I can't take much more of this. I'm tempted to challenge him but I hold myself back. I don't want to start anything with the others here. It can't be anything to do with…

In that moment, I hate the lot of them. Smug in their status as married couples. Their good jobs, their self-improvement. They're all working class louts at heart—Al doesn't even try to hide it. But Keith, and even Jan, they obviously believe they're better than anyone else. Better than me, anyway. But they're not. I don't aspire to what they aspire to, so why should I consider myself a lesser person? They make me feel that way. Keith especially, but Janice too. She's always had that attitude. Treated me in that slightly patronising manner—as if I have to be chivvied along, given special treatment because I'm not quite up to scratch. Oh, I expect she means well but like they say—the road to hell is paved with good intentions. Well, not my road. My road to my personal hell is paved with bad intentions. Intentionally bad intentions. Don't make excuses for me. I do what I do because I want to, not because of the past, my childhood, my mother—Manda did what she thought was best. She had to survive. We both had to. I'm not Jan's poor relation but that's how she treats me. Poor Monica. What a rough start in life, losing her mother like that and no dad to speak of. Wearing hand-me-downs and having to live with that horrible old aunty. She doesn't know the half of it. And I'll never tell her. Never tell anyone. My secrets are my own.

'You look positively murderous, Monica,' Keith says with a grin. 'Honestly, it was just a joke. You're no Cushie Butterfield. Too skinny. And I bet you don't even drink beeeor.'

'Keith!' Jan warns him with her eyes. 'What's got into you today?'

'Just letting off steam, man,' Al says. 'It's this ripper case. It's getting to all of us down at the station.'

Ripper case. Couldn't they come up with something more original?

'Not so much a ripper,' says Keith, 'more a piercer. Straight up into the brain.'

Peggy lets out a breathless 'Oh!'

'Jesus, Keith,' Jan says. 'Was that really necessary? We're trying to have a relaxing afternoon here.'

I jump up. 'Sorry. I'm going to have to go.' I didn't know I was going to do that but now I've made the move, I'll have to go through with it. I put my cup and saucer down on the coffee table.

'Mon,' Jan says, getting up. She puts her hand on my back as we move to the door and it's all I can do not to shove her away. In the hallway, she gives me an apologetic frowny smile. 'I really don't know what's the matter with him today. He was fine last night, when you were round. He was okay to you then, wasn't he?'

I shrug-nod, not trusting myself to speak.

'It's this case he's working on,' she says. 'He's been on edge since he got home in the early hours. Al's right, they're all wound up with it.'

'Doesn't have to take his frustrations out on me,' I mutter through a clenched jaw.

'I know, pet. I'm really sorry.'

'Not my fault they're getting nowhere.'

She sighs. 'Oh, it's not that they're getting nowhere. They did find something last night.'

I lift my head to look into her face.

'I'd better not say any more, though. Not that I know much.' She pats my arm and I want to punch her. 'Why don't we have a catch up one lunchtime,' she says. 'I don't like leaving it like this, with you so upset.'

I nod once and turn away.

Chapter Four

Heart racing, I dab a hanky on my brow but shiver at the same time. How can I be both cold and hot? Everything is clenched—fists, jaw, stomach. It's fair to say I've not felt like this in a long while. I'd like to go out now and—but I can't. And yet, why not? I don't have to abide by any rules. I make my own rules. I want to run, to escape, to get away from the area and myself.

A yellow bus lumbers up as I reach the stop. Wrong one but I don't care. I'll jump on, wherever it's going. I want to be away from here as fast as possible. I climb aboard and run upstairs. Throwing myself into the back seat, I scrabble for my cigarettes. I'm not much of a smoker, really, only smoke for effect usually, but I feel the need now. I light up and draw the smoke deep into my lungs. Proffer my coins to the conductor without saying anything. He seems to sense my mood and gives me my ticket without comment.

The bus takes me into town and I hop off at Haymarket. The bus station is thick with diesel smoke and the stench makes me queasy. I pause by the war memorial. The town is quiet. Not quite six on a Sunday. Pubs still closed. Only the Tatler Newsreel Cinema is open. A place where people waste time when they've nothing else to do. I pay my ninepence and go in. Moving through the dim light, I slip into a seat near the back. The screen shows images of a dog show on

Pathe News. It doesn't interest me. Nothing interests me. Only my beating heart occupies me; my pounding pulse. I try to calm my breathing. Light up another Craven 'A'—two inside an hour. Another record. The tobacco calms me a little and I settle into my seat. The news ends and a cartoon comes on. Tom and Jerry. I stare at it uncomprehending. The characters flash past on the screen and the music taunts me. It isn't funny. Not to me. Nothing is amusing. I want to hurt someone. Myself if necessary. I dig my nails into my palms until it stings.

As my eyes adjust to the darkness, I peer around. The cinema is sparsely populated. No more than a couple of people in each row. Mostly men. The odd middle-aged couple—filling time while waiting for their bus back to the sticks no doubt. Been to the Hancock Museum, maybe, and a walk in Exhibition Park. A turn on the boating lake. Innocent days. I close my eyes and lean back in my seat, letting the sounds of the cartoon drift away. The lights and colours flicker on my eyelids. I could sleep now; my rage has exhausted me. I want to remove myself from consciousness. Slip away into a dream. My cigarette hangs slack between my fingers and I can smell the smoke curling upwards. I could drop it on the floor. So what if I set fire to the place? What does it matter? What's it all for, anyway?

I become aware of a shuffling sound further along the row as someone gets up to leave. I try to ignore them but am on edge as they approach. Why couldn't they leave by the other aisle? Why do they have to disturb me? The forward movement ceases as someone slumps down into the seat next to me. Oh no. I know what will happen next. I've been here before. I keep my eyes closed, hoping I'm mistaken but sure enough, a hand creeps onto my knee. I stiffen. Why can't they leave me alone? Why do women have to put up with this? Some pervert getting his kicks from touching up a female stranger. The hand slides up my leg, pushing my skirt upwards. The cotton rasps as it slides over my nylons.

I knock his hand away but he puts it right back. Pinches my thigh painfully so that I squirm. 'Fuck off,' I whisper, without looking at him. The man takes a sharp breath in. Gets off on bad language, does he? I take a draw on my cigarette and bring the lit tip down hard and fast on the back of his hand, twisting it into the flesh.

He hisses and yanks away. 'Cunt,' he says under his breath.

I keep my eyes down and my face expressionless as he stands up. He kicks my legs as he squeezes past into the aisle. Heads turn. Shhhh! The usherette shines her torch on me. On me! 'Dirty old man!' I spit after him, as he stumbles up the incline. The usherette tuts. At me. Of course, it's my fault. I must have encouraged him. I throw my broken cigarette to the floor and grind it into the sticky carpet. I'm trembling and I hate myself for it. My heart is racing again, my pulse pounding once more. I hate myself. I hate myself. I hate myself.

I want to leave but I can't go yet. Have to let him clear off first. Make sure he's not still outside waiting for me. A newsreel about Churchill's retirement is starting. I'll watch it through, though the topic holds no interest for me.

And after that? When it's dark enough? I don't know. I don't know. Don't want to be rash—but then…

*

Later, outside in the cool of the evening, I wander along Percy Street. The pubs are open, noise and light filtering out into the street whenever a door is opened. Blasts of stale beery fug. I never venture into pubs. Can't. A woman alone can only be one thing. I swing past, energised again after my apathy. Anger is energising. Rage makes for strength and purpose. Stupid drunken faces all around—drunk on company and anticipation, if not yet drunk on alcohol. I don't need alcohol but a rum would be good right now. I won't go in, though. Never. I won't lay myself open to their sneers and assumptions. I'll go home and drink there, on my own. No one to see or comment or judge.

My muscles ache from tension, because I've held myself so tight for so long. A rum will relax me and take away the ferocity of my anger. Loosen me up. Then maybe I'll sleep. Maybe. I remember Charlie again—Charlie and his Navy Rum. The first time I smelled it, I loved it. Dark and with a hint of vanilla. Or was it almonds? Perfume. Charlie was all right. Treated me well, mostly—apart from that last time. Such a shame. I wish he was here now. What would he say, if he was? You don't need them—not Janice, and certainly not Keith. Cut them loose. Get out from under them. They make me feel so dirty. Grubby and stupid. Yet I'm better than they are. Cleverer. Superior. My star will shine brighter than theirs ever will.

I catch myself thumping my palm with my other fist. A young couple—arms linked—stare at me. They catch each other's glances and smirk as they pass. Home! Home and away from this. I can't bear the idea of another bus—lit up and crowded—so I walk. It's not far. Walker Road is barely two miles from the city centre. I cut along Blackett Street, New Bridge Street, down Pilgrim Street. My energy surges and I speed onwards, crossing the main road just before the Tyne Bridge, the Holy Jesus Hospital on my left, falling into ruin. Quickly past Manors and along City Road. Not far now. My breathing is rough and irregular. I run, walk, run, walk as the evening turns to night.

When I get in, I can hear one of the kids upstairs wailing. I want to bang on the ceiling, batter at their door to make it stop. I turn on the wireless to drown it out and music pours through the flat. Eddie Calvert—*Cherry Pink and Apple Blossom White*. The soaring trumpet soothes me a little.

The rum. I pull the bottle out of the old sideboard in the kitchen and pour a shot. A large shot. Tip it down in one. It hits me immediately and relief spreads through me with the warmth of the spirit. I pour another one. And another. It's the only way I will get through this night. The only way I'll stay safe. I can't allow myself out when I'm like this. For what I do, I need to be calm. Cold. Precise. And I will be again.

Soon.

Chapter Five

Fever. Sickness. I can barely open my eyes. I know—it's the rum. Partly, anyway. But it's more than that. I've been attacked. Wounded to the core. I'm sensitive to slights. Barbs go deep with me. All I can do is lie here until it passes. Until the violence of it is subdued. I don't know how long I've slept—a night and a day? Is it Monday still, or Tuesday? I don't care. I'm weak, my limbs heavy and lethargic. I need to eat but I don't want to. The very thought sickens me. I'm ethereal—light and empty—and that suits me. I am a wraith. Maybe I will die here. Maybe that would be for the best. I can't think—daren't think. My thoughts torment me. Words whirl around my head. Words, phrases, insults, responses. I want make them stop. I want to kill anyone—everyone— who has ever hurt me with their words or deeds. If I could kill them all, that would make the memories stop. The words would cease if there was no one left to say them. If the voices were wiped out, then the words would no longer matter and I would have won. Triumphed over them. I exist—you and your hateful words do not.

But there are too many of them—too many people who have insulted me. I can't kill them all. I no longer know where half of them are. Aunt Mill. I could start with her. She's long deserved my attentions. Janice and Keith—Keith certainly, but best if Jan goes too, or she'd be a constant reminder.

Others from the past—old school friends. Hah—friends? Enemies, rather. Sly, backstabbing, tale-telling bitches. I could track them down; they can't be too difficult to find.

And teachers. Evil old witches, with their 'could do better' and 'Monica will never amount to much'. I could easily find them; they won't be far away. Probably still spilling their poison into the ears of other sensitive girls. Intelligent, beautiful girls, worth ten of them. Girls who rouse them to jealousy, like me.

Employers. There've been a few. Flabby, greasy men, for the most part. They won't be missed.

All the men who've ever laid hands on me. Wipe them out. When they cease to exist, their words and actions cease to exist. I will be clean again—renewed.

For a few moments I am energised by the thought of getting rid of them all. I sit up. A sweep of the hand and I could knock them all down.

But how many are there? How long will it take? Will I have to go on suffering until it's done? My head thuds and the sickness returns. I slump back on my sweat-damp pillows. It's no use—it could take years. And all the time the voices would be nagging at me: You're worthless. You're selfish. You'll amount to nothing. Little Madam. Show us your tits. Go down on me, Cunt.

I won't take it any longer. I can't. It has to stop. It has to be put a stop to. But how? If I can't kill them all, I'll have to silence the voices some other way. Kill the source of them.

But the voices are in my head. The source is me.

I have my answer, then. I have my solution.

*

A grey greasy dawn and the sea a queasy verdigris. Tynemouth Longsands. The gulls miaowing overhead, the sand damp and hard-packed, stretching away to Cullercoats. The smell of brine, of seaweed. No one in sight. This is the essence of loneliness.

Slack tide, the water sickly and lethargic. On the turn. I'm right at the edge, far from the ice cream stand and the shuggy boats—all closed anyway. I hear the slop-slop of wavelets lapping at my feet.

How did I get here? I have no memory. A night bus? An early workers' special? The first train from Manors? I search my pockets for clues—a ticket maybe—but find nothing.

As I walk along the wet sand, I gaze down at the frill of water. Bubbles and froth, gathering energy to surge back in. I look back up to the distant road, across the stretch of beach. The road seems miles away. No one to see me. No one to stop me. I could walk into the sea now, walk as far as I can until I'm out of my depth.

I don't know how long I stand there, in a trance on the shoreline but when I come to, the sky is lighter and the tide coming in. I put one foot into the water. My shoe fills and the icy North Sea chills me. The other foot now, and soon I'm up to my ankles, shivering. My calves. My knees. It's so cold, my flesh tingles. My skirt clings to my thighs as I wade further in.

On the horizon a tanker appears—a dot, heading for the Tyne. Another drifts a mile out, swaying as the tide turns. Choppy now. Waves up to my chest. So cold. So cold, I want to scream. I throw myself forward into the swell and an incoming wave knocks me back towards the shore. I'll have to swim further out. Swim until I'm exhausted. But though I'm a strong swimmer, the waves are pushing me back. Great rollers hurtling me to the shore.

Stupid stupid stupid. Trying to do this on an incoming tide. I should have been here earlier. Or later, so I could be swept out on the ebb. No planning. No thought. Stupid!

Useless. Can't do anything right. Amount to nothing. Suck me, Cunt—it's all you're good for.

My limbs grow weak. Can't be bothered any more. Take me. Take me or return me. I won't make any more decisions.

*

Consciousness slowly returns. My first sensation is of intense cold. I shiver violently, my teeth rattling together. When I move, I am stiff and awkward. My eyes flutter open. Blue sky and a figure, blurred, off to one side, manhandling me, turning me over. My stomach heaves and ejects salt water, my guts contracting again and again. It takes a while and when it's over, I sink face down, depleted of energy. My lips taste of vomit and salt and my hands scrabble uselessly on grit and shale.

Voices. Figures crowding me in. Hands on my forehead, on my arms, my legs, pulling my skirt down. The sound of the sea rushes in my ears. Something is thrown over me, a blanket, a coat? Smells musty. Sirens in the distance.

Everything fades.

*

Lights blinding my eyes. A stethoscope cold on my chest. I realise I am in a hospital gown and cast a glance around for my clothes. The doctor glares down at me. 'Well, that was a foolish thing to do,' he says. 'Do you know how much trouble you've caused? Emergency services called out. A hospital bed taken up. Silly girl.'

I say nothing. Am truly speechless.

'The police have decided to turn a blind eye,' he goes on. 'They're accepting it as an accident. Think yourself lucky, you could have been prosecuted.' He reaches down and widens one of my eyes with a finger and thumb, and I flinch at the sudden attack. 'Keep still.'

Green curtains enclose the bed and I hear sounds of the ward beyond them. My wet clothes must have been taken away. I shudder, wondering who undressed me.

'You think we haven't got enough to do without pandering to hysterical young women?' the doctor goes on. 'What was it all about? A tiff with the boyfriend?'

'Didn't ask to be brought here,' I mumble, my lips numb.

'Well, you were, and you should be grateful. By rights you should be in a prison hospital. Attempted suicide is a crime, you know.'

I know he's only trying to frighten me. To make me feel guilty. He'll have to be added to the list of those to dispose of.

A nurse pushes through the curtains carrying a blanket.

'Temperature checks every half hour, Nurse,' the doctor says. 'She swallowed more than she inhaled so her lungs are fine. Keep her in overnight for observation, though. If all's well, she can leave first thing in the morning.' He scribbles something on my chart. 'The boyfriend's outside, by the way,' he says. 'Needs to give you a good slap, in my opinion. Causing everyone so much bother.' He yanks back the curtain and I hear his rubber footsteps recede.

The nurse tosses the extra blanket over me and tucks it in. As she gets out her thermometer, I open my mouth obediently. After recording the details, she gives the thermometer a shake. 'Do you want to see him, then?' Her manner is brusque. 'He's been waiting ages.'

'Who?'

She tuts. 'Who do you think? Your boyfriend.'

'I… I don't…' I start, but she ignores me.

'He can come in for five minutes,' she says, 'then he can get away home. He must be worn out, poor lad.'

She rattles the curtains aside, revealing a dozen or so other beds. The occupants in the nearest ones, glare at me and I shrink back from their malevolent stares. Closing my eyes, I try to drift away but am jerked out of my reverie after a few minutes.

'Hello,' says a voice. 'How you doing?'

I open my eyes and he smiles down at me.

'Are you all right?' He pulls a chair nearer the bed and sits down. 'Daft question. You still look a bit green around the gills.' He shuts up for a minute while we observe each other. He's pleasant-looking, fair-haired, with a fresh open face. His lips are full, like a girl's, and there's a cheeky glint in his hazel eyes. 'Not every day I find a mermaid washed up on Tynemouth sands.'

'You…? Found me?'

'I did. Spotted you when I was taking the dog for his early walk. We both galloped down to see if you were all right, while some woman went to the phone-box to dial 999.'

'Sorry,' I say, though I'm not sure what I'm apologising for.

'No bother, pet. It was a bit of excitement. I'm glad to have helped.' He sticks his hand out. 'Bobby. Bob.'

I touch his fingers briefly with my own. 'Nice to meet you, Bobby-Bob.'

He grins. 'Oh, we've got a live one here.' He smiles at the sour-faced hags in the beds on either side of me and they can't help responding to his charm. A nice lad will always be preferable to a hysterical female.

'And you are?' he says.

'Monica.' I pause. 'Monica Brown.'

'Well, I'm pleased to finally meet you properly, Monica Brown,' he says. 'Robert Wilson at your service. Mermaids rescued, dogs walked, and coal delivered.'

I raise my eyebrows and he goes on, 'Aye, I scrub up well, don't I? For a coalman.'

I guess he's about the same age as me, maybe a little older. There's a softness about him, I find appealing, and a cheerfulness that counterbalances my deep despair. His smile is warm and wide.

'Why aren't you at work, delivering coal, then?' I say.

'Skiving,' he says. 'Rescuing a damsel in distress has got to be a good excuse to have a day off. The best excuse, I should think.' He takes my hand and chafes it. The heat of his palms radiates through me. 'Seriously, though,' he says, 'I wanted to make sure you were okay.' He pauses. 'And, since I quite liked the look of you, I didn't want to let you slip away.'

Chapter Six

When I'm about to get dressed on Wednesday morning, in rushes Janice, all windswept and breathless. 'Oh, Monica, pet. What happened?'

'What are you doing here? How did you…?'

'We heard it on the wireless last night and I rang the hospital. Are you all right, pet?' She peers into my face and I turn away.

'I'll be fine.'

'The nurse said you'd need some clean clothes, so I've brought you these. It's just an old dress of mine and some underwear.' She examines my clothes laid out on the bed, stiff and smelly as if they've been dried in a boiler room. 'They may not fit perfectly but they'll be better than those.'

'Thanks,' I say, taking the hold-all she proffers.

'Keith's outside in the car,' she goes on. 'He's on lates this week, so that's handy.'

'Very,' I say.

'We've been so worried about you. I hardly slept a wink last night.' She puts on her concerned face. 'They're saying it was an accident, but how on earth…?' She looks as if she's about to embrace me, so I move away and twitch the curtain.

'I'd better get dressed. They need the bed.' I open the bag and wait until she steps away so I can draw the curtains.

As I pull on the loose cotton dress, I hear her talking to the woman in the next bed. Lovely day out there. Better than yesterday. The usual platitudes. Janice hasn't brought footwear as we're not the same size, so I have no option but to squeeze my bare feet into my sodden shoes. Someone has stuffed them with newspaper in an effort to dry them out but they are still unpleasantly cold and damp. After throwing my own clothes into Janice's hold-all, I yank back the curtains and squelch out.

'Ready, pet?' Janice says.

I nod. The woman in the next bed eyes me warily as if I might do something unexpected. I point a smile at her. 'Hope you're better soon,' I coo. Her mouth purses and she glances across my vacant bed to my other delightful neighbour. I don't bother to look back as we head down the ward to the door. The Staff Nurse gets me to sign some papers and finally I am free of them.

As we approach the car, Keith lowers his head so he can peer up at me through the side window. Jan opens the door and ushers me into the back. 'Here she is,' she chants cheerily. Keith turns to look at me as I squeeze into the back seat of the old Rover. 'Monica,' he says with a nod.

'Keith,' I respond.

'Feeling okay?'

I twitch my head. 'So-so.'

'Let's get her home and get a nice cup of tea into her,' Jan says. 'You'll come back to our house, won't you?'

'No.' I realise my reply is abrupt so I soften it with a smile. 'I'd rather go home. I need a warm bath and a lie down. Hospitals are so noisy though the night.'

Keith pulls away down Hawkey's Lane and heads for the Coast Road back to Newcastle.

'Aren't you supposed to be at work?' I ask Jan.

'I've rung in to say I'll be late,' she says. 'Told them it was an emergency.' She swivels in her seat to give me a sympathetic smile. 'But I can take the whole day off to stay with you, if you like.'

I shake my head. 'I'm fine. Really.'

'Maybe you should talk about it, though…'

'No, honestly. All I need is a good sleep.'

We say nothing for the rest of the journey, though Jan keeps turning to check on me and I can see Keith peering at me in the rearview mirror. When I get out of the car on Walker Road, he's still looking at me from under his brows. He's been very restrained in his comments. Janice has obviously told him to mind his manners. She gets out of the car with me. 'Should I not come in with you?' she says. 'I can stay for a while. Get you settled. Keith can pick me up later.'

I have to make a conscious effort not to get annoyed. 'Honestly, Jan,' I touch her arm. 'You've done enough. I'll get these clothes back to you as soon as I can.'

'Don't worry about that.' She brushes the idea away with a flap of her hand. 'Did you talk to someone at the infirmary?'

'Yes,' I lie. 'I had a good chat with one of the doctors. It was an accident really, you know. I didn't mean to go that far out.'

The look she gives me says she wasn't born yesterday. 'Are you sure?'

'Sure, I'm sure.' I get my keys out. 'Go on. I'll be fine.'

'Well, I'll go in to work, then,' she says, 'but if there's any problem—any problem at all, ring me. I'll come straight over. You've got the number, haven't you?'

'I'm sure the gas board is in the phone book, if I don't,' I say, opening my front door.

'Or you could ring Keith. He'll be home till four.'

I turn to look at him. He's still peering up at me from the car. I can't quite read his expression. He's the last person I'd call, emergency or not.

'Has somebody rung your work, by the way?' Jan says. 'I can call them for you, if you like.'

'What? Oh yes—yesterday. Don't worry, it's sorted.' Too many questions being asked. I need to get away from them.

'Take care, then, pet.' This time she does manage to embrace me and I suffer her hug with Keith staring at me, his eyes boring into me like he's scouring my thoughts.

*

I have my bath and climb into bed. It's my safe place, my haven, and it's neat and clean just how I like it. Whatever I was doing the other night, it didn't take place in the bedroom. The empty rum bottle is on the wooden drainer by the sink. Even in my debaucheries, I'm tidy.

I lie for a while but I can't get off to sleep. I'm not really tired as I slept deeply last night, despite what I told Jan. Must have been exhausted after my seaside adventures. I remember nothing of the hospital night—almost as if I switched myself off like a light. Wish I could do that every night. Stop the nagging, repetitive voices. I make a cup of tea and take it back to bed. I'm not hungry, though I don't know when I last ate. The gnawing, emptiness soothes me. I hate to be full, filled up, stuffed. I am a vessel—hollow and echoing. Full only of potential—which is a kind of emptiness, a waiting for something worthy of my embrace.

Bob comes into my mind. Robert Wilson. What a plain ordinary boring name. Almost as bad as mine. Bobby. I haven't thought about him since yesterday. Had forgotten about him, almost. What about him then? Who is he? Why does he want to see me again? For we have made a date for the weekend. A date. Ah, how sickly sweet that sounds, like the other kind of date—with the hard stone in the middle. I've not been out with anyone since Charlie, though what we had couldn't exactly be called dates. Not towards the end, anyway. Meetings of mutual destruction, maybe. Nights fueled by rum and violence. Enjoyable in a way. In many ways. But unsustainable. I miss Charlie sometimes. Regret what happened—sometimes.

And Bob? Bobby? He's no Charlie. He's too nice. Far too nice for me. It won't come to anything—he'll soon realise I'm not the pretty little girl next door type. He needn't expect me to pander to his whims, like Jan does with Keith. But I'll go along on Saturday evening. Meet him under the clock at Northern Goldsmiths, where he'll be hanging around waiting with all the other young hopefuls eager for coupledom. I suppose I owe him one evening out of my life for saving me—though if he hadn't been the one to find me and help get the water out of my system, someone else would have. Maybe it would have been too late by the time that someone else came along and I'd have quietly expired there on the shoreline, with the waves crashing over me. Maybe I'd have been swept back out to sea and never found again, left to rot on the seabed with fish nibbling at me.

Don't be so morbid, Mon! I hear Jan's voice reprimanding me, the way she does. She'll be over here again before too long. Curiosity will bring her to my door, tonight or tomorrow, eager for the 'chat' she thinks I need. She wants to know why I did it. Why I walked out into an incoming tide and made a fool of myself. I'd like to know too. I'm oddly elated, despite knowing I've been a bit of an idiot, which normally I can't bear. But I survived, you see. I survived. I'm not exactly pleased or relieved or grateful but the experience has changed me in some way. Washed something out of me and left me cleansed. I am renewed.

Maybe I can start again. With a smile on my face, I close my eyes and drift off. Start again? As what? A coalman's wife?

Chapter Seven

As expected, Janice turns up on Thursday evening. I know—she's concerned about me and being a good friend etc etc but I could really do without her poking her nose in right now. I've always kept myself to myself as much as possible and our meetings have been on my terms. It's me who contacts her—she knows that—but lately she seems to think she can show up whenever she wants to. Still, I knew she'd be over before too long, so am ready for her.

'How are you today, pet?' she says, handing me a bunch of yellow tulips.

I'm not sure what to do with them. Don't even know if I've got a vase.

'Do you want me to put those in some water for you?' she says, noticing my hesitation.

'No, no. I'll do it.' Does she think I've gone doolally or something? 'You sit down. Tea?'

'Thanks.' She follows me into the kitchen and gets in my way as I search for something to put the tulips in. I find an old earthenware jug under the sink and use that.

'Take these through, will you,' I say, 'and sit down.' There's barely room for one person in the kitchen, let alone both of us. She takes the jug of flowers and does as she's told while I put the kettle on the stove and tinker about getting the tea things ready.

'I came straight from work,' she calls through, as if I couldn't have worked that out for myself. When I glance into the front room I can see she's peering around, looking for clues to my state of mind, perhaps? She'll find nothing that gives any of my secrets away. I'm very careful about that.

'So, are you all right?' She pauses. 'After your … mishap?' She tries a little smile, wry and restrained, as I bring in the teapot.

'I'm getting there.' She wants me to be weak and wobbly and show I'm suffering for my foolishness. I play along and put on a hangdog expression. Have to throw her some titbits, after all.

'What on earth were you thinking, Mon? Honestly?' Her eyes are soft with concern. 'Were you trying to …?' She leaves the words unsaid. The words 'commit suicide'. As that doctor pressed home to me, it's a crime. Self Destruction. How idiotic is that? If the perpetrator is successful, they can't exactly prosecute and why would they want to make some poor sap suffer even more for making the attempt? The law's out of date, of course. Based on some old religious tenet. Thou shalt not kill—thyself.

I decide to give Jan a bit more of what she wants. 'It was a moment of madness,' I tell her, all regretful and earnest. 'I knew that, even as I was doing it. I didn't really mean to do away with myself. Yes, I thought about it … but I didn't really want to do it.' I go back into the kitchen to get the cups—and hide my smile.

'I went out a bit too far, that's all. Got knocked over by a wave.' I put the cups and saucers on the coffee table and slump into a chair. Oh, I can do pathetic when I want to.

'Was it a cry for help?' She pours the tea out and hands me a cup.

'Playing to the gallery, as Aunt Mill would say?' Sardonic.

'Don't be so hard on yourself. You must have been in quite a state. Can I do anything to help? Is there a … a problem?'

The way she says it and glances down suggests she thinks I'm pregnant.

'Of course not,' I say, blowing on my tea. 'We were only talking about … you know … the other night.'

'I know, and you were happy enough then, weren't you?' She puts her cup down on the saucer with a chink. 'Oh God, Mon, it wasn't because of what Keith and Al were saying on Sunday, was it? Oh no, it couldn't be, surely.'

It couldn't be? Well, that's me told. I say nothing and stare blankly, blowing across the surface of my tea, making little waves.

'Tell me it wasn't that. You're not that sensitive, are you? What did they say that was so bad?'

'It wasn't that.' Well, it wasn't. Not only that, anyway. 'It was a combination of things. I've been feeling a bit strange lately.' That's certainly true. And acting a little odd, if truth be known. 'Dwelling on the past too much,' I say. Thinking of all the things people have done to me, and said to me. Thinking of all the things I've done.

'I wish you'd told me. I would have helped, if I could. You know you can come to me any time.'

'Thanks,' I say. I sip my tea and she sips hers. 'I felt ridiculous and couldn't bear anyone knowing …'

'Oh Mon, I'll never judge you, whatever it's about.'

Oh really? I bet that's not true.

'By the way,' she says, 'what's the name of your company, again?'

'What?'

'The place you work. What's the firm's name?'

'Why?' I'm instantly on edge. This is not safe ground.

'I tried ringing you today on the number you gave me ages ago. It made the unknown number noise, you know...'

'Really?' I cut her off before she makes an attempt at the sound.

'Then I tried looking it up in the phone book but I couldn't find it. I must have got the name written down wrong.'

'Why were you ringing?'

'I thought you might have gone in today—though I'm glad you didn't. Wanted to check before I came over. I know you usually finish a bit later than I do.'

'No, I'm taking the rest of the week off.'

'So what's it called—where you work? I thought it was Chapman, Fisher and somebody but I couldn't see anything like that in the phonebook and the Operator hadn't heard of them either.'

'I'd rather you didn't ring me at work, you know that. They don't like us getting personal telephone calls.'

'But… well, okay.' There is a silence as we contemplate our teacups.

'Oh, here,' I say, remembering the clothes she lent me. I hand her the hold-all. Didn't bother to wash them as I only had them on half an hour.

She takes it and puts it beside her bag.

'How's Keith's case going?' I say after a moment. 'Any advancement? What did the new evidence turn out to be?'

'Oh, some old tramp saw the victim, earlier, apparently,' she says, 'with a woman.'

'A woman?'

'Eeh, Monica—I wasn't supposed to tell you that.' She tuts. 'Don't let on to Keith.'

'As if I would.'

'He'd been asleep in a doorway,' she goes on. 'Woke up to relieve himself and that's when he first saw the man.'

'Wasn't it misty that night?'

'I don't know. Was it?'

'I thought I read somewhere… Well, it often is down by the river.'

'The man went past a lamppost, so the tramp saw him quite clearly. Saw him approach the woman and saw her face in the flare of a lighter. So Keith says.'

'Can he be trusted?

'Who, Keith?' She laughs.

'The old tramp. Been drinking very likely. What is it they drink? Methylated spirits?'

'All I know is that the police are taking his evidence seriously.' She puts down her cup and saucer. 'It just goes to show, we shouldn't take our lives for granted. Life is precious.' And here comes the lecture. 'That poor man who lost his life. And the others. Four of them now. Their poor wives.'

'If he was with a woman, he probably wasn't thinking about his wife,' I say.

'We don't know that. We don't know anything for sure.'

'Did this old tramp manage to describe them? Are they sure it was the same man?'

'He gave a reasonable description, as far as I know,' she says. 'Enough for the police to accept it was probably the dead man he saw.' She shudders. 'It's all so awful.' She pours herself another cup of tea and holds the pot up with a look of enquiry.

'Yes, please,' I say, stretching across to get a refill.

'Their poor families,' she goes on. 'What must it be like for them?'

They weren't worried about their families when they were out wandering the quayside in the early hours. Their wives and children were the last things on their mind.

'What do you think they were doing out at that time of night?' I say. Janice seems to imagine I'm the naïve one but it's very much the other way around. 'Where had they been? Where were they going?'

'I don't know. A night out with friends?'

'Where were these friends then?'

She shrugs. 'You don't seem very sympathetic towards them.'

'Why would I sympathise with men who are out looking for … for women? Cheating on their wives?'

'They don't deserve to die for it, surely. And we don't know they were all out for that reason, just because this latest one may have been.'

Oh, I think I do know that. 'So did this tramp describe the woman?' I say.

'I believe so. Keith didn't go into details. They've been out looking for her though. That's why he's been on lates. Questioning streetwalkers and acting as decoys.'

'Agents Provocateurs,' I say. Just as well I've not been down there lately.

'Not really,' she says. 'Posing as potential clients, that's all. Waiting to be approached.'

'That's not always how it works.'

'How do you know?' She huffs out a laugh. 'Got friends down Dean Street, have you?' She puts down her cup. 'Don't look so shocked, Mon, I'm only joking.'

I'm shocked all right. Shocked that I've broached this topic. What am I thinking?

'They need to find this woman and see what she knows,' Jan goes on. 'Where they went and what time she left the poor man.'

I've had enough of this now. I get up in order to change the subject. 'Just going to the …' I nod towards the back and go out.

In the outhouse, I'm seething. Stupid. Yet again. Stupid. What is wrong with me? I take a few minutes to calm myself down. When I leave the lavatory, I look up and see the woman upstairs gawping down at me. They've both given me funny looks each time they've seen me. They must hang about near the back window especially to check on me. Maybe they imagine I'm going to hang myself by the lavatory chain. The thought makes me smile as I go up the few steps to my back door.

I catch Janice glancing at her watch when I go back in. 'You get off home,' I say. 'I'll be fine.'

'No, it's okay. Keith won't be back till first thing tomorrow.' She lifts her cup, looks into it and puts it back down. 'Have you eaten?' she says. 'I could go and get us some chips. Fish 'n' chips, if you like.'

'I wouldn't want you to feel you were slumming it, Janice,' I say with a straight face. 'I'm sure you'd have something much more exotic if you were at home.'

She laughs. 'Don't be daft. We only stretch to spaghetti and wine when we have visitors. I'd probably have a boiled egg since I'm on my own. What do you normally have?'

I lift a shoulder. 'The same, maybe, or a tin of soup. I don't bother much.'

'I can see that,' she says, eyeing me. 'You're looking quite rangy these days.'

Rangy? What's that supposed to mean? I'm slim—why can't she say that. Jealousy, I expect.

'So,' she goes on. 'Fish and chips? Where's the nearest chip shop? My treat, of course.'

'I couldn't eat that much.'

'Fishcake, then?'

'If you insist.' I obviously won't get rid of her until she's seen me eat something. 'The nearest chippy's on Raby Street.'

'Come with me?' she says. 'You look like you could do with some fresh air.'

I sigh. 'Very well, Janice. I'll get my coat.'

The walk to the chip shop is uneventful and we don't have to queue as it's not busy. Thursday, you see. If it was Friday, the queue would be around the block.

'Plenty of scranchums,' Jan tells the woman serving. She may be on her way up in the world, but she still likes her bits of crunchy batter.

We carry our warm parcels home under our arms and I have to admit the greasy, vinegary smell sharpens my appetite. When we get back, there are a few minutes of pleasant companionship as we eat our chips and lick our salty fingers. Then Janice starts up again.

'Simple pleasures,' she says, 'that's what makes life worth living.' She gives me that earnest look as she crumples up the wrappings. 'Don't take it for granted, Mon. you have so much to live for.'

'Do I?'

'Of course you do. You're young and attractive. You'll meet someone one day.'

Ah, so I have to have a man in tow in order for life to be really worth living. That's what it takes for the magic to start happening.

'I already have met someone,' I say.

'Have you?' Her eyebrows go up. 'Who? When?'

'His name's Robert,' I say. 'He's the one who saved me from an untimely death on Tynemouth Sands.'

'It's no laughing matter,' she admonishes. 'He saved you? What? He pulled you out of the sea?'

I smile at the thought. 'No, I managed that bit myself. Or at least the waves did. Robert gave me the kiss of life. Quite romantic, in a way.' I'm embellishing, of course, but she needn't know that. 'His kiss awoke me, like Sleeping Beauty.' I wipe my fingers on a tea towel. 'What do you think of that, then?'

Jan sinks back in her chair. 'I… I… well, it's wonderful, of course.' She stutters over her words as if she can't quite take it in.

I can't help a little glow of triumph as I sit observing her. She doesn't know how to react to such unexpected news. I've floored her.

'When will you see him again?'

'Saturday,' I say. 'Seven thirty under the clock.'

'Wonderful,' she says again, her voice faint. That's knocked her off her perch. She's got too used to thinking of me as being on the shelf.

'Where's he taking you? And what will you wear.' She warms to the idea. 'Must be so exciting for you.'

'I've no idea what he has planned,' I say. 'I'll wear something attractive but demure. Don't want him getting any ideas.'

'When do I get to meet him?'

'Oh Janice! Let me get to meet him first. I have to get to know him. Anyway, I don't know if anything will come of it.'

'It'd be lovely, if it did,' she says. 'You haven't been out with anyone for ages.'

'How do you know?' I tease. 'I don't tell you all my secrets.' Hah. I don't tell her any of my secrets. If she only knew …

'Well, if you have, you've not said anything. Not since that awful, whatsisname … Charlie?'

'Charlie was okay,' I say quickly. 'I liked Charlie.'

I may even have loved him. The feelings were strong on both sides. Tempestuous, you might say.

'Whatever happened to him, anyway?' Jan says.

I get up and take the chip papers through to the scullery and put them in the bin. 'More tea?'

'Thanks,' she says. 'I'll have a quick cup then head off for my bus before it gets too dark.'

'You don't imagine you're at risk from the killer do you, like that silly friend of yours.'

'Peggy?' she says. 'No. But I like to get home and get the lights on. So, what did happen to him?' she goes on, when I come back with the teapot. 'That Charlie?'

I'd hoped she'd leave that subject alone. She can never let things rest. I don't want to talk about Charlie. Don't even want to think about him. About what happened. It's too upsetting. 'Oh, we just called it a day,' I say, heading back for the cups and saucers I've just rinsed.

'He wasn't was very good for you, was he? You were… strange… when you were seeing him.' She gives the teapot a vigorous stir with a teaspoon. 'I only met him the once, I think, but I can't say I liked him. Weird eyes.'

Deep blue eyes, oddly piercing. Could pin you to a card like a butterfly.

'A bit like Keith, then,' I say, possibly more tartly than necessary. 'He stares at me sometimes in a very unnerving manner.'

'You don't like Keith much, do you?'

I pour the tea. 'He doesn't like me.'

She takes a deep breath. 'He does…' Her voice is a little whiney. 'But… oh you know what men are like. Jealous of anyone their woman is friendly with.' She tries to make light of it.

Is she seriously saying it's acceptable for men to be jealous of female friends? I don't believe that. I know Charlie was a little possessive… a little overbearing… that's what did for us in the end, really… but it can't be right. Can it?

When she's gone, I tidy away the tea things and feel oddly flat. The room seems emptier than usual. Janice has left a negative presence behind—or rather, an absence. How annoying. I'm used to being on my own; used to having no visitors, most of the time. I like it that way and have made sure that that's how I get to live. My choice—to have my days to myself and my nights—well, most often to myself. Only occasionally crossing the paths of others.

Suddenly weary, I decide to go to bed. I am still recovering, after all. A nightcap would be lovely but I have nothing in and though I could go to the off-sales at the pub, I won't. I don't need alcohol. I'll get through tonight without it, as I did last night. As I do most nights. I can sleep perfectly well without it. I don't always dream.

Chapter Eight

Saturday evening. I've dressed carefully—a bottle green rayon dress and the necklace of pale green glass beads that used to belong to my mother. Aunt Mill gave them to me— I don't know how she came by them. Manda must have lent them to her at some point. Amanda and Millicent. I try to picture them as young girls, getting ready to go out as I am now—swapping clothes and jewellery; giggling and talking about their young men. Did they do that? I can place Manda in this picture but Aunt Mill is harder to visualise. Difficult to believe she was ever young. And what age is she—fifty? Fifty-five? She looks ancient, I know that—in her brown crepe tea-dress and owlish round spectacles. Why does she still wear wire-framed National Health specs? She can afford better, surely. I try to imagine her in the upswept catseye frames now popular. The idea is so unlikely, I have to laugh.

I dab on a little Max Factor and smooth it into my face. A touch of red lipstick, a squirt of Evening in Paris—the citrus top-notes perfectly set off the floral mid-tones. Black court shoes, gloves, and my best leather handbag, and I'm done. Pausing, I look at myself in the dressing-table mirror. Am I really going through with this? Am I really going to hop on a bus into town and meet a young man for an evening out? How quaint. Janice was right—it is a long time since

I've done this. I'm out of practice, not that there was ever a time I was very practiced at it in the first place.

When I met Charlie, I was young and naïve, an ordinary girl—well, as ordinary as I ever could be. Charlie saw the extraordinary in me and brought it out. Nurtured it. We were two of a kind, Charlie and me. He found the darkness in me, located it in some hidden part of my soul, and revealed it to me. And then he showed me his darkness and joined it to mine. We rolled it into one big ball and lived inside it. We revelled in our murkiness, our lightless abyss.

You'd think when I got free of him, the darkness would dissipate, recede, but it didn't. It wasn't replaced by light but by a deeper blackness. A blackness that sucked the brightness out of everything. I cherished that deep dark place and I cherish it still. I can't let tow-headed Bobby banish it altogether, that would never do, but maybe—I fight the idea but it forces its way into my mind—maybe he will allow a little chink of light to enter, a tiny trembling shaft of dawn to poke a finger into my night.

*

'Well, hello there, Miss Mermaid,' he calls as I cross the road towards him. I'm relieved he's there first. Though I made sure I was a little late to avoid getting there before him. I'd have gone around the block a couple of times if he hadn't been there, of course.

He comes to greet me, takes both my hands in his and pecks me on the cheek. I draw back a little. 'We already French kissed on the beach,' he says, a cheeky twinkle in his eye. 'Too late to be coy now.'

'That was not a French kiss,' I say. 'It was purely medicinal.'

'It seems to have done you good,' he says. 'You're looking a lot less green than you were the other day.' He pulls back to take in my dress and necklace under my open coat. 'In the face, anyway. Everywhere else, green suits you.'

'Thank you. So glad you approve.'

'Oh, I think you'll find me full of approval.' He sticks out his elbow and I take it. 'Right, miss, where to? What do you fancy doing?'

'I'll leave that up to you.'

'Dangerous ground,' he says, winking.

I roll my eyes.

'So what's it to be—pictures, dancing, an alcoholic beverage? Have you had your tea?'

'I'm not especially hungry,' I say.

'How about a few twirls at the Oxford, then?' he says. 'And if you get peckish later—we can peck.'

I try to give him a disapproving look but the truth is, his innuendoes are innocent and I find myself amused.

We wander along New Bridge Street to the Oxford Galleries arm in arm and he pays us in. After we check our coats in the cloakroom, we go into the ballroom. The hall is dim and lights twinkle. The band isn't on yet but a disc jockey in a booth plays the latest records—Dickie Valentine and Ruby Murray. Bobby ensconces me at a table and goes to get a drink. 'Orange squash, please,' I say.

'Shot of gin in it?'

'Absolutely not.'

A mirrored ball turns and coins of light spin around the room. A few couples are dancing, making slow movements backwards and forwards, with only one or two pairs attempting anything more formal. The music doesn't lend itself to a waltz, anyway, and I don't know why they bother. Showing off, I expect.

When Bobby returns with the drinks, he sits down, takes out his Players and offers me one. I take the cigarette and he produces his lighter. The sudden flare startles me—the wick, and therefore the flame, is far too long. 'Sorry,' he says, and adjusts it. 'Didn't burn you, did I?'

I smile tightly and shake my head. As he lights my cigarette, my heart pounds. Few men light cigarettes for me and usually they are… I shudder.

'Somebody walk over your grave?' he says.

'I'm fine,' I say, pushing the thought from my mind. I am here, now. I will not be that other person. I am Monica Brown, demure, respectable.

'Tell me about yourself,' he says, taking a sip of his brown ale.

'What is there to tell?' I toy with my glass of orange squash. Can't stand the stuff but I don't want him imagining I can't enjoy myself without alcohol. 'You know my name. And you know I like swimming in the sea at dawn.' I've decided I'll address the 'incident' head on. Make a bit of a joke of it. Otherwise, it will lurk between us forever. There but not spoken of.

'Have you fully recovered?' His voice is low, tender, and I know he doesn't just mean the near drowning.

'I have,' I say. 'Fully and completely. Taking to the water was a moment of madness. It will not be happening again.'

'Glad to hear it.' He raises his glass to me and I respond. I take a sip and put the glass down. We turn towards the dancefloor and watch the dancers in silence for a few minutes.

'The band comes on at half past eight, I think,' he says. 'George Evans tonight. We'll have a dance then, yes?'

'Yes.'

'So, who are you, Monica?' he goes on. 'What do you do? Where do you work?'

Always the first question anyone asks. Is there nothing else to know about a person but where and how they earn their living?

'I do reception and telephone duties,' I say. 'But I only work part time at present, in a temporary capacity.' I'm going to give myself a bit of leeway. I don't want him catching me out like Janice did. I know she won't leave it to rest. She'll be trying to get information out of me next time I see her. I'm going to have to stay out of her way for a while. Out of their way.

'Part time?' He raises his eyebrows.

'My aunt gave me a pair of flats,' I say. 'I live rent-free and get a bit of income from the rent on the upstairs flat.'

'A property owner, eh?' He grins. 'Not one of these slum landlords, are you?'

'I certainly am not.' I am pert, arch. 'I'm very considerate towards my tenants, I'll have you know. A model of propriety.'

'I can see that.' He takes another slug of his beer. 'You have an aunty, then. Parents as well?'

I shake my head briefly. 'My mother died in the war. The night they bombed St Peter's. My Aunt Millicent brought me up after that.' I look down at the squash—horrible, sickly, saccharine stuff. 'I don't know where my father is. He may be dead as well, for all I know.'

'Sorry.' His hazel eyes are tender again. 'Didn't mean to upset you.'

'You haven't. I miss Manda, of course—that's my mother—but it was a long time ago. I hardly remember her really.'

The high-pitched whine of a microphone cuts through the noise of chatter and we look towards the activity on the stage. Musicians are setting up their instruments, moving here and there in the semi-darkness.

'Looks like they are about to start,' Bobby says.

I'm tempted to say something smart, like, I never would have guessed, but I bite it back. He's bringing out the niceness in me, it seems. I'm amazed there's any to unearth.

'And you?' I say. 'Are your parents…?'

'Yes. Both alive and kicking. Dad's a coalman, like me. Me mam's a housewife.'

'Following in father's footsteps.' I smile.

'Aye. He owns his own business and I'm the eldest son and heir. Got my own wagon and everything.'

I put my head on one side. Not just an ordinary working man, then.

'A property owner and a business tycoon,' he says. 'We'll go far.'

*

When the band strikes up, Bobby takes my hand and pulls me to the dancefloor as if he thinks I'll be reluctant and honestly, I am, a little. I've not displayed myself in public like this in a long time. Not since we—Jan and me—used to go out together on a Friday night. That all came to a stop when she met Keith and that must be four or five years ago. I met Charlie not long after. He was recently back from doing his National Service and raging about the loss of two years of his life. His fervent intention was to wreak revenge on the society that turned him into a squaddie and forced army life on him.

I didn't see Jan so often then as I was taken up with my affair with Charlie and she was dithering about in an on off relationship with Keith. Keith was finding his feet in the police then, so there was dithering on his side as well. Careers come first. Idiots. Anyway, they eventually got engaged—a long engagement. It's barely a year since they got married.

Weddings. I don't know how I feel about them. Certainly not keen on the whole white dress and big party aspect. If I was ever to get married—and how unlikely is that?—I would want to elope. Avoid all the fuss. Or a registry office, with just the two of us and a witness brought in from the street. Jan asked me to be a bridesmaid, along with her sister, Jeannie, but I wasn't keen. I don't like being on display, especially if I'm done up like a dog's dinner in peach taffeta. I don't want people staring at me—the very idea makes me cringe. I hummed and harred so much, Janice let me off the hook and asked Betty Barton instead.

I'm okay dancing with Bobby like this, though, because it's dark and cramped and we're moving slowly, blending in with the crowd. He has his arms around me and is inching steadily closer to me. A moment of panic grips me and my steps falter. He draws his head back to look at me. 'All right?' He's so caring, damn him. So gentlemanly. I find it all a bit ridiculous. Smiling, I take control of myself and we continue our dance. Round and round we go, shuffling backwards and forwards under the mirrored globe. The flickering lights are hypnotic; our rhythmic movements soothing. The whole experience is soporific—the warmth of his embrace, the stuffiness of the dancehall, the faint trace of brown ale on his breath. Round and round and round.

I enter into a sort of trance and in that trance, I inhabit a different world. A world where nothing bad has happened; where all is pure and light and innocent. I am pure and innocent. But when I close my eyes, I see scenes from my life flit past, as if I am dying and my life is flashing before me. Childhood, Manda, memories I don't want to look at. She was the perfect mother. She was. She was. She couldn't have done those things, those terrible things I remember. She couldn't have made me do them. She couldn't. She didn't! I hiccup out a slight cry and Bobby is instantly attentive. 'What's wrong? Do you want to sit down?' He takes my hand. 'Come and sit down.' I let him lead me from the dancefloor while the coins of light swirl round and round and round.

*

'You need something a bit stronger than that,' he says, as I gulp my orange drink. 'I'll get you a brandy.'

'No. No really. I'm fine.'

'You say you're fine, but you're obviously not.' He pats my hand. 'What's up?'

I shake my head. There's nothing I can say. I can't tell him. What is there to tell, anyway? I'm making something out of nothing. Looking for attention, Aunt Mill would say. I stare into my glass as the music crashes around us—drums and cymbals. It's a faster number now, and the dancers are lively, almost jiving some of them. I'm aware of them twirling past, aware of the heightened atmosphere of people having fun. The tempo increases and there is laughter. Joy, exuberance. Innocent pleasure and the pleasure of innocence.

I look up into Bobby's eyes, see the concern there. Why would anyone be concerned for me? It's too late for that.

'I'll get you that brandy while it's not busy,' he says, peering over to the lighted bar. 'There's only a couple of people waiting.'

I say nothing, which he takes for acquiescence—they always do—and I sit alone at the table for a few minutes, watching the couples fling themselves across the floor, grins on their stupid faces. When Bobby comes back, I've pulled myself together. I don't want the brandy but I toss it back quickly.

'Looks like you needed that,' he says. 'Didn't touch the sides.'

'I don't need alcohol.'

'Maybe not, but it sometimes helps.'

'Sorry,' I say, 'I don't know what happened before…'

'Don't apologise for having a funny turn,' he says, pouring a fresh drink for himself. I stare at the bottle with the blue star on the label. So many nights…

'Eyeing my beer now, are you?' he says.

I jerk my head away. Beer. Bee-or. 'Can't stand the stuff,' I say.

'Whoa, there, I'm only joking.' He takes my hand and though I want to pull it away, I don't. I let him hold onto it, pat it, stroke it. I know he's giving me that soft-eyed look, though I've turned my head away.

'Howay, pet,' he says. 'Tell us what's wrong.'

'Nothing.' I shrug. 'Felt a bit peculiar, that's all. Probably the heat, lack of air.'

'Do you want to go outside?'

He is so absurdly solicitous, it's becoming irritating. Before the annoyance overwhelms me, I jump up. 'No. let's have another dance.' The brandy must have sparked something in me. That's the trouble with spirits. Fire water. This time, I grab his hand and yank him onto the floor. I'll show him.

I've never jived before—not properly. Charlie used to get me to try it—not in a dancehall but at home with the chairs pushed back. Not enough room for a proper fling. There's room now though—I'll make room. Some of the other couples are rock 'n' rolling, the lads twirling the lasses, the lasses ducking under their partner's arms. I attempt something similar and Bobby accommodates me. Seems to know what to do. Nobody is watching—they're all too busy enjoying themselves. Anyway, I don't care. For once, I do not care. Bobby's grinning like mad as he spins me around. He doesn't attempt anything too outrageous—no lifting me in the air, or sliding me between his legs, like some of them are doing. Our version of rock'n'roll is fairly sedate. The dance exhilarates me, though. My heart is going ninety to the dozen and my hair flies about my head, apart from the strands stuck to my damp face. There's a bead of sweat running down Bobby's temple as well.

The music ends with a flourish of horns and we all come to a shambling halt, breathless, laughing. The girls dab hankies on their faces, smooth their hair. The lads get out their combs. The band troops off for the interval and we all trek back to our tables. I feel odd, as if I've been part of something. I joined in, that's what it is. I joined in, as if I'm a normal person. An ordinary lass.

Chapter Nine

After the delightful whirl of the dance—and I have to admit, it was delightful—we sat for a while sipping our drinks. Bobby got me another squash and was on his third bottle of brown ale. I hope he's not going to turn out to be a boozer. I won't put up with that—him sozzled with drink every weekend. Or even worse—every night. He doesn't have that look about him though. He's fresh-faced but the pink in his cheeks is not from alcohol. Probably from him being out in all weathers delivering coal. I smile to myself. A coalman. Whatever next? Janice will turn her nose up—until I tell her it's his own business. She'll still be a bit sniffy, I expect. Being a coal merchant isn't a profession. Well, we can't all be police sergeants and office supervisors. I can't imagine anything worse, personally.

It occurs to me there's something I haven't asked Bobby. 'Is it,' I say, 'a horse and cart you have for the coal, or a motor vehicle?'

He grins. 'Hoss and cart,' he says. 'But we're planning to motorise shortly. Elsa's getting on a bit, now.'

'Elsa?'

'The hoss. Elsa and Jimmy. Jimmy is dad's horse. He's even older than Elsa. Time the poor old nags were put out to grass.'

'What will you do with them?'

'Retire them to the countryside,' he says, 'or more likely, the glue factory.'

'You wouldn't!' The stink of the boneyard in Low Walker comes to mind. The sickening smell of bones being rendered down.

'I don't like the idea. Grown fond of the auld nags over the years. They're working animals, though, and keeping them going when they're no longer useful would be an expense.'

I don't know why I'm so shocked at the potential deaths of a couple of horses I don't know. I've never even ridden a horse, though I remember being on a donkey once, at Whitley Bay. Still, the dispatching of a creature you've had personal dealings with seems too brutal. Like drowning a cat because it keeps having kittens. Funny I don't feel the same way about humans. There are plenty of them I could happily dispatch. I've never had an animal, of course. No pets allowed in Aunt Mill's house. Nasty dirty beasts that smell and make a mess. And Manda never bothered, even though I remember begging for a kitten when I was five. Please Mammy-Manda. Pleeeeeeese. But it wasn't to be. 'You've got a couple of teddies,' she said. 'Pretend they're cats.' I've never really been an animal lover though.

'You look very thoughtful,' says Bob. 'It's not like the horses'll suffer. In fact, they're better off out of it when they get old.'

'Would old people be better off out of it?' I say.

He puts his head on one side. 'There is an argument that suggests they would. If they're suffering. Some people advocate euthanasia.'

Euthanasia? He's had an education, then. 'Isn't that what the Nazis believed?'

'That's what they called it. But euthanasia means "a good death". The Nazis believed in killing willy-nilly—of folk they didn't like, anyway. Or anybody who was defective in some way. They were also interested in eugenics. Breeding to produce a superior race. Getting rid of the misfits before they were ever born.'

'Would that be a bad thing? Surely there are people who would have been better unborn?'

'You mean cripples?' he says. 'Spastics and mad people and suchlike?'

I mean people who are swines and manipulators and evil so and so's, but I simply shrug.

'Dangerous to go down that road,' he says. 'Where would you stop?'

'I was thinking more about people who hurt others. Who do horrible things to them. Make them do things … cheats and liars and perverts …'

'Well, you might have a point, there, like.' He takes a mouthful of ale. 'Like this fella who's going around stabbing people. He'd have been better off not being born. Or at least, the poor sods he's killed would have been better off if he hadn't been.'

'How do you know that, though? Maybe the men he killed were unpleasant in some way themselves. Cheating on their wives. Spending money on …' I stop. I'm saying too much.

'You seem to know a lot about it.'

'My friend Janice's husband,' I say quickly, 'he's a policeman. Working on the case. He lets things slip. I shouldn't have said anything. Ignore me.' I gulp down some squash. 'Another dance?'

He's giving me a quizzical look but he shakes himself out of it. 'Aye. Aye, another dance would be lovely.'

*

He walks me to the bus stop and waits with me, though I tell him he needn't.

'No, pet,' he says. 'Don't want you standing around on your own while this cracker is going around stabbing people.

'It' only been men…' I start but shut myself up. Everybody seems to imagine the 'cracker' will start on women sooner or later. There are plenty of other people at the stop anyway but I can't say I'm not pleased to have Bobby accompany me. I was half-expecting him to pull me into a shop doorway for a cuddle but he hasn't. Not sure if I'm pleased about that or not. Is he always this much of a gentleman? Or is it because he sees me as being fragile, a special case? The lass who tried to drown herself and may go loopy again if he tries anything on? He has his arm around me, loosely, as we stand in the queue.

'Been a nice night,' he says. 'Want to do it again sometime?'

It has been a nice night—mostly, and I think I would like to do it again. I smile. 'Love to.'

'Could go to the pictures through the week,' he says. 'If you fancy it.'

I've not been to the pictures for a while, not the proper pictures anyway. There was that horrible episode last Sunday at the Tatler but that wasn't a film. I haven't seen a film in ages. 'That'd be lovely.' I push the memory of Sunday away, as my rage rises. If I ever see that man again…

'Smashin',' Bobby says. 'Wednesday? Same time, same place?'

I nod. 'Here's my bus.' The yellow trolleybus trundles to a stop and the queue moves forward. I turn towards him. 'Night, then. Thanks for a lovely—'

He kisses me quickly, on the lips, and I jerk away. 'Sorry,' he says, 'I… didn't mean…'

'It's fine,' I say, but I'd rather he hadn't. Not like that, in a rush, at the bus stop. I'd rather he'd found some quiet place and lingered over it. I back away as the people ahead are piling onto the trolley, but pause, lean forward and give him a quick peck on the mouth. Good lips. Dry and warm, faint smell of beer but pleasant enough.

'See you Wednesday,' he calls, as I run to hop on the bus before it pulls away. I see him standing there, with his hands in his pockets, watching me as I watch him.

The trolleybus wheezes along City Road and into Walker Road. It's not far, so I sit downstairs. I've had problems upstairs on buses before now. You get all sorts up there late at night—drunks and perverts. There was a man wearing lipstick upstairs on the 34 one night—a while back now. Red lipstick! Can you credit it? Didn't stop him rubbing his leg against mine, though. That was another time my Craven 'A's came in handy. I only had to threaten him with it and he was up and off to a seat nearer the front to pester some other girl. Never actually laid a hand on me, luckily for him.

Anyway, this time there is no trouble and I hop off at my stop just before the bridge. There's a light on in Mrs Dack's shop on the corner and I hesitate. I could nip in for some rum. But no, surely they can't still be open at half past eleven. I check my watch. Nearly quarter to twelve, actually. Maybe they're doing a stock-take or filling the shelves up. Funny woman, Mrs Dack. Gives me the look up and down every time I go in there, which is as infrequently as possible. She obviously wonders why I'm at home through the day, with me not being married or having brats in tow. None of her business. I don't have to explain myself. Best I don't go rattling their door now though, that would really bring the sneer to her face.

I turn my key and go into the flat. It's always nerve-racking coming into the place when it's dark and empty. There's an echoey feel to it—dank and depressing. I hate it, quite frankly. Sometimes, I'd rather not go out at all, than have to come back to this. The silence; the lack. Because it is a lack—of companionship, of another human being. I'm not exactly a social butterfly but I do feel the emptiness and it's particularly obvious when I've been with someone I like. This is why I don't go out much. It's different after my occasional forays down to the quayside. I barely register getting home those nights. Nights or mornings, whatever it may be. I don't always know. Something happens to me those nights. I'm lifted out of myself, have a heightened awareness, an animal sense of risk and danger and excitement that sharpens my senses for a while. I hear every tiny sound, see every tiny movement. I'm alive then—filled with vibrant life and fearlessness. Offering myself up to the lurking men, enticing them in, acting as if I'm the vulnerable one, the one they can make use of to play out their fantasies. But all the time, I'm using them. Making them pay.

When it's over, I go into a sort of amnesia. My mind blurs and I'm never quite sure where I've been or what I've been doing.

My heart beats wildly as I stand in the dim front room, lit only by the streetlamp outside. It's Saturday night. The only night I venture out down Dean Street. Should I? I'm tempted, though it's only a fortnight since the last time. Too soon, perhaps. I draw the curtains closed and flick on the light to dispel the atmosphere I've built up with my thoughts. Too soon. Too risky. Wouldn't want to run into Keith or his cronies. I remember the tramp who saw me—so he says. I didn't see him. How could I have missed him? My sight, my hearing, all my senses, are so acute when I'm down there, there's no chance I could have missed him. Maybe it wasn't me he saw. Some other girl going off with some other man, maybe? And his description of the man just happened to sound like the dead man. That must be it. They're all so similar, anyway. All the same type. Yes, that's it, it was someone else. No need to worry about that any longer. Jan didn't mention what the woman looked like but maybe Keith didn't tell her. If the woman had sounded at all like me, he would have said something, even if only to make a joke of it. No, it wasn't me that stinking old tramp saw, couldn't have been. But the way Keith looked at me last Sunday. Those dark brooding eyes.

I shiver as I take off my coat and hang it in the tiny hallway. Turning off the light again, I go through to the bedroom and undress in the dark. I pull on a nightie, though I don't always wear one, and snuggle down under the covers. Bobby comes into my mind, banishing the unpleasant thoughts. Bobby. What am I going to do about him? He's no Charlie. He won't get a thrill from my exploits, I'm pretty sure of that. He's far too nice. Far too ordinary. Yet I like him. I do. As I pull the covers up over my ears, I sigh. Whatever will become of us?

Chapter Ten

Sunday morning and the usual clamour of kids in the back lane. I don't mind them this morning as I'm peaceful and rested. Slept well last night. No alcohol, which is unusual for a Saturday night. Didn't want to drink when I was with Bobby, though. Don't want him to get the wrong impression. Yet, what impression do I want to give? I'm doing my best to make him think I'm virginal but of course I'm not. And he'll find that out one day. This thought stops me in my tracks. He'll find out I'm not virginal, will he? I've already decided, then, that I'll let him have his way with me. Maybe it will be a little like it was with Charlie and be enjoyable, if not as exciting. Then again, maybe it will be exciting in its own way. Maybe 'it' is always exciting if done properly. What do I know? I may not be exactly virginal but my experience is limited. There's only ever been Charlie. Well, if you don't count the others—but they're different. They definitely don't count.

I get up and potter about. I had my bath yesterday before I went out, so I'm not entirely sure what to do with myself. Maybe I could go for a swim. Get back in the water, like getting back on a horse after you've been thrown. Though my experience last week hasn't put me off water. Not in the least. Water doesn't frighten me. Never has. That's why it was so stupid to try to use it as a method of… I laugh to myself. Well, the balance of my mind was disturbed. That's what they'd have said if I'd been successful. 'Took her own life while the balance of her mind was disturbed.' I'm glad I wasn't successful. I'm so much happier this week than last. Is that because of Bobby? I suppose it must be. Funny how things can change so quickly. Just goes to show, you should never give up—you never know when things will turn themselves around. Yet, if I hadn't done what I did, I'd never have met Bob. Bobby-Bob. So how's that for a complex situation? Can we ever know whether the outcome of our actions will be for the good or for the bad? Sometimes things that seem evil, are anything but.

I realise I'm hungry. We didn't eat last night and it must be yesterday lunchtime that I last had anything. I make myself some toast and tea. Maybe I'll go out for a walk. I do some tidying first, then have a quick wash and get dressed. Pale blue cotton dress with a full skirt and sandals for a walk out. Where shall I go to? Walker Park? Heaton Park—hmm, no—don't want to run into Jan and Keith playing tennis again. Could go into town and have a wander around the boating lake in Exhibition Park. Haven't been there for a while. I could even have a stroll around the Hancock Museum. In an instant, I feel flat. These are things I should be doing with someone else. With Bobby. I wonder why he didn't ask to see me today? A Sunday afternoon out. Did he think it would be too soon? Make him seem too keen? Maybe I'd have thought it was too soon. Would I? I don't think that now.

While I'm dithering over this and getting myself wound up over why he might not have wanted to see me today, there's a knock on the door. My heart lifts. He's called round to see me— I immediately deflate. It can't be him; he doesn't know my address. Does he? I don't recall telling him. Maybe…

The knock comes again and I go to answer the door. It's Janice. Of course, it is. I stare at her as if she might magically change into who I want her to be.

'Jesus, Mon, why do I always have to knock twice? Didn't you hear it the first time?' She says all this with a little laugh, to take any sting out of her words.

'I was getting ready,' I say, without smiling back.

'Are you off out? Where are you going?'

I step back to let her in. For a mad moment, I consider telling her I'm seeing Bob. That'll get rid of her. But I hesitate too long. 'Thought I'd have a walk out somewhere,' I say at last.

'I'll come with you,' she says. 'How are you? I wanted to come over to make sure you were all right. Everything okay?'

She wanted to come over to find out how it went last night—that would be closer to the truth. Wants all the gossip about my 'date'. I'm reassessing her lately. She is nosy.

'All well,' I say, picking up my dark blue duster coat and a cream clutch bag. 'Trying to decide which park to go to.' Now she's here, I've gone off the idea anyway. 'Or we could do something cultural. Art gallery. Science museum.'

'Marvelous,' she says. 'Let's do that. As long as you're feeling well.'

'I'm fine. Don't fuss.' I pull the door closed behind us as we step out into the street.

'You went through a traumatic experience last weekend,' she says, her face serious, 'it's natural that I'd be worried about you.'

'No need. All is well with the world.' I reward her with a smile. 'Why aren't you at home dishing out Keith's Sunday dinner, anyway?'

'He's working today.'

'He's always working,' I say.

'Yes, he is. Lots of overtime. I'm getting fed up with it. Hardly seen him this week.'

'Found more clues, have they?'

'He won't say much but yes, they're making progress.'

Ha! Progress? I'll believe that when I see it.

'So,' she says, as we stand at the bus stop, 'did you go last night? How was it?' She even nudges me.

'Fine,' I say, fiddling in my purse for change.

'Fine?' she says. 'Is that all?'

I can't help myself. I smile—and it's a genuine smile. 'It was lovely,' I say. 'He's… lovely.'

'Oh, Mon, I'm so pleased for you.'

'Early days still,' I caution. 'Best not get ahead of ourselves.'

'But you're seeing him again?'

'Wednesday,' I say and I really cannot help the grin that stretches my cheeks. 'Pictures.'

When we get off the bus, the town is quiet. No shops open, of course. Jan links my arm. 'Well, this is nice,' she says. 'It's been a while since we've been out together like this. Reminds me of the old days, when we were young.'

'Young and daft,' I say, smiling.

'Before I met Keith,' she says, 'and you got involved with that Charlie.'

That Charlie! Still, nothing seems able to spoil my mood right now. 'When we were young and fancy free,' I say.

'Yes. I hope Bob is better for you than that Charlie,' she says. 'What did you say happened to him?'

'We stopped seeing eye to eye,' I say. 'It was no longer…' I pause. 'No longer much fun.'

'I'm surprised it was ever much fun. He was a strange one, as I recall.'

'It was fun while it lasted,' I say. And it was. Fun and exciting. For a while. 'Anyway, that's all over now. And I do think Bob will be good for me.' I hesitate about calling him Bobby in front of her. That's my name for him. Mine alone.

*

We decide on the Laing Art Gallery and walk up from Mosely Street, arm in arm. Very cosy, the two of us giggling like the teenagers we used to be. The Laing isn't busy and we wander through the galleries, pausing in front of this and that, making comments. It's as if I'm a normal person, with normal friends. I feel benign towards Jan—she's not that bad really. Caring, friendly, intelligent enough. What on earth can be wrong with me? It hits me suddenly. Could it be that I am in love? Surely not. Not so soon, so fast. And if it is love, it has a different character to anything else I've ever thought of as love. But the signs are there—a certain dreaminess, a sense of wellbeing, benevolent feelings towards others. Stars in my bloody eyes. Spring fever, as the song says. *It mi-ight as, we-ell be-e, spring.* I'm laughing now, hysterical, and Jan peers at me.

'Mon?' She looks from me to the painting we're in front of—one of those melodramatic John Martin seascapes, all crashing waves and apocalyptic visions. 'What's so funny? Nothing much amusing in this, that I can see.' She examines the painting again, for hidden depths of humour.

I collapse on one of the leather benches, overcome by the hilarity of my situation. Can I ever be an ordinary person, in love with an ordinary man, with ordinary friends, living an ordinary life? How is that possible? How can I—me— possibly expect all to go well when it never has before? It can't ever happen. Even if I tried really hard, went all out for it, embraced it, decided firmly on living a new, a different sort of life—how long before I succumbed to my true nature? How long before I drifted back into my old ways? I leap ahead through the years—Bobby and me, a married couple lying in bed together, reading our library books, cocoa on the bedside table. How long before I waited for him to doze off, so I could get up and go out on a Saturday night? How long before the accusatory looks on the Sunday morning? The demands to know where I had been, what I'd been doing out at that time of night. I can hear him now: You're my wife! I have a right to know.

Do I want to allow him the right to know all about me? What if there were children? I could be so lulled into security by this new life that I ignored my strictures not to reproduce myself. To perpetuate my evil in the world. But no, wait, those weren't my strictures, but Charlie's: No getting away from it, Monica, you're a cold bitch. Unnatural. Not womanly at all, 'cept between the legs. Oh dear, Monica, don't ever have kids. You'd be a terrible mother. You ever find yourself up the duff, stick one of your knitting needles up there and work it loose. Do the kid a favour.

The hysteria turns to sobbing.

'Mon, Mon, Jesus, what is it?' Janice sits beside me, arm around my shoulder, patting, rubbing, comforting. 'I knew you couldn't be all right. I knew it. I said to Keith… it's too soon. You can't possibly be okay. Not so soon. Not yet.'

Her chafing irritates me and I look up, give myself a shake. I see a gallery attendant approaching and wipe away my tears. Sniff, sigh, take a deep breath. Sitting up straight, I steady my voice. 'I'm fine now. Let's go. I'm okay now.'

Janice nods to the assistant. 'Sorry,' she mouths, 'she got a bit upset…'

Understatement of the year, that. The assistant takes himself off but not before casting me a glance that tells me to stop making a fuss in a public place.

'It's that painting, isn't it?' Jan says. 'The sea? I should have realised–'

'It's not that.' Hysteria bubbles in me again. As if a stupid painting could have that effect on me. Still, it would be a good excuse. I consider retracting the statement. I could take the easy way out, blame the sea. But I don't. Something has changed.

'Let's go outside,' Jan says, 'and sit on the steps, get a bit of fresh air.'

I feel a click in my chest as we park ourselves in a patch of sunshine. Around my heart area, as if something has opened up. I don't know what it is but it makes me raw and vulnerable. It also makes me want to tell Janice things I've never told anyone before. It seems so right. It's the perfect time. The only time. I don't even try to resist the urge. The desire to tell her—to tell someone—is so strong.

So I tell her.

Chapter Eleven

'I've been remembering recently,' I say, 'my mother, my childhood. Incidents.'

She peers at me, concerned. 'What incidents?'

'Men,' I say. 'Men and Manda.'

'What do you mean?'

'There were always men around. Lots of men.'

'So she was a…' She hesitates. '…a good time girl? Had a lot of boyfriends?'

I huff out a laugh. 'Boyfriends? No, they weren't boys and they weren't friends. Not really. Paying guests maybe.'

'Paying…? You mean…?'

I nod, sniffing and dabbing my nose with my hanky. The scent of lavender wafts from it and I bury my face in the delicate linen. One of Aunt Mill's Christmas presents, the box of three handkerchiefs unopened until this morning. Little lavender sprigs embroidered on them…

'So, she… I mean…' Jan stumbles over her words. 'Did she…? Did you… see anything?'

I look up. Did I see? Oh yes, I saw.

'I saw, yes. I more than saw. I…'

'What?' Shock has whitened her face. 'Oh God, Mon, what?'

'She made me… she told me to….' Tears trickle down my face, though the sobbing has stopped. Janice puts her hands over her mouth. Both hands, as though the sound she might make must be kept in at all cost.

'I had to… participate.' The little hanky is soaked now and I don't have another with me. Jan rummages in her bag and gives me hers. I stare at it for a while as if I don't know what to do with it. Little pink roses on hers but no perfume. Slight smell of Omo, maybe. 'Thanks.' I wipe my face.

'What. Did. You?' Staccato words. Jan has never been so tongue-tied.

'Everything,' I say. 'Everything you can imagine. Probably things you can't imagine.' I twist my lips. 'Still, I got teddies and dolls and half-crowns…'

'But you were so young,' Jan goes on. 'How old…?'

'Don't really know when it started. Four, five, maybe. Maybe younger. Don't remember.'

She gasps.

'Remember when it stopped though. Those bombs in 1941. Every cloud has a silver lining, eh? So they say.' My lips curl again. I want to hurt, spit vituperation, snarl obscenities, use spite and sarcasm but I stop myself. Not Jan's fault. Save it for the true perpetrators.

'Oh Mon. Oh God, Mon. You were a baby. A little girl. How could…? How could it even be possible?'

'Are you saying I'm lying?' Hackles rise. Maybe she does deserve the sharp words.

'No. No, of course not. I can't imagine it, that's all. How anyone could… how your own mother could… Are you sure?'

'Yes, of course I'm sure.' I glare at her. 'How could I not be sure?'

'Well, memory can…' She stops. Bites her lip.

'Nothing wrong with my memory. And I'm not making it up. It happened.' I wish I hadn't said anything. Kept myself to myself, as always. 'Knew no one would believe me.' I make a move to stand up but she stops me.

'I'm sorry. I do believe you. But it's so… I don't know what to say.' She's trembling, tears rolling down her cheeks now. I give her back her handkerchief, damp though it is. She sniffles into it. 'All these years. You've never said anything. Why…?'

'Only recently started to make sense of it, that's why. Barely remember really. Flashes of images, incidents, words, sensations… pain.' I draw my lips back, exposing my teeth in a grimace of a smile. Jan's eyes flicker. Maybe she imagines I'm going to bite her. 'Last few months, that's when it's started to come clearer. Ha! Must be getting old. Recalling delightful childhood memories in my dotage.'

'Don't, Mon, don't.' She touches my arm.

'Childhood,' I go on, 'when all summers were long and sunny. Carefree and lighthearted days, seen through the golden mists of nostalgia. I don't think!'

'Don't torture yourself.'

'Oh, the torture was over long ago.'

Jan is crying seriously now. Her sleeves are wet where she's mopped her eyes. So are mine. Mascara everywhere. And snot. I realise people are looking at us as they stroll past, their pleasant Sunday afternoon disturbed by two wailing women.

Jan notices too. 'Should we go back into the gallery? Find the ladies?' she says. 'Need some lav paper to blow my nose. Hope it's not that shiny Izal stuff.' She attempts a watery smile.

'In a minute.' I need to pull myself together. It's a common saying, pull yourself together, usually meaningless, but on this occasion, I do need to gather my forces. Bring my arms and legs and brain back into service. Dispel the weakness in my limbs.

'I don't know how you've kept this to yourself so long. It must have always been there—under the surface. Oh Mon.' She reaches out and hugs me and I stiffen. I'm not a hugger. Physical contact is strictly rationed where I'm concerned. But I succumb for a moment and let her comfort me. Though of course, it's herself she's comforting. As I pull away, I say, 'Don't tell Keith. I don't want anyone else to know.'

'Oh, of course not. No. I won't say anything.' She pats me. 'But I wonder if you should talk to someone? A professional?'

'A doctor? Psychiatrist, do you mean?' My spikes are up again. 'No. I don't think so. Probably wouldn't believe me anyway. Taken me all my time to convince you.'

'I'm sorry. I do believe you. I do. Maybe see some sort of … counsellor, then?' She's probably trying to say I should see a priest.

'Telling you has helped,' I say. Time to stroke her ego. 'You're a great listener.'

'Any time, pet, any time.' She looks into my eyes with her serious expression on. 'I mean that. Any. Time.'

I nod, though I can't imagine Keith would be best pleased if I turned up at their door at three o'clock in the morning whingeing about my life.

She shakes her head sadly. 'I cannot imagine how she could have done that to you. Your own mother. Jesus, Mon, I'll never be the world's best mam—prospect terrifies me if I'm honest—but I could never do that. Never. Her own child. Any child.'

'And yet I loved her.'

She gazes at me for a moment. Nods slowly. 'I know. I know. You've said so often enough. And she praised you, you've said, told you how beautiful you were, dressed you nicely. She must have loved you—in her way.'

'Warped kind of way, but yes, I believe she did. I don't think she saw what she was doing as being wrong. It's not her I blame. Or if I do, I can contemplate forgiving her. No, it's them. The men. They must have encouraged her. If they hadn't wanted it, she wouldn't have had to do it. Or make me do it.'

'I suppose not. But still... she must have known it was wrong. Surely.'

I shrug. 'Maybe. We are all capable of deluding ourselves as to our crimes.'

'Blind to our sins,' she says, the lapsed Catholic in her coming to the fore. 'Evil, that's what it is. Pure evil.' Her voice goes up a notch, falters. Reminds me of Manda, her weak voice and cracked cries under the rubble, and I smile.

'Let's get some of that lav paper now,' I say. 'I'm drenched.'

*

We're subdued as we head out, naturally enough.

'I'll come back with you,' Jan says but I shake my head. Perhaps too vigorously.

'No. No. I'm fine. I'm going to be fine.'

'You're not fine,' she says, 'and I don't mind, honestly.'

'No. Please, Janice. I want to be on my own.'

'Really?'

'Really. I need to think things through. Sort myself out. I may not go back to work tomorrow. May give it up. Take on a bit of temp work, maybe.' How is it so easy for me to lie to her when we've been so close? Another of my many talents.

'I understand. Yes, that might be best. Have some time off. Get yourself fully recovered.'

As we part, she kisses me on the cheek. Well, that's new. And not to be encouraged. She's earned it though, I suppose. 'I'll come over again soon,' she says. 'Or you come to me. ANY TIME.' And there it is again, in capital letters.

'I will,' I say, though I probably won't. 'And remember.' I put a finger to my lips. 'Not a word to Keith.'

She smile-frowns. 'Of course not.'

I wave and head off before she hugs or kisses me again. My heart is palpitating so loudly, I'm surprised others can't hear it. Or see it even, swelling and thumping in my chest. I get a few odd looks from people passing. Maybe it is visible, or more likely, I have a strange expression on my face. I'm glowing. If I'd known confession was this pleasurable, I'd have done it years ago. Those left-footers are definitely onto something.

Chapter Twelve

Tuesday morning, a letter from Aunt Mill turns up in the first post. She reports that she's heard some disturbing news about me. She's seen a small passage in *The Journal*—shown to her by her next-door neighbour, because she doesn't deign to read such rags—about my misadventure at Tynemouth. She trusts I'm now fully recovered and have seen the error of my ways but is somewhat surprised I have not yet been to see her. She would have preferred to hear the news from me rather than get it second or third hand. She had thought, she goes on, that I would be fit enough by now, after my ordeal, to at least pay her a visit over this last weekend, Sunday afternoon particularly lending itself to such an opportunity. Not being apprised of my current state of mind and body, she would wish to see for herself that I am, indeed, fully recovered IN ALL SENSES—she has capitalised and underlined this last bit. Therefore, she adds, she would be much obliged if I would come over to Beech Grove at my earliest opportunity, in order to set her mind at rest. Failing my appearance within the week, she will have no alternative but to trek down to Walker Road herself to check up on me. Signs herself, 'Your loving aunt, Millicent Hargreaves.'

Well, receipt of this arrant nonsense makes me fume and I am positively murderous. How dare she order me up to Forest Hall—a journey requiring two buses—when for all she knows, I could have caught influenza from my soaking in the sea and be at death's door. Why didn't she get off her skinny behind and come to check on me before now, if she's so concerned for my wellbeing?

On the other hand, I think, after a moment's reflection, I do not want her coming here and poking around—which she would do, as she acts as if she still owns the place. I certainly do not want her sticking her enormous nose into my affairs.

I suppose I'll have to go and see her 'within the week' as she stipulates but I am not about to rush over there 'at my earliest convenience', there being no such thing. It is not convenient and never will be convenient. I'll have to go but will leave it as long as possible. Depending on what I have arranged with Bobby, I'll go next weekend. She can twiddle her thumbs until then.

*

After further reflection, I decide I'll not wait until the weekend to see Aunt Mill. Bobby's likely to make plans and I want to be available for whatever he comes up with. I'll go today and get it out of the way. Turning up fairly soon after having received her letter has to get me into her good books, surely. Maybe she'll slip me an envelope with a few pound notes in it. It has been known, though not often.

Anyway, I take the 19 up to the end of Coach Lane and jump on another bus to Benton Station. The day is pleasantly warm, but not hot, so I've got my duster coat on again over a neat pastel pink twin set and lightweight brown skirt. I considered adding a string of pearls (twenty-first birthday present from Aunt Mill) but changed my mind. I don't want to go too far down the compliance route. She's always thought I was something of a beatnik and, though nothing could be further from the truth, I like to tease her by not being totally conventional and predictable.

Millicent Hargreaves. Married Jim Hargreaves when she was fairly young—he was a good bit older. Uncle Jim's long gone now but he left her comfortably off, thank you very much. Did well for himself in tin boxes or some such. I remember him going on about it when I first went to live with them. Boring as anything, especially to an eleven-year-old girl. Think he had me earmarked for taking over the company, seeing as they had no kids of their own. Of course, that was never going to happen.

Aunt Mill doesn't care to spend much, so I'm assuming there's plenty of cash stashed away for when I get my hands on it. Whenever that may be. She's only in her fifties though, so it could be a few years yet. I smile to myself. Maybe I could hurry her along a bit.

The house has an enclosed porch but the main door is always propped open, so I step in and ring the doorbell. After a few seconds, I see Aunt Mill through the inner glass door. That's always unlocked as well and I could go right in—especially as this used to be my home—but I observe the niceties and wait for her to open it. 'Come in, come in,' she says. 'Don't stand there gawping.'

I follow her into the back room—the dining room, though she uses it as her little sitting room, leaving the big front room for favoured guests. Of which I am not one, obviously. There's a paltry fire going in the grate and the room is stuffy and dim. I'll have the French windows opened up once I'm back living here, and tidy up the yard. Get a few geraniums in pots, a bit of colour.

'Wasn't expecting you to come over so promptly,' she says. 'You're usually somewhat tardy in your visits. Do you want some tea?'

I nod and she goes off to the kitchen to put the kettle on. I hear it whistle after a few minutes and she's soon back with the brown betty teapot encased in one of her knitted tea-cosies. Brown and green stripes with a pompom on the top. She puts the pot on the hearth and goes back for the crockery. 'As I said,' she says when she comes back with the cups and saucers—and it's not the Crown Derby, I notice. 'As I said, I wasn't expecting you yet, so I've not much in. There's a couple of fig rolls there, if you want them.'

She's a tall woman, nearly as tall as I am, and thin and rangy. Her salt and pepper hair is scraped back in a tight bun that must surely give her a migraine. I've only ever seen her wear two different dresses—both crêpe de chine forties' numbers. Today she's wearing the dark green one. The other is brown. Her colours. A Victorian cameo at the neck is her only concession to personal adornment. Apart from her wedding ring. She did wear a black dress for Uncle Jim's funeral, now I come to think of it, but I've never seen it since.

She pours the tea and hands me a cup and saucer. 'You're not saying much, Miss,' she says. 'So, what's all this nonsense about, then?'

I take a fig roll. It's soft and slightly damp. 'What?'

'What? What? You know fine well what. You. In the sea. What was all that all about?'

'It was an accident. I went in too far.'

'Accident, my foot,' she says. 'What were you doing down at Tynemouth at that time in the morning?'

I have no answer to that, so I remain silent.

'Ah, I thought so,' she says, taking a slurp of her tea. 'Playing silly buggers, were you?'

I'm not sure what she means by this so I shrug.

'Hmph. So what was behind it all? Some lad, I expect. Dumped you, did he?'

'No!' I'm annoyed that I sound like a sulky kid but this is what she does to me every time. Every time I see her, I'm fifteen again, and in some kind of trouble.

'You don't want to go drowning yourself over some daft lad,' she says. 'Plenty more fish in the—' She stops, the irony of her words occurring to her, perhaps.

'It wasn't about a lad. Why would it be about a lad?' I'm hunched, defensive. That stupid doctor thought the same. As if I'd do that over some man.

'What was it about then?'

'I… I don't know. I just… I felt… Oh, I've no idea. I'm fine now, though.' Thanks for asking, I mutter under my breath.

'What's that?' she says.

'Nothing.'

'Should know better at your age. Time you got yourself settled down. Have a couple of bairns. Then you won't have time to be dousing yourself in sea water in the early hours.'

'*You* didn't,' I say.

'Didn't what?'

'Have children.'

'I had you,' she says. 'Frankly, you were enough.' She pulls herself up straight and sniffs. 'Though it is to my great regret that I had none of my own. But it was not to be.'

She's not particularly religious but if she were, this is the point she would say it was God's will. She has that long-suffering, pious look about her.

'I did my best for you, Monica,' she goes on. 'We treated you as if you were our own.' She puts her cup down on the little table to one side of her chair. 'I don't know what went wrong. You were bad enough as a girl but you've got worse, not better. Time you grew up.'

I grew up long before you ever got your hands on me, I think.

'Not enough responsibility, that's your trouble. You've had it too easy. We went through two world wars and a depression and still did all right for ourselves. And you're the one reaping the benefit.'

I turn away so she can't see me raise my eyes. Here it comes.

'Nobody gave us a pair of flats at your age. We had to work for what we got. Jim put in umpteen hours a week to build up the business. And I did my bit.' She sniffs again. 'He might have lasted a bit longer, poor Jim, if he hadn't worked himself to the bone.'

To the bone! That's a laugh. He was a big beefy man, bursting out of his grey suit. Huge tan shoes on huge feet. Terrified the life out of me, at first. Though, to give him his due, he never did anything to me. And he was genial enough in his way. More genial than she ever was.

'Pull yourself together, Monica, and stop acting like a spoilt brat. You've got everything ahead of you. Be grateful for your lot in life. There's folk with much worse.' She squints at me and I squirm in the spotlight of her attention. 'You're not…?' She casts her eye at me meaningfully.

'No!' Why does it have to be about lads, or pregnancy? Is there nothing else a woman can get upset about?

'Well, that's something.' She sips her tea in contemplation for a moment. 'It wasn't money worries, was it?' she says eventually. 'Couldn't be, surely. You're working, aren't you? And it's not as if you've rent to pay. Plus, you get a few bob from them upstairs. They pay up regularly, don't they?'

'I've lost my job,' I say, inspired by her comments. 'They don't want me associated with the company after… the sea thing.'

'Not surprised,' she says, picking the teapot up. 'You've brought it on yourself. Will you get something else?' She pours us both more tea. Thick and treacly it is now. She was always heavy handed on the tealeaves. Her one extravagance.

'I'll pick up some temporary work, I suppose. I'll be all right.' I pause. 'Might be a week or two before I get something, though. And before I get paid.'

She sighs and stands up. 'What are we going to do with you?' Her purse is on the sideboard and she opens it with a snap and fishes out a fiver. She pauses, then pulls out another. 'Will this keep you going for a couple of weeks till you get sorted?'

I take it, a little shamefaced, but smiling underneath. 'Thanks,' I mutter. I raise my head and look her in the eye. 'Thanks, Aunt Millicent.'

Chapter Thirteen

Wednesday and it's time to get ready to meet Bobby. The temperature's dropped and the sun hasn't been seen all day. Looks like rain, in fact. Again. I decide to wear my grey costume—calf-length pencil skirt and little jacket nipped in at the waist. White rayon blouse underneath. I never wear a corset, these days—not even a roll on. Don't need to. I contemplate myself in the mirror. Look like an office girl, but that's what I'm supposed to be, isn't it? The skirt is slim enough to be flattering rather than dowdy and when I slip on my new black patent stilettos the effect is very alluring, if I do say so myself. We'll be sitting down, as we're off to the pictures, so I can slide the shoes off if necessary. They give me added height but Bob's not going to complain, as he's a good six foot.

I'm pleased to be updating my wardrobe. Maybe I'll use the rest of the money Aunt Mill gave me to buy a new dress—something to wear on Saturday, if we go dancing again. There's plenty left over. Apart from the shoes, I only bought a few groceries yesterday, and the rum.

Once I've got my hair up in a French pleat and I'm all made up with a dab of *Soir de Paris* behind my ears, I shrug on my shortie wool swing coat as it's likely to be chilly later, and trot off to get the 34. I don't have to wait long and I'm in town by quarter past seven. I get off the bus on Mosely

Street and walk up Pilgrim Street, twitching my gloves into place. I must be a little nervous. Edgy. I don't know why. We've arranged to meet under the clock again but when I get near the Northern Goldsmiths, I peer ahead and it doesn't seem as if he's there yet. I cross over to Cook's Corner and linger there a moment. I can't see him approaching from any direction, so I stroll up Northumberland Street to Fenwick's to have a look in their windows. Give him a chance to turn up. Hate arriving first.

I spend a pleasant few minutes window shopping, seeing if there's anything I might want to buy. I spot a rather swish gown in Fenwick's—emerald green silk, but too expensive for me, sadly, and where would I wear it? Lovely though. I've always suited green. I browse the rest of the displays but, apart from a pretty candy-striped sundress, there's nothing I'd want. Even the sundress isn't my style, if it comes to that—too pink and girly. I go for a more sophisticated look these days.

I wander back to Cook's Corner, keeping a look out for Bobby, but can't see him yet. Couples meet and kiss on both corners and go off arm in arm. I check my watch against the Northern Goldsmiths' clock. Nearly half-past seven. No, I won't go and stand there first. I'll wait until I see him. A thought strikes me: what if he doesn't come? I shake it off. Of course, he'll come. He was very keen last weekend. Of course, he'll turn up. The nerves have got to me now though. What if he stands me up? Leaves me waiting here like a fool? Couldn't accept that. Can't allow it. I'll go now before— before what? Before it becomes obvious that he's not coming. Before it's a certainty. That way, I'll be the one to leave him standing. If he comes at all.

My stomach heaves and I prop myself up against the wall as the nausea makes me light-headed. How dare he? How dare he treat me this way? I'm not some silly schoolgirl to be kept hanging around. I won't put up with it. I won't. I spin on my heel, clopping away, no idea where I'm going, going anywhere to get away from the vicinity of our meeting place. Supposed meeting place. My eyes blur as I stride up Northumberland Street, brushing people out of my way or stepping off the pavement to avoid them, ignoring the blare of horns. The traffic fumes catch my throat and I gag at the stink of diesel and petrol. My new stilettos hinder me, make me wobble as I walk but I surge onwards.

A hand grabs my arm and I swing around ready to strike with my handbag.

'Whoa,' he says. 'Where are you rushing off to?' Bobby, his hands up as though warding me off. 'Saw you from the bus so I leapt off to catch up with you. Where are going?'

I'm speechless and he must see something in my face as contrition appears in his.

'Sorry if I'm late. I'm not too late, am I?' He checks his watch. 'Just gone half past by my watch. Sorry. Did you think I wasn't coming?'

I glare at him, not trusting myself to speak.

'Got a lift from a mate as far as Sandyford,' he says. 'Hopped on a bus the rest of the way. Traffic was snarled up. Sorry, should have walked.'

Couples are pushing past from both directions, staring at us. Nothing but bloody couples. I want to hit out at something. Him, perhaps. I don't want to hear his excuses, his constant apologies. I stiffen as he takes my arm.

'I'll always turn up if I say I'm going to,' he says. 'Wouldn't leave you standing there like a lemon.'

The terminology infuriates me. What a ridiculous, facile thing to say.

'Do you want to nip into the Percy Arms for a brandy? Look like you could do with one.'

Saying nothing, I allow him to lead me through Prudhoe Street to Percy Street. We go into the lounge where he parks me at a table while he goes to the bar. I'm simmering still, but simmering down. I can't blame him for what never happened. He didn't stand me up. He's here. He arrived more or less on time. He's not to blame in any way, yet I do blame him. Blame him for wanting to be with someone like me. Someone who goes off halfcocked for no reason. Now he'll see me as even more of a liability, even more fragile and broken. I don't want to be this person he's turned me into.

'Why do you want to be with me?' I ask, when he comes back with the drinks. 'What do you see in me?'

'Well,' he says, 'you're beautiful, for a start. And… intriguing. You're not like other lasses. You're different. Fascinating.'

'Don't make fun of me.'

'I'm not,' he says, his eyes widening in innocence. 'I mean it. I find you interesting. Compelling, if you like. I'm drawn to you. Moth to a flame.' He's smiling but there's an honesty about him. 'You're gorgeous, Monica. And intelligent and… altogether wonderful. There you go. Good enough for you?'

'You don't know me,' I say.

'I want to,' he says. 'I want to get to know you. You'd reward years of study, you would.'

'Stop it!'

'I'm not teasing you, honest. Well, not really. I could gaze at you for hours. Investigate your hidden depths. Will you let me do that?'

'You wouldn't like what you found.'

'That's for me to decide.'

'Is it?' I sip my brandy. Surely, it's for me to reveal or not as I see fit?

'There's no rush as far as I'm concerned,' he says. 'I'm happy to study you indefinitely.' He looks into my eyes. 'I want to know you, Monica. Feel I half know you already… like we've met before.'

'We haven't.'

'In a previous life, maybe?' He grins. 'Do you believe in reincarnation?'

'No.'

'Neither do I, really.' He laughs. 'But you never know. Be nice if we came back, don't you think? As somebody else. Or something else.'

'No, it wouldn't be nice at all. I'd hate it.'

'You're a funny one. But I…' He trails off. 'Whoops. I nearly said… I shouldn't say it. Not yet. Too soon.'

'What?'

'You know. Three little words.' He takes a gulp of his pint. 'Sorry. Don't want to frighten you off. It's far too soon.'

I look to one side. 'Far too soon,' I agree. 'You don't know anything about me.'

'I know. I'm a daft ha'porth,' he says. 'But I have to admit I am much enamoured of you, young lady.'

'Don't be silly. We barely know each other.'

'Aye, I know. I'm getting ahead of meself. Ignore me.'

But I can see he's smitten. It's there in his shining eyes, in his fresh open face, in his big soft demeanour. Somebody loves me. Somebody. Loves. Me.

*

We go to the Haymarket Cinema to see *Three Cases of Murder*. Bobby finds seats a few rows from the back. I'm pleased he didn't choose the back row. Can't be bothered with all that nonsense. We've missed the Pearl & Dean advertising and most of the Pathe News but we get ourselves properly settled in before the big film starts. It's a trilogy of stories, enjoyable enough, if a bit far-fetched at times, and my attention wanders. I get caught up watching cigarette smoke curling above the heads of the audience. We're in the stalls, which is fine by me and the flickering light and dark hypnotises me. Bobby takes my hand and I let him hold it for a while, though I get irritated if I can't have full control of my own limbs. I remove myself from his grasp—a dry grasp, thankfully— after a little while but make sure I give his hand a pat when I let go of him. He grins at me, and in the darkness his teeth gleam.

I'm glad I had the brandy earlier; it's taken the edge off my nervousness, so it only jitters at the edges of my consciousness now. I dislike feeling nervous; it makes me think bad thoughts and plot bad deeds. I don't believe I'll ever have to do bad things to Bobby, though. I hope not, anyway. I wouldn't want it to end the way it did with Charlie. That was such a dreadful day.

*

We'd been out in Charlie's car—a 1948 Hillman Minx he got cheap from someone who owed him a favour. Sort of sage green, it was. He even let me drive it sometimes. Taught me the basics, though I never took the test. Charlie didn't care about that—preferred it when I drove badly or wildly. Danger thrilled him and he encouraged me to go fast, though you couldn't get much speed out of an old Minx.

We'd go off into the wilds of Northumberland, overtaking the green bus to Alnwick on the A1, careening around lanes to out of the way villages, racing over the moors. I loved those days out—days and nights sometimes—not getting home till dawn. I don't like remembering that last trip though. I don't let myself dwell on that.

I push Charlie out of my mind and force myself to concentrate on the film. Soon, my heart rate settles and Bobby takes my hand again.

*

By the time we come out, I'm much calmer, relaxed and refreshed. Walking back along Percy Street, he pauses beside the entrance to an alleyway and gives me a querying look. He must read acquiescence in my eyes because he eases me into the shadows, a few steps beyond the lights of the main road. I breathe in his smell—Wright's Coal Tar soap, a hint of bay rum maybe, the lingering sourness of the beer he had earlier. It's pleasant. That and his warmth. We stand inches apart, seeing very little until our eyes adjust. He's nothing but teeth and eye-whites, and closeness of skin. When he kisses me, it reaches to my depths. The jolt—down there—is shocking but delightful. The tingle spreads between my thighs. His kisses are dry and warm, not sloppy, soft at first, increasing in pressure and urgency. I respond. I can't help myself. He slides his hands inside my loose coat and clasps me around the waist, his fingers stroking the back of my costume jacket, sliding down over my hips then back up again. I lean into him and there it is again, that pang of—lust—I suppose, desire, want. And like the other day with Janice, my heart expands and once again I am raw and open, vulnerable and exposed. Strangely, I don't mind. He goes no further than kissing and I'm glad of that. What we have—what's developing between us—is too important for a back-alley fumble.

We make arrangements for the weekend—Saturday definitely and with a hint of something for Sunday perhaps. On the trolley home, I'm not sure I want us to go out again. What I'd like to do, is stay in. But of course, I can't suggest that. Not yet.

Not yet.

Chapter Fourteen

Three weeks now, we've been together and we've been models of propriety, walking out together—courting—with Bobby being the perfect gentleman. We've been dancing, seen films, been to cafés, pubs, had a walk in the park and a visit to the Hancock Museum. We are exclusive, a couple, in love. We've linked arms, walked hand in hand, kissed in doorways. Soon, I hope, we will seal the deal in my bed. He's not pushed me on this but if he doesn't make a move soon, I may have to push him.

Bobby wants me to meet his family. I'm not sure about this but I've agreed anyway. I'm going over next week, next Sunday, for tea. But I'll see him before then as we're meeting Janice and Keith tonight. I've seen Jan once or twice recently and she has worn me down with her demands, so I've agreed they can finally meet Bob, as they call him—Bobby is the name only I use.

We meet in The Old George, off the Cloth Market and everyone is on their best behaviour—even Keith. It's all hello, how are you, lovely to meet you, and such like. Keith gets the first round in—beers for the men, Babychams for me and Jan. I find the drink a little sickly but it's inoffensive and women are allowed to drink it without being considered tarts. We get ourselves settled at a table and all smile around at each other.

'I hear you're on the coal,' Keith says to Bobby, to break the silence that threatens to settle in. 'Hard graft, eh?'

'Oh aye,' Bobby says. 'Maybe not as hard as what you do though. Chasing after criminals.'

'A lot of it's down to brainpower,' Keith says. 'Studying information. Perusing evidence until things click into place. With any luck we don't have to chase anybody—they'll give themselves away and all we have to do is pick them up.'

Jan and I listen politely, sipping our spritzing drinks. The chatter and chink of glasses grows louder as the pub steadily fills up.

'Must be interesting work, though. Bit of excitement now and again.' Bobby picks up his pint. 'You're working on this ripper case, aren't you?'

'Yes. Plenty to keep us occupied on that right now.'

'Oh, here we go,' Jan says. She raises her eyes in a long-suffering look.

'We came by some new information on it recently, as it happens,' Keith goes on. 'Been very helpful.' He glances at me. I bite into the cherry from my Babycham and give him a slight smile.

'A man's come forward,' he says. 'Tells us he was threatened with having his throat ripped out by a woman three or four years back.'

'A woman?' Bobby puts his glass down. 'On her own?'

'Oh, she had a pimp lurking in the background. She came on to him but all they really wanted was his money.'

'Three or four years ago?' I say. 'What took him so long to come forward?'

Keith smirks. 'He was embarrassed. Ashamed. Didn't want his wife to find out.' He takes a slurp of his beer. 'The wife died recently, though, and he's racked with guilt.

Decided he should do something worthwhile in her name, poor sap. So he's come forward in case there's a connection.'

'And is there?' Jan says, caught up despite herself.

'Maybe. Can't say at the moment.'

'Can't or won't?' I say.

'Bit of both. We're still working on some of the details.'

'It's a bit much when there's a woman involved,' Bobby says, frowning.

I give him a look. Oh yes, crimes are always much worse when they're done by a woman.

'She relieved him of his wallet while the pimp held the knife under his chin.' Keith goes on.

'So it wasn't the woman who was threatening to rip him open, then,' I point out.

'Well, that's a relief,' Bobby says. 'God help us if the lasses start doing that sort of thing.' He chuckles.

Jan shakes her head. 'What kind of a woman gets involved with something like that?'

'She was a blonde lass, apparently. Quite young. Twenty maybe. Twenty-one at a push.' Keith looks at me across the top of his glass. 'Tall girl, the bloke said. Good looking. Couldn't believe it was happening to him.'

'Here!' Jan says, in an accusing manner. 'You said it was all to be kept under wraps. You told me not to—'

'Some details aren't being revealed yet. But things move on, Jan. The rest'll be all over the papers tomorrow.' Keith pauses. 'We're revealing this much because we want to encourage more men to come forward. The more accounts there are, the more detail we get.' He takes a long draught of ale. 'They're bound to have done it before, this pair… and since.' He wipes the froth from his lips. 'Bloke said they seemed to have it all planned out.'

'Definitely not the first time, then,' Bobby says.

'No, and probably not the last. There'll be other poor sods out there that it's happened to.'

'They didn't kill their victims, though?' I say.

'No. And there may be absolutely no connection with the latest attacks.' Keith picks his pint up again. 'On the other hand, they may be the forerunners to them.'

'Didn't you say the current killer wasn't using a knife?' I sip my drink. 'I'm sure you said that.'

'Aye, that's right,' Keith says. 'Well remembered.'

'So what is it he's using then, this ripper guy?' Bobby says.

'Like I said, some details aren't being revealed just yet. Details of the weapon are still being held back.'

'Is that because you don't know what it is?' I say, twisting the stem of my cocktail glass. The gold Bambi printed on the side catches the light.

Keith scowls. 'It's being thoroughly investigated and we have our ideas.'

'But is there a reason they're not letting on?' Bob says.

'It's not for me to say.' Keith slams down his empty glass. 'We've all been told to keep schtoom so I'm keeping schtoom.'

'Schtoom?' Jan says. 'Never heard that before.'

'Means keep quiet. All the cons use it. German or Yiddish or something.'

'Only following orders, eh?' Bobby says with a grin. 'Another pint? Babychams again, lasses?' He stands up and goes to the bar.

*

'He's a bit intense, is Keith,' Bobby says, as we walk down the Cloth Market to my bus stop.

'Yes,' I say, 'I find that, too. I always feel like he's accusing me of something.'

'Must be him being a polis, I suppose,' he goes on. 'I've got a pal in the Force and he can be full of it at times.'

'Full of… what?' I say, with a smile.

'Cheeky!' he says. 'Girls aren't supposed to think naughty things like that.'

'Are we not?' I'm flirtatious and feminine, teasing him because I can. He's not perfect in every way—of course, he isn't. He's a man, how can he be? But he's close to being exactly right for me. For me as I am now.

And he's hooked, I know, and that makes me feel beautiful and powerful. I remember Manda telling me, 'You can do anything you want, my gorgeous girl.' Of course, I also had to do things I didn't want, but I won't dwell on that. Things have changed. A sea change, that's what they call it, and it was. When I went into the sea, everything changed. I'm no longer the person I was before. Can we be held responsible for what we did when we were different people altogether? I'm not responsible for what she did—the me before the me I am now. I am innocent. Reborn out of the sea like—who was it? Venus? Yes, Aphrodite to the Greeks. I'm Bob's mermaid, with the emphasis on maid, risen from the foam.

Before we reach Moseley Street, he pulls me into an alleyway and we kiss. We kiss deeply and there's that pang again, that longing. I cling to him like I've never clung to anyone before. Our breath is hot and fast and we can't keep our hands off each other. 'Should I…?' he says. 'Should we…?' I nod silently. 'Your place?' he says, and I nod again.

*

When I wake on Sunday morning, he's gazing at me, his head propped on his hand. There is nothing but love in his eyes.

Adoration. It frightens me a little but last night… last night was so good. Nothing bad can come of this. This isn't like before.

Chapter Fifteen

Whit Sunday, and I'm going to Bobby's house for tea, to meet his parents. I've been dancing on air all week. He came over on Wednesday night and we—well, you know—but didn't stay over because of work the next day. And we were together Friday and most of Saturday. Still, it seems as if I've not seen him for ages. A whole twenty-four hours!

He meets me at Tynemouth Station and we walk back along Tynemouth Road towards Shields. The Wilson family live in one of the squares off the main road. The weather is getting very warm and I pat the sweat from my brow with my hanky as we reach the house.

The front door opens as we walk up the path. 'Hello. You must be Monica. Well, who else would you be?' Mrs Wilson, all homey and flour-dusted, spreads her arms in welcome. 'Come on in. Tch, look at me, still got me pinny on.' She wipes her hands on the floral pinny covering her soft plump body. 'What am I like?' she says.

I give her my best good-girl smile. 'How d'you do?' I'm nervous and that makes me vicious sometimes. I must not be vicious today. 'Lovely smell,' I say, sniffing appreciatively at the baking aromas emanating from the kitchen.

A dog appears in the hallway and woofs a welcome. 'This is Paddy,' says Bobby. 'Was the two of us spotted you–' he breaks off and I catch a glance between him and his mother.

I'm not a dog-lover but I know people can be sentimental about their pets, so I let it sniff my hand. Seems good-natured enough. Mongrel, of course, a mix of black and tan with spindly legs.

Mrs Wilson shoos us into the big back room—bright and comfortable, with a dark red three-piece suite and an upright piano by the window. 'Shift up, you two,' she says, flapping her pinny at the two lads occupying either end of the big settee.

The younger one—thirteen or so, by my guess—is sprawled out, reading *The Beano*; the older one—sixteen, maybe, and trying to look grown up—is perusing a paperback.

'This is wor Jimmy,' Bobby says, pretend-cuffing the younger one around his head. 'Don't take any cheek from him. And this is our resident intellectual, Tom. Tom's taking exams. He's got prospects, unlike the rest of us thickos.'

The boys grunt their greetings and I see Tom eyeing me with interest. They both get up and move to less comfortable seats—the comic-reader lies on the floor next to the dog and the intellectual sits back to front on a wooden chair, resting his book on the backrest.

'I don't know what you're doing clocking in the house on a day like this, anyway, the pair of you.' Mrs Wilson says. 'Away outside and get some sunshine. And take Paddy with you.'

'I'm waitin' for me tea,' Jimmy says. 'I'm clammin', man.'

'Oh, it'll be a half hour yet. Your dad nipped out earlier for "a pint of fresh air" as he calls it,' Mrs Wilson tells Bobby. 'It's well past chucking out time so he must have gone to Geordie Fraser's place to look at his new bike. He better not be too long getting back.'

Bobby settles me on the couch. 'Dad likes his lunchtime session at the Club,' he says. He hitches his trousers up at the knee and sits beside me, crossing his legs. An inch of bare white shin shows above his sock. 'Where's wor Angie, Mam? Is she not part of the welcoming committee?' His accent has coarsened, I notice, since he stepped through that front door, but I don't mind.

'Upstairs,' says his mother. She backs into the hallway and bellows: 'Angie! Howay down and meet Monica.' Putting her head around the door again she says, 'I'll get the kettle on shortly. Just let me get this cake out of the oven and knock up a few sandwiches.' She bellows again: 'Angie!' and there is movement upstairs.

'My other sister, Josie, should be over soon,' Bobby says. 'They always come for their tea on a Sunday.'

'The married one?'

'Aye,' he says, 'got a baby now as well.'

I can't help shuddering slightly. Will they be bringing it with them? I wonder. Well, of course they will. I give Bobby a tight smile. This is all somewhat overwhelming, I have to admit.

A girl appears in the doorway. Seventeen or so, at a guess. She stares at me sullenly. 'Here she is,' says Bobby. 'Angela: Monica. Monica: Angela.' She nods and I nod back. Not exactly a great welcome but so what. Females of that age don't interest me. Let's face it, females of any age don't interest me. Seems she is of the same mind. She perches on the piano stool.

We all sit twiddling our thumbs for a while, with Bobby attempting the odd hail-fellow well-met bluffery. His conversational openings fall flat, as might be expected when the recipients of his gambits are three teenagers. The girl rolls her eyes at his jokes and turns around to play *Chopsticks* on the piano; the *Beano*-reader picks his nose and scans his comic avidly; and the intellectual peers at me—maybe even leers at me—over his dog-eared paperback. It's D H Lawrence, I notice. *Sons and Lovers*. Doing it for his exams, I expect.

After ten or fifteen minutes of this awkwardness, Mother Wilson comes back in. 'Your dad's back,' she says. 'He's just putting his bike away. It's a wonder he can stay upright on it, after a session down the Club.'

'He doesn't drink that much, man,' Bobby says. 'He's a lightweight.'

I am startled when an older version of Bobby presents himself in the doorway. The same smiling bonhomie, the same blond mop—though greyer than Bob's—and the same fresh complexion, reddened by a couple of decades of boozing and being outside in all weathers. He sticks his hand out and comes to greet me. I make a half-hearted move to stand. 'Nah, nah, don't get up, pet,' he says, reaching down to shake my hand. 'By, you're a bonny lass.' He grins at Bob. 'Done well, there, son.'

I fear I may throw up if this continues but make a real effort to smile. Noooo, I'm saying to myself. I don't want this. I can't cope with this. I catch Bob's eye and he sees my alarm. He pats me on the knee. 'It's all right, Mon, none of us bite.'

Mrs Wilson pokes her head around the door again. 'Giz a hand with these sandwiches, Angie.' The girl slumps her shoulders and drags herself away from the piano. Thank God that tinkling racket has stopped.

*

When the older sister turns up, she is indeed accompanied by an infant, plus a husband, both of whom are called Simon. The kettle is duly boiled and we all troop through to the dining-room where the table is laid out with the cake and the sandwiches mentioned earlier. There are also home-made scones, open-topped baps featuring an egg and cress mixture and Penguin biscuits, encased in shiny blue and red wrappers.

'Eeh, I better make myself decent.' Mrs Wilson unties her pinny at the back and hooks the straps over her head. Her curly greying hair is caught up in it and Bobby goes to the rescue. 'Thanks, son.'

Nobody says 'FHB'—there is no scarcity at this table, so no need for the Family to Hold Back. They all dig in, including Bobby, and I modestly help myself to a triangle of ham sandwich.

'So, where is it you live, Monica?' says married sister Josie.

'Walker Road,' I say, 'between St Peter's and Ouseburn.'

'Ah right. Quite close to the town.'

I nibble my sandwich and nod.

'Do you work in Newcastle, then?' she goes on.

I take a moment to swallow. 'Usually. I'm only part-time... temporary... not doing much at the moment, really.' See? Work is the first thing people ask about when they meet someone new. Tedious.

'She's a property owner, is Monica,' Bobby says with a note of pride. 'Owns her own flat and the one above.'

'Eeh, that's smashin',' says Mrs Wilson.

'So she doesn't need to work full time.' Bobby adds.

'What do you do all day, then?' says Josie. 'When you're not working?'

I hate these conversations. I'm afraid I stutter a little when replying. 'Oh... I... I find things to do, you know. I read a lot.'

117

'I'd get bored, me, like,' says Simon—the husband, obviously. 'I like to be busy.'

I purse my lips into something resembling a smile.

Josie says, 'So do I. I'm not working at the moment, because of this little one.' She jogs the infant up and down on her knee. 'But I'd like to go back when he's a bit older. Get sick of my own company.'

That's because you've no imagination, I think. No rich inner life.

'I never worked,' says Mrs Wilson. 'Well, I worked enough at home. Hard work, an' all, looking after all this lot. Shopping, cooking, cleaning, washing, making their clothes. It's a full-time job.'

'You can get these new electric washing machines now, man,' says Simon. 'And vacuum cleaners.'

'I'm getting a washer,' says Josie. 'Need it for the nappies. It's coming next week.'

'Blummin' expensive,' says Simon.

'You young 'uns don't know you're born,' says her mother. 'Cold water in the back yard, when I had yours to wash.'

'Ye can even get knittin' machines,' says Simon. 'Cost an arm and a leg, mind.'

'Do you knit, Monica?' Mrs Wilson says.

I start at this. 'What? I mean … sorry?'

'Knit,' she says, louder, as if I'm a foreigner. She makes knitting movements with her fingers.

'No. No, but my Aunt Millicent taught me. I don't have much call for knitting.' I still have the wool and the needles she gave me, though.

'Are you more of a dress-maker, then? Sewing?'

'Not really, no…'

'I used to make all my own clothes,' says Josie. 'I'll start again, when I get some time. Make some romper suits for his lordship, here.' She puts her face close to the baby's and makes babbling noises.

'I made all their clothes when they were bairns,' Mrs Wilson says, glancing round the table at her offspring, the males of which are stuffing their faces. 'Have another sandwich?'

'Er... I...' She shuffles another ham triangle onto my plate, though I haven't finished the first one yet. 'Got to be quick with this lot around. Gannets, the lot of them.' All the males grin and carry on scoffing. Angie looks huffy. Josie helps herself to a bap.

'I'm feeding the baba myself,' she says, 'so I can eat what I like, these days.'

'Aye, Monica, dig in,' says Dad Wilson. 'Don't stand on ceremony.'

Jimmy wipes his nose on his sleeve and takes a scone. Tom has his book on his knees below table level; his eyes are fixed on it while he chews ponderously. Angie cuts her sandwich into smaller and smaller pieces. I recognize my own behaviour in this and hate her for it. Right at this moment I hate the lot of them.

'Did you see to the horses today?' Dad says to Bobby.

'Why aye. I was there first thing and I'll go over again later.' Bobby looks affronted.

'Just asking. Keep your hair on.'

'Well, I wouldn't not go, would I?' Bobby turns to his mother. 'Can I cut that cake now?'

'Here,' she says, wielding a carving knife, 'I'll do it.'

Josie notices Tom reading. 'Put that book away, Thomas. What bad manners, reading at the table. And when we've got guests an' all.'

'Got exams,' he mumbles through a wodge of bap. 'Anyway,' he goes on, giving me the sort of under-brow look Keith does so well, 'there's only one guest.'

Pedant.

'You can spare us half an hour out of your busy schedule,' Josie says. 'Manners cost nothing.'

Angie rolls her eyes. Jimmy snickers like one of the horses mentioned and tosses a piece of ham to the dog.

'You can shut up, an' all,' Josie goes on. 'Have you not got a hanky? And look at the state of those hands! Mam! Have you seen his hands? That's disgusting.'

Jimmy hides his paws under the table. Mrs Wilson shakes her head. 'Eeh, you need eyes in the back of your head to keep on top of this lot.'

'Eat your tea, Josie, and leave the lad alone,' Bobby says. 'Always was a bossy-boots,' he says to me in an aside.

She's probably a couple of years younger than me but she both looks and acts much older. If that's what marriage and babies does for you, I'll give it a miss, thanks.

Dad Wilson helps himself to the biggest slice of the cake now it's been cut. Angie picks up the knife and shaves herself off a paper-thin slice.

'Watch what you're doing with that knife,' Josie says. 'Mam, you cut it for her.'

'Oh honestly!' Angie glares at her sister. 'I am perfectly capable of cutting cake myself.'

If this is what families are like, I'm glad I don't have one. Jimmy picks up the knife as soon as Angie puts it down and waves it about like a Samurai sword, making swishing noises. 'Shoof shoof shoof.'

'Cut that out, lad,' says his dad, 'before you decapitate somebody.' He grins at me. 'What must you think of us, Monica.'

120

'She must think we're barbarians,' says Josie, dabbing the baby's brow with a flannel.

'I'm pretending I'm the ripper,' the boy says. 'Shoof shoof shoof.'

'That's enough!' Mr Wilson takes the knife away. 'You don't want to be like that cracker. It's awful what's gannin' on.'

'Aye,' Simon the husband agrees. 'It's not safe to be out.'

'I used to work down Dean Street,' Josie confides, as if she has inside information. 'In an insurance office.'

'Well, I had an interview at a place near there, once.' Angie is not to be outdone. 'The dole sent us.' She draws back in an aggrieved manner, as if the Labour Exchange had made a deliberate attempt to put her in danger. 'Didn't get it, thank heavens.'

'It's us fellers that need to be worried,' says Simon. 'The murderer's not interested in the ladies, it seems. Maybe he's one of those.' He flaps a limp hand, which raises knowing chuckles from the older males.

Mrs Wilson and Josie do synchronised tuts.

I eye the knife, smeared with strawberry jam, and clamp down the hysterical laughter that rises in my throat.

Chapter Sixteen

'I think they liked you, pet,' Bobby says as he walks me to Tynemouth station.

I say nothing but look at him in a manner he may well take for adoring. He has his arm around my shoulder and hugs me closer, so I'm stifled. I like him, I do. I more than like him. But his family. Any family. I'm torn.

This isn't me. This is not how I am. This soft, soppy female, ready to swoon into the arms of the first handsome man who comes along. I hate being like this—as though I'm blending with him, merging into him, becoming a mushy, amorphous mass with no separate existence. Where have my sharp edges gone? My brittleness? Where is my discrete self, my independence of mind, my sarcasm, my vicious humour, my underlying nastiness? I miss that in myself. I want myself back.

And yet, when I consider it honestly, I didn't much like who I was before. Oh dear, Monica, you silly cow, you're having an identity crisis. I can almost hear Charlie's voice berating me. Get yourself back on track. Away out and do something mad. Something bad. You know you want to.

Does it matter, in the end, what I do? It's all one, anyway. I remember my Shakespeare: there's nothing either good or bad but thinking makes it so.

*

I dress in dark clothes and slip into my new stilettos. I pack my flatties into my bag for walking home at dawn. As usual, I wait until the last bus back into town. It's almost empty, the few passengers tired and uninterested. People going home to the west end after visiting friends and relatives in the east end. Late night cleaners, shift workers—sleepy people on a slow bus. This may well be the last time, if things go well with Bobby, and it seems they might. Maybe for once I will allow my life to run smoothly. Be normal. God knows it's time. But I have to keep something for myself. Something to remember in the staid and stable future that may be ahead of me.

I get off near the bottom of Grey Street and wait until the trolley has trundled off and the few late pedestrians disperse before I turn the corner into Dean Street. I'm glowing with energy and power. I must have this. It's become essential to who I am. Not the full thing—I can stop before it gets to that stage. I'm confident in my abilities to play the part just right. I have a plan in mind. A way to get myself out of any awkward situation. I'll conjure up Charlie. Oh no! I'll cry, when the punter fumbles at my blouse. My boyfriend's here. Look! And I'll point into the darkness. That's all it'll take. He'll run off, I can guarantee it, even though he sees nothing, though I'm pointing at no one. They won't take the risk of an encounter with another man—boyfriend or pimp. They'll be off. I can do it more than once, if I feel like it. If I don't get enough of a thrill the first time. I have all night.

I linger at the bend at the bottom of Dean Street, opposite Dog Leap Stairs. I love the smell of the night—the river, rank and salty. Tide must be out. A quarter moon scuds through the clouds. Walking slowly, I go round into Side, find a doorway halfway along, so I can see both bridges, the platform of the Tyne Bridge outlined against the sky on one side, the sooty arch of the High Level Bridge on the other. My eyes adjust quickly to the darker doorway, where I can watch without being seen—until I'm ready to show myself. I'm aware of my heart pumping steadily, if a little fast; aware of my breath catching in my throat, my perfume, my pulse. So thrilling—hiding in the darkness, the cool nocturnal air a caress on the back of my neck.

Distant sounds as the city settles for the night: traffic noise quietening, the odd rev of a car engine, the clang of a fire engine far away. Sound carries on still nights like this. Laughter across the river—lads walking up Bottle Bank, home to Gateshead and beyond. Then the slow deepening silence as midnight passes. St Nicholas' Cathedral chimes the half past, the quarter to, then the single lonely toll of one o'clock.

I love this. I love this; this waiting, nerves tingling, trembling with anticipation. I don't even need a punter to entice, to play with. Being here, the thrill of it, is enough. But I'll wait a while. See who happens along. If I can tease and frighten one of them back to his wife and family, why not do it? I'm doing society a service.

I hear footsteps somewhere up Akenside Hill; somebody coming down from Pilgrim Street probably, past All Saints. Then there are more footsteps, on the opposite side, coming down from the Cathedral this time, echoing on the cobbles. I tense, my pulse fluttering, my bowels clenched. I'll wait until one of them goes past, moves on. Shrinking back into the shadows of the doorway, I hold my breath. What a thrill it is. What a thrill.

*

Monday morning. I am elated. Clear-headed. Different from how I usually am after a night down there. A Sunday night rather than a Saturday—different feel in the air, different atmosphere. Charged with something—or maybe that was just me.

I lie in bed late, though not because of a hangover. I barely drank anything last night. Didn't feel the need. Not the same, you see. More innocent. No need to block out the memory of some fumbling man and his bodily fluids. This is the way forward. I see it now. If I can keep this, then I can be with Bobby. Of course, it will have to be an occasional thing—a treat once in a while. And I'll have to think up an excuse. Staying over at Jan's, or with Aunt Mill. I'll come up with something when the time comes. Maybe I'll be able to sneak out and back without him knowing. Depends how heavy a sleeper he is; how early we go to bed. It makes it possible, though. Makes it bearable. The life I will have as a married woman. If it ever gets that far.

*

When I slept with Bobby, it was the first time since Charlie, and I considered myself an honorary virgin. Thirty-three months, I was celibate—longer than I was with Charlie in total. Charlie was my very first, if you don't count those others, and I don't count them because they do not count. They were not by choice and I was too young to know what was happening, except I did know, in some way. Knew it was wrong, knew it was hurting me, knew it was damaging me in a way far beyond physical pain. Manda said it was okay, though, that it was all right to do that. That I had to be a good girl for the nice men.

Afterwards, when they'd gone and we snuggled together in her big saggy bed, she made up for it. Cuddled and comforted me and told me how beautiful I was, how loved I was, how adorable they all thought me. When I was calmer, we would laugh and giggle together and play 'King of the Castle' until I grew too big. I remember the way the quoits and springs of the old metal-frame bed jangled. We didn't use her bed for… for the other thing. We kept it for us. It was our sanctuary. Our private place. The place where only she kissed me and wrapped her arms around me. Yes, she made up for what I suffered, to some extent. She loved me, I know that, despite everything.

Yet that night—the night they bombed St Peter's—something clicked in my head. I was eleven, coming into consciousness of my femaleness and my sense of self. Manda told me I might soon bleed and become a woman. A big girl, anyway, and we all know big girls don't cry. So that night, after the bomb fell, when I heard her whimpering as the dust settled and a last brick toppled from the cracked wall, whimpering in the same way I did when they made me do those things, the way I'd whimpered since I was barely more than a baby—something snapped in me. When I heard her faint cries coming from beneath the table, where she was trapped, that faint, weak voice stirred something in me and the thought entered my head that this was a way for her to experience something of what I felt. To cry softly, to protest without hope of preventing the inevitable, to plead for help with no expectation of a saviour—she must be feeling something of this, since her bleating cries were so like mine. So I let her feel it.

I wriggled out from under the table, filthy with plaster dust, hands and knees raw from crawling over the broken glass and crockery and splintered wood. I was out and free. I clambered over the rubble of our downstairs flat, the whole house now open to the sky, and wandered into the street.

Chaos all around. People shouting, screaming, groaning and yet with an eerie silence behind it all, after the noise of the raid. Flames lit up the night sky. A man with blood on his face, dazed and wandering like me. A child's legs, sticking out from a pile of bricks and broken lintels. Maybe someone I knew—a schoolfriend, a playmate.

I wandered away from Janet Street down to Walker Road, not too far from where I live now, I suppose. An Air Raid Warden stopped me but I told him nothing. Said I couldn't remember where I lived, couldn't remember who I'd been with. He handed me over to the Red Cross or St John's Ambulance people, who wrapped me in a blanket and fed me bread and marge with watery cocoa. I stayed numb and confused until it suited me to be otherwise. Or maybe I really was numb and confused. I no longer know what was the truth and what wasn't.

When the confusion, or my affectation of it, passed, I told someone my address and they sent off for information. They found Manda eventually but it was too late. Perhaps it was always too late and I could never have saved her. I'll never know. That's what I tell myself, though. When I need to.

Chapter Seventeen

A Sunday morning in June and we're out on Tynemouth Longsands taking Paddy for a walk. I've got my swimming costume on under my blue poplin dress and plan to have a dip, though Bobby has expressed concern. Not surprising, given the way we met.

'I'll be fine,' I tell him. 'I'm a good swimmer. I won't go out too far.'

The sky is the same colour as my summer dress and the sea is dark blue and sparkling. The perfect day. Wisps of clouds drift high in the sky and the beach is not too crowded yet, though it'll soon be packed, no doubt. I prefer it in winter when there's no one around but it will be lovely to have a swim.

Paddy leaps about chasing a ball, up and down the beach, in and out of the water. He has a smile on his doggy face, his tongue lolling, his breath hot when I reach down to pat him. I've become fond of Paddy. I don't quite know how that happened but who am I to question it on such a gorgeous day? I toss his rubber ball into the sea and it bobs happily on the waves. Paddy lunges after it with a yip, grabs it in his teeth and comes bounding back. When he shakes himself, glittering droplets fly from his coat, soaking the pair of us. Bobby grins at me, seemingly delighted that I'm having such a good time entertaining his dog.

I pause, a thought occurring to me. 'Is Paddy your dog, Bob?' I ask. 'Or is he the family pet?'

'He's mine, I suppose. But it's a fine line between that and him belonging to all of us.'

'So, would he live with us, if…?'

'Aye, if you like.' He throws the ball along the wet sand and Paddy races after it. 'I wasn't sure you were that keen. Didn't think you were a dog person.'

I ponder this. A dog, hmm? 'I'm probably more of a cat person, though I'm not big on animals generally.' I grin. 'Unless they're on a plate.'

'Aye,' he says, 'with a bit gravy.'

We chuckle together over this, and everything is perfect. Everything is wonderful—the sea, the sky, the sand, the dog. Even the families arriving and filling up the beach—mams and dads laden with picnic bags, kids with buckets and spades—none of it bothers me.

This is contentment.

We stroll hand in hand along the hard sand, dipping our toes occasionally in the wavelets frilling the edge of the water. All at once, I want to be in there. Submerged.

'Right, I'm going in now.' I unbutton my dress before he can dissuade me. I whip it over my head and he whistles when he sees my turquoise costume. Piped with white, it is the most flattering swimsuit I've ever had. Marilyn Monroe wears something similar on the cover of this month's Photoplay. I'm not as curvy as Monroe but Bob says I'm just as pretty, maybe even prettier. But then he would say that, wouldn't he? He's a man in love and biased. I rummage in my beach bag for my swimming cap and pull it on, making a face when the rubber tugs at my hair.

Bobby kisses me on the nose. 'Go on, then, Esther Williams,' he says. 'Get some synchronised swimming done.' He pats my behind.

'You've got to come as well,' I say. 'I can't synchronise on my own.'

It's his turn to make a face as he reluctantly strips off. He fastens a towel around his waist before he unbuckles his grey flannels. Dropping them, he looks around to check no one is watching, before wriggling out of his underwear and pulling his trunks on. I leave him to it and skip into the waves. How different this is from the last time I was here. How can life change so rapidly? A few short weeks and I've gone from a miserable neurotic wreck, to a woman in full command of her life, filled with joy and love. And all because of this lad, now dipping his feet in the sea, now cautiously venturing up to his calves.

'Come on!' I yell. 'Stop being such a cowardy-custard.'

He plunges in, going under and thrusting up, shining water streaming from his hair. We swim side by side, round and round, back and forwards, until at last he grabs me by the waist. 'Come here, mermaid. My mermaid.' We kiss and I taste the salt on his lips, feel the jolt of desire tingle through me, cling to him and sense the answering pulse in his body. He glances towards the shore and I know what's on his mind.

'No! Bobby! We can't.'

'Divven worry, pet,' he says, breaking into broad Geordie to amuse me. 'The watter's ower caad for that. I'm nae bigger than a shrimp, man.'

Paddy swims past, greeting us with his eyes. He turns and paddles towards the beach.

'You're shivering,' Bob says. 'Howay, let's dry off and warm up. You got that flask of tea in your bag?'

'I have indeed.'

Yes, the perfect day. This, surely, is happiness.

*

We run out of the sea, bodies tingling from the chilly water, and lie on our backs side by side, letting the sun dry us. Children splash in the shallows, the girls in cotton costumes sewn with shirred elastic to fit their sturdy bodies, the boys in minuscule trunks. Lads roll up their trouser bottoms for a plodge and lasses slip off their peep-toe sandals to join them. The older folk slump in deckchairs munching their egg and tomato sandwiches. The buzz of conversation and the shouts of the kids on the shuggy boats, is softened by the rush-rush of the sea. Bobby smells of brine and seaweed and I breath him in.

We rarely did this, Manda and me, but I recall the odd occasion. The excitement at the sight of the electric train with 'Coast' on the front approaching the station. My delight at the first sight of the sea and the cold crash of waves on my body. We didn't do it often enough. Aunt Mill never took me to the seaside. Too sandy and uncomfortable for her, but I came by myself when I was old enough. This is my element. How fortunate I am to be with a man who lives near the sea, who may one day make a home for me near the sea. If I'd known I could ever be this happy, I would never have done the things I did.

Does love last? I wonder, as I stare up at the almost cloudless sky. Will we still love each other like this in five years, or ten, or twenty? I have nothing to judge it by. Are Bobby's parents still in love? Maybe not in the full throes of passion, but I sense affection there. They don't seem to hate each other, anyway. I'm changing my views about men, somewhat. They aren't perfect and they aren't always strong, but they *can* feel. They do appear to be capable of feeling the softer emotions as well as the harsher ones. I've seen Bobby with dewy eyes when he gazes at me. I've seen his rough affection for his siblings, and his respect, as well as love, for his parents. I don't think I'm mistaken in this. It looks similar to the way it's portrayed in films, written of in books, if a little more prosaic and coarsened by reality. The only thing I have to judge love by is Manda's warmth and cuddles, but I was a child then, a very young child, for those comforts slackened off as I grew older. To tell the truth, I'm amazed that there is a thing that can be called love, pure love, untainted with other complex emotions.

I shake myself and sit up. Of course, it won't stay like this, that's impossible. It's too intense to last. It must fizzle out eventually. But might it change into another kind of love? Gentler, maybe deeper, longer lasting? I hope so. I do hope it will.

No, they aren't perfect, the males of the species, but maybe they are better than perfect. They are human. I see that now. I gaze down at Bobby, dozing beside me. Bob is ordinary, normal, and that normality is what it's all about, isn't it? If he grows older like his dad, he won't be too bad. Dad Wilson is genial, easy-going—Mother Wilson rules the roost, that's easy to see. Matriarchal society. There's no evidence he hits her or abuses her. These things are often hidden, I know, but she's cheerful and kindly in her manner towards him, and I don't imagine she'd be so relaxed if it were otherwise. So Dad must be okay to live with. I'm sure I'm reading the situation right. Come to think of it, that Josie rules her husband—Simon—with a rod of iron, from the look of things, and he doesn't seem to mind. Mother and daughter have picked the same type of man for their husbands. Bobby's made from the same mould. Men can be—well, nice, I suppose. I do hope I'm not fooling myself, being blind to something obvious. I don't think I am.

Wondering about Bob's dad makes me wonder about my own. That mystery man. He's not even on my birth certificate, I know that much. Never married my mother. I stare out into the North Sea, watching a ship on the horizon. In the past, I despised my father, blamed him for everything. For Manda being the way she was. For me being the way I am—the way I was, anyway. But what if I'm wrong? I made the assumption he hurt Manda, led her into doing what she did, or left her with no other option. But what if that's not how it was? What if Manda made him leave—either by telling him to get lost, or by her actions. What if she was the one in the wrong and my father was the innocent victim of her evil ways? I have no idea. No way of finding out. I could ask Aunt Mill how much she knows. Now there's a topic that's never been broached. I could say I need to know because it's only fair to Bob, if we're going to get serious, etc etc. It's her duty to tell me, if she knows anything. I'll go over and ask her. She surely cannot refuse me that.

Chapter Eighteen

The next Friday, we go to a nightclub. It's a place Keith and his police colleagues frequent, apparently, and we've been invited, presumably to seal our friendship as couples. Peggy and Al are coming too. We are now part of a circle, it seems. Bobby asked his friend Will, who's also a policeman, if he wanted to come along with his wife, but they couldn't get a babysitter.

We meet at eight outside the Carliol Club. Jan and Keith turn up almost immediately with Peggy and Al in tow. Introductions are made and I can see little Peggy is impressed by Bobby. She looks up at him with admiration in her eyes. When we're settled at a table with our drinks, the conversation flows—between Jan and Peggy and the two of us, anyway. Keith is his usual surly self, though, and gangly Al is subdued. I catch them both giving me curious looks— looks, that is, that have a touch of curiosity in them, as if they are puzzling something out. I find that odd and eye them surreptitiously. I'm far too happy to worry about them though and chat happily with Jan and Peggy, pleased to be showing Bobby off.

Bobby asks me up to dance and we swirl around the tiny dancefloor, swaying to David Whitfield, *Beyond the Stars*, our movements slow, gentle. Our steps are measured, backwards and forwards. The music is heady, enveloping, the

Mantovani strings sweep us along, and the Martini I've had promotes wellbeing and warmth. Yes, the night is warm, the room is hot, warmth in all senses suffuses me. The warm glow of tenderness, of passion, of love. All that went before is brushed aside, the slate wiped clean. *Tabula rasa*, if I remember my smattering of Latin. The blank page, that's what I am. My life began again on that chilly morning at Tynemouth Sands. I can't go back. I won't go back. I've decided. No more Dean Street for me, however thrilling it is. Last week was the last time. No more waiting in the shadows for the right mark to come along. That's all done with now. My new life with Bobby will be enough.

We sit down and after a few minutes Jan and Keith also come back to the table. Peggy and Al are still dancing.

'Phew,' says Jan, wafting her face with her palm. 'I'm boiling. Should we have a few minutes in the ladies, to cool off?'

'Okay,' I say. I too, could do with splashing my face, so off we trot like good little girls. We pause by an open fire-escape to get a breath of air. The night is balmy and there are stars above the sordid barrel-filled yard. At least, I think there are. I may be romanticising. The seedy backyard is transformed in my eyes. I see beauty in ugliness, the sacred in the profane. I've been touched by something wonderful and Jan sees I'm bursting with joy and pleasure.

'He's lovely, Bob,' she says. 'Such a nice lad.' She laughs. 'You are so smitten, Mon, it's seeping out of your pores.'

'Oh, that's sweat,' I say, deliberately bringing myself back to earth before I float off into dreamland. I'm in love! I want to shout, but don't.

'You're in love, aren't you?' Jan says, reading my mind and I'm incapable of keeping the huge grin off my face. 'Mon-ica's in lo-ove. Mon-ica's in lo-ove,' Jan chants. She hugs me before I see it coming, though I probably wouldn't have avoided it even if I had. 'He's in love with you, too. You can see it a mile off.' She plants a kiss on my forehead, standing on tiptoe to do it. 'Good for you, pet. It's about time. I'm so pleased for you.'

Right now, I am in love with everyone and everything—the world, the universe, the entire population of the earth. This is my moment. Now, I will fly. My soul, if there's such a thing, soars into the mid-blue night sky. Translucent clouds shine—on my horizons, if not on the real ones—and the nights are short and filled with light. There is magic in the air.

We visit the ladies and do what we have to do, splash our faces, reapply powder and lipstick, then head back to the table. Jan's eyes are shining and I know mine must be, too. Her eyes are shining for me and so will Bobby's be, when he sees me returning to him. The look he gives me sometimes is toe-curling in its adoration.

It's a disappointment, therefore, when he doesn't look up as we approach. His eyes are downcast and he's turning his glass round and round on the damp table top. Keith is the one who is looking at us, watching us from under lowered brows, me in particular. His dark eyes are unreadable apart from a hint of hostility—hostility I thought I saw earlier but dismissed as imagination.

Jan senses something is amiss. 'What's happened?' she says. 'What's the matter with you pair?' She's still bouncy and lighthearted but there's anxiety in her voice.

I say nothing but watch Bobby closely. He still hasn't looked at me and the shock of that has set me shaking. I concentrate on his hands as he turns his glass round and round. Attractive hands and clean nails, considering his job. Gentle and soft. He wears gloves at work, he's told me, huge leather gauntlets. Round and round and round he turns the glass.

'Keith?' says Jan. 'Is one of you going to tell us what's up? You look like somebody's died.' She attempts a laugh.

'Oh, a few people have died, 'Keith says, 'in the time you've been away. What is it? One every second somewhere in the world?'

'Cheerful,' says Jan, still trying to lift the mood.

Bobby finally looks up. 'D'you mind if we go?' he says, not catching my eye. 'Or… well, you can stay, if you want but I'm gonna have to go.'

'What?' I say. 'What is it? Has he…?' I shoot a glance at Keith. What can he have said? What does he know?

'I'm not feeling too grand,' Bobby says. 'I need to get out of here. Are you coming?' He stands and I see his fists are clenched, his jaw too. 'Actually, no,' he goes on. 'You stay. You stay here but I've got to get out for some air.' He strides off across the dancefloor, which is half empty, and is soon at the other side and out the door.

I stare at the table and at his unfinished drink. A pulse starts up in my temple and a tremor runs the length of me. It crosses my mind to rush after him but no, I won't do that. If he doesn't want me with him, fair enough. His loss. Ah but no, it's my loss. My terrible loss. I sink into my chair.

'What just happened?' Jan says. 'For God's sake, Keith—what happened?'

I raise my head to see Keith's reaction. He shrugs, twists his mouth. 'Told him a couple of things he needed to know.'

Janice's face reddens. 'You told him…? What? What did you tell him? God, Keith, what have you done?'

He doesn't answer her but instead directs his response at me. 'You've been seen, Monica,' he says, 'by a reliable witness. Down Dean Street, late at night.'

'What?' Jan says.

Keith turns his gaze towards her. 'And here is that witness,' he says, as Peggy and Al come up behind her. 'Right, Al? And neither of us can think of any reason why a woman would be down there at that time of night, unless…' He pauses. '…she was on the game.'

*

Not quite ten o'clock and I'm home. No point in hanging around since the evening has been curtailed. Though the night air is mild, I am cold. Cold with a crisp clarity that pierces my brain and chases away the fog. I slip off my wrap and let it slide to the floor, tossing my little beaded clutch bag down on top of it. I was seen—by Al, it seems—last week when I ventured to my old stamping grounds for one last look. One last chance to choose a mark, to reel him in. It was only a game. All I was doing was laying the past to rest. Nothing else. I was fishing but I let the fish go. Nothing came of it that night. I was untouched, virginal, innocent, and I touched no one else.

I kick my wrap and bag furiously across the floor. The bag explodes against the wall, spilling lipstick and mirror, handkerchief and comb. Coins roll into the corners and beads scatter like buckshot. I throw back my head and howl. Deep from within come discordant notes of despair, echoing around the dark room. My eyes are dry. I have no tears, only rage. I snarl and scream and stamp until a movement upstairs makes me pause and I stop my wailing. Back where I started. That's it, then. Back where I started. There will never be another Bobby. I'll make sure of that.

No, nothing came of that night last week—but this night… this night is young. This night I will not be seen, not be recognized in any way.

I change quickly, a sudden thrill of anticipation trembling to my fingertips. Despite this excitement my hands are steady enough—or will be when necessary. Off comes my new dress, so pretty and feminine, and on go the black clothes so I won't stand out in dark. The skirt is split to the thigh, the blouse low-cut, showing a hint of lacy brassiere, the heels high and spiked. I rummage in a drawer for the unfinished pack of Craven 'A' I know is in there. I've not needed a cigarette for weeks now—either for show or for comfort, so they'll be dry, a little stale, maybe, but they'll do. The bottle of rum is more than half full but that's for later, when I get back. It's also left over from that other life—the one I thought I'd left behind. There'll be enough.

I catch a late bus into town. My plastic mac covers my outfit and a headscarf hides the wig I'm wearing, from too close an inspection. There are the usual dozing passengers on the bus, going home. I'm simply one of them, heading back to Denton Burn for all they know. They don't notice me getting off at Mosely Street and if they do, I don't care. I could be going for the last bus from Worswick Street, heading back to the sticks somewhere.

The wig makes me sweat and I'm glad of the cooling night air. It's a cheap one, a dark brown nylon thing I saw advertised on the back page of *Women's Own* for 39/11d. Had it a while now. Overpriced for what it is—no great quality to it, but it'll do. In the dark it'll pass and in the dim light of the bus it's not obvious. Tonight, I must not be obvious. My bright blonde hair must not give me away this time. I'll be safe anyway—no Keith on duty tonight and no Al either. No one to recognise me and any description of me will be of a dark-haired woman. I'll be safe, though a slight hint of danger adds a salty tang to the taste of the night. It is the condiment for the meat to come.

*

I see him as soon as I reach the corner of Sandgate, there under the High Level Bridge. The night is clear and calm but there's no one else around that I can see. He spots me, nods and we're on. That's all it takes. We go off to perform the usual rites.

Good. Tonight, I'm happy with a fast result. No lingering in the way of prying eyes. The thrill will come later.

Chapter Nineteen

Saturday afternoon, lying in bed recovering, the empty rum bottle on the floor. Could have done with a little more alcohol, but my head is pounding, anyway, and I'm disoriented. I may lie here forever, unmoving, arms by my sides, staring at the ceiling. Faint music throbs above—*Listen on Saturday*—probably, on for the kids. Radio's turned down low, thankfully. I'd be banging on the ceiling if it wasn't, though after my shrieks last night perhaps I should allow some leeway. What I'm feeling is apathy. Anti-climax. My veins don't trill with the usual high-pitched hum and my excitement is abated, never really got going this time. The thrill was nonexistent and the work was simply that—work. Toil. Tedium. I may as well stop altogether if there's to be no spark to it—no 'buzz', no 'kick', as they say. I got more of a thrill last week when I did nothing but watch and tease. Well, it's probably time to call a halt anyway, now that I've been seen. No point in prolonging it—too dangerous, though the money will be a miss. I'll have to call on Aunt Mill more often—either that or, horror of horrors, get a job.

I'm pondering these matters when the knock comes on the door and, for a moment, I'm terrified that it is 'the knock'. I look around the room—everything is in order. I soaked my plastic mac in the bath last night and put it on a hanger. I'm always good that way, I do it automatically, even through the haze of the afterburn, even when I'm barely aware of what I'm doing. Discipline, you see—got Aunt Mill to thank for that. Discipline and routine—once they are instilled into you, it comes naturally.

The knock comes again. Probably Janice wanting to see I'm still alive and haven't hurled myself into the sea again. I won't answer. Can't be bothered. She's bound to be on Keith's side and Keith is the enemy. No more fraternisation. The letterbox rattles as it's pushed open. 'Monica?' It's not Jan, it's Bobby. I sit up. The shout comes again. 'Mon? are you in there? Open the door.'

I debate the point and my thinking is clear, despite my banging hangover and lack of interest in life and all its doings. I won't answer and that's that.

'Mon,' he shouts louder. 'Come on. I know you're in there. Open the door.'

Damn him. He'll have the neighbours out soon and I don't want that. I get up and push the rum bottle under the bed with my foot. It rolls away into a far corner. Naked, I slip on a loose dress rather than my dressing gown. It slides over my damp body, catching on my nipples, on the way down. Erect nipples? I even shock myself sometimes.

'Mon. I'm sorry,' he calls, as I cross the front room. When I open the door, he's slumped against the frame, all six foot of him, looking somewhat hangdog. He even shuffles his feet. 'I'm sorry,' he says again. 'Can I come in?'

Pulling the door open, I step away and he follows me into the dim room. I don't bother opening the curtains. There's enough sunlight straining through the worn cloth for us to see each other. God knows what I look like—death warmed up probably—but I don't care. He's had the best of me, now he can have the worst—though my true worst is considerably worse than this.

He's staring at me and I realise he can see my contours and protrusions through the thin cotton dress. He glances to the bedroom door. Oh? He thinks I'm with someone? Because I'm aroused? What fools men are. 'I'm alone,' I say, my voice sharp, my manner curt. I go into the kitchen for a glass of water, running the tap till it's cold, making the old pipes judder.

'Can we talk about…you know…?' he says when I step back into the front room.

I lift my shoulders. Perch on an armchair. 'Sit down,' I say, 'you're making the place look untidy.' I see he's surprised at my manner. He's not used to this aspect of me. Well, he'd better get used to it if he wants to hang around.

He slumps on the couch. 'Look,' he says. 'Last night…' He spreads his hands, palms up. 'I didn't leave because of you. I left because I'd have bloody-well punched that Keith, if I hadn't.'

I say nothing, merely observing him dispassionately.

'If I'd stayed another minute, I'd have smashed his smarmy face in. Him and that long drink of water who backed him up.'

I still say nothing. I notice a stray bead from my bag, on the lino beside his feet. Missed it when I was tidying up last night.

'I didn't believe him, Monica—course, I didn't. But what he said… what he told me… Riled me up something rotten. I had to leave. Didn't want to get into a fight with a polis. I'd get pinched, even if he was off duty. His pals would make sure of that.' He points his face at me—his fresh, pink, open face—appealing to me to forgive him. It's a face I thought I loved. A face that brought me delight when I saw it close up and anticipation when I saw it in the distance. A face I cupped my hands around. A face I kissed with passion.

A stupid, pathetic, gormless face. 'You left me to deal with it on my own. People were staring at me, smirking, even if they didn't hear what was said. I needed…' My voice falters, curse it. 'I needed… an arm around me. Words of comfort… to know you were on my side…' I bang my empty glass down on the coffee table. 'I got nothing. I had to face Keith and Al alone, with their insinuations. I had to walk out of there, on my own, with people laughing at me. Poor lass, her boyfriend's stormed off and left her. Yes, I heard someone actually say that.'

'I'm sorry.' He puts his head in his hands.

Sorry he may be, but when it counted, he was gone. Our first hurdle and he tripped on it. Left me to face the disgust and triumph on Keith's face; the embarrassment on Al's.

He lifts his head and he's red in the face and there's a glint of a tear in his eye. 'But why did he say it? What was he playing at? Why the hell would he say something like that… if…'

'If?' I say. 'If what? If it wasn't true?'

'No… I don't mean…' He shakes his head. 'I love you, Monica. I want to know the truth, that's all.'

My heart is so hard, my carapace brittle. 'I'll tell you the truth,' I say. 'The truth is that Keith Burgess is a nasty so-and-so… and he's always hated me. Doesn't want his darling wife associating with the likes of me. I'm not good enough for them and their fancy new middle-class ways.'

'But why would he say… that? I mean, why say something like that?'

'Because Janice must have told him…' and I know this for certain now '…that I was made to do things as a child. Horrible things.' I should have realised earlier, remembering how she blushed when Keith said he'd told Bobby things he thought he should know. She thought he'd told him about

Manda and my childhood activities. So much for secrets between friends. She betrayed me the first chance she got.

'What things?'

I look him in the eye and can't keep the contempt off my face or out of my voice. 'I was forced to participate in… sex, sex things…' I am brutally honest. 'By my mother. As a very young child. Will that do?'

He's horror-struck. 'Your mother? She made you…? No.'

I smile and nod. 'Yes, astonishing, isn't it? But I survived. Here I am, perfectly normal and not filled with hatred and anger at all.'

'I'm so sorry,' he says, and that lurking tear rolls down his cheek.

I can't stand the sight of men crying. What have they got to cry about? I stand up. Go and get more water and swallow a couple of aspirin. He's on his feet when I come back.

'Monica. Mon…' He moves to wrap his arms around me but I back away.

'No. Don't touch me. I'm not ready for that yet.'

He lets his arms hang slack by his sides, the picture of misery. 'I don't know what to say,' he says, all puppydog eyes and pathos. 'I can't believe it…'

'Believe what you like.'

'I don't mean that. I mean—it's just so blummin' difficult to understand.'

'That's the trouble. Anybody would find it hard to understand. That's why I've never said anything. Till now.'

'And it definitely happened? You didn't…?'

'Imagine it? No, I didn't.'

He still looks bewildered. Something occurs to me. 'And I didn't invent it either, to make you feel sorry for me.' I glower at him from under lowered brows. 'It's true. I'm telling you the truth.'

'I'm sorry. I'm not doubting you. Honestly, Mon. It's… I can't… I mean… Oh God, I'm so sorry.' He shakes his head making his fair hair fall loose over his brow and I almost—almost—feel sorry for him. I know it's a lot to take in.

I make us a pot of tea and we sit down again, both silent for a while, contemplating our own thoughts. Eventually, he lifts his head. 'What did she make you do? Your mother.'

My eyes are deadened when I look at him. 'If you're after salacious details, you can forget it,' I say. 'I'm not raking up my miserable past for your titillation.' My intention is to hurt, to bruise, to draw blood if I possibly can.

'Mon. You know that's not the reason. Don't be like that.'

'Like what?'

'You're being so… so hard. It's not like you.'

Hah, little does he know. Charlie taught me to be hard. Weakness was not tolerated in that partnership. That was a lesson I learned well, as Charlie found out to his cost.

'I don't want to cause you more pain,' Bobby goes on. 'You don't have to tell me about it, if you don't want to.' He sniffs and brushes his hand under his nose. 'I should know, though, shouldn't I? So I can help you through it.'

'I am through it,' I say, and I'm starting to believe that. Something has changed. I've been through the furnace and come out the other side, stronger. I'm more assured now, have a clearer sense of myself. I sip my tea. My headache has gone and I'm calm and clearheaded. Powerful. 'I am through it,' I repeat. 'It's over. It's in the past.'

'It's something we should talk about, though,' he says, 'if we're going to be… you know.'

'What?'

'Married.'

Chapter Twenty

Bobby looks surprised as if he wasn't expecting that word to come out of his mouth. 'Ah, what a mess I've made of it. I should have asked properly. Should I go down on one knee?'

'Don't you dare!'

He's crestfallen. Looks as if he might cry again. 'You mean… you don't want me to ask? Ever?'

'Oh, for heaven's sake, Bobby, this isn't the time.' What on earth is he thinking? So much for romance.

'Ah, no,' he says. 'Yes. No. I mean… of course it isn't. I know.' He clunks himself on the side of the head. 'Dozy bugger, me. That's thick coalmen for you.' He tries to make light of it, forcing a smile, but his heart's not in it. He's so miserable, so down-hearted, it's plain on his face. He looks idiotic, and I want to laugh. I turn away so he can't see the mirth in my eyes. Silly so-and-so. Charlie would never have acted like this, been so vulnerable. He never allowed me to get one over him—not until that last time. But he didn't see that one coming.

I open the curtains as Keith's old Rover rattles up outside. Oh no. What does he want? I relax slightly when Jan gets out and Keith pulls away. She spots me at the window and gives me a half-hearted wave but I don't wave or smile back. I wait until she knocks before going to the door.

'I got Keith to drop me off,' she says, 'because we need to clear the air.' I let her in. 'Oh,' she says, when she spots Bobby on the settee. 'Bob. Didn't know you'd be here.'

He nods to her but I give her my deadeye look, which I'm perfecting of late.

'Well, of course I didn't know. How could I? Haha.' She sputters on like this for a minute but neither of us say anything to help her out. 'I wanted to... well... apologise, really.'

My my, two people turning up at the door to apologise, in one day. That must be some kind of record.

She licks her lips—hasn't forgotten to apply her red lipstick, I note—and clears her throat. 'Could I have a glass of water?' She eyes the teapot. Still saying nothing—why should I make it easy for her?—I get another cup and saucer and bring her a glass of water. She glugs it down while I pour the tea. 'Thank you.'

Well, isn't everyone so polite and formal today?

'I know you must be mad at Keith,' she says, placing the glass carefully on the coffee table.

My glance is enquiring. No! Really? Why? I sit next to Bobby on the couch and point Jan to the armchair, where she perches. Bobby glowers at her and still neither of us speak. She bites her bottom lip and some of the lipstick coats the edge of her teeth. She forces a smile and spreads her hands like Bobby did, appealing to both of us.

'I have to apologise for Keith,' she says. 'He was out of order saying what he did. Al must have been mistaken. He can't have seen you...' She falters and Bobby steps in.

'He wants to be careful what he goes around accusing people of,' he says. 'If I'd stayed a minute longer last night, I'd have...' He clenches his fists.

'I was mortified,' Jan says, 'and so was Peggy. I don't know what's got into Keith lately, and Al, well…' She shakes her head. 'I don't know why… what …' She looks at me. 'Say something, Mon.'

'What do you want me to say? "Oh, don't worry about it, it's nothing, an easy mistake to make?"' Oh, how I enjoy watching her squirm.

'Course not.' She takes a sip of her tea, which is cold and stewed by now, though she drinks it down as if it's nectar. I keep my eyes on her, increasing her discomfort. She's apologised for Keith, which is something he should have done himself, but she's not mentioned her own peccadillo. I decide to remind her.

'So, you told Keith everything I told you at the gallery. About me and Manda. Things I told you in confidence.'

She flushes and I have to tense my facial muscles to stop myself grinning. Red of face, lips and teeth. Poor Janice.

'I'm so sorry. So so sorry.' She blinks, frowns, realising she hasn't actually told me about spilling the beans to Keith. 'How did you know?'

'I guessed. I saw it in your face, last night. You thought that's what he was going to come out with.'

She chews at her lips again. 'Sorry. I swore him to secrecy. I didn't think he'd say anything. Well, he didn't, did he? Not about that.'

She's trying to justify telling him. Passing on my private information is fine as long as he keeps it to himself, is it?

'No,' I snap, 'but it added verisimilitude to the story Al gave him.' Verisimilitude. That's an Aunt Mill word. I turn my laugh into a cough.

Bobby twists his hands, straightens his tie. 'I'm sickened by what Monica's told me… about her mother,' he says. 'Sick to my guts. How anybody could…'

'I know,' says Jan. 'I know. So was I. Horrified.'

'When you've both finished picking over the ruins of my childhood,' I say, 'can we move on?'

Bobby pats my thigh. 'Sorry, pet.'

I stand up, mainly to stop him touching me, and surprise myself by what I say next. 'I have some news.' I smile down at him. 'We have some news.'

They're both in the dark, and look it. I glance from one to the other of them, finally settling my loving gaze on Bobby. 'We're getting married.'

Now they are both stunned. Bob obviously doesn't believe what he's just heard and isn't sure whether to be happy or terrified. Janice is clearly what is known as 'gobsmacked'.

'M-married?' She turns to Bob. 'Well I never.'

'Bob's only just this minute asked me,' I say, affecting pride, joy, love. 'I was about to give him his answer when I saw you outside.' Sitting down next to him again, I take his hand. 'The answer is yes. Yes, of course, I'll marry you.' I flutter my eyelashes and try to force out a tear. They both sit there open-mouthed.

Bobby pins a grin on his chops. 'Ah… that's… that's… Aah.'

I toy with his fingers like a coy schoolgirl, simpering up at him every now and then.

Janice's eyes are perfect circles. 'I'm so pleased,' she says, sounding anything but. 'So happy for you. Both.' She gives Bobby a wary look. His expression is that of a man on his way to the gallows, trying to show appreciation for his last meal. Perhaps he was somewhat hasty in his cack-handed proposal earlier.

But no, he pulls himself together. 'Ah, Monica, I'm over the moon.' He plants a kiss on my nose. 'This calls for a celebration. Have you got any of that rum left?'

I grit my teeth. 'No. I had a drop last night,'—now there's an understatement— 'and I knocked the bottle over.' I fix him with a sad smile. 'I wasn't very happy, you know…'

'I'm sorry, pet,' he says. 'I should never have gone off and left you like that.' His fists clench again. 'So why hasn't he come to apologise? Burgess?' He lights a cigarette and blows a stream of smoke towards Jan. 'Where's your husband? It's him who should be grovelling on his knees to Monica.'

'I know,' says Jan, 'but he's had to go to work.' She sighs. 'Of course, you won't know… it's not common knowledge yet. They've found another one.'

'Another one what?' Bob says, frowning.

I go very still.

'Body. Down by the quayside. Looks like that killer's been at it again.'

Chapter Twenty-One

'Well, that goes to show what rubbish your man was spouting,' Bobby says. 'Monica is much too sensible to go wandering about down Dean Street when there's a lunatic on the loose.' He drapes his arm around me 'You're not daft, are you, pet? No chance you'd be putting yourself in danger. Bloody idiot.' This last is directed at Keith, presumably.

Jan examines her fingernails—also blood-red, like her lips. Left over from last night, though I can't say I noticed then. 'No,' she says, 'I suppose you're right.'

'Course I'm right.' Bobby sticks his cigarette into the corner of his mouth and stands up. 'I'm away to the...' He nods in the direction of the back yard. Too much tea, maybe. Or probably the couple of pints of Dutch courage he's had before coming here.

Jan is still examining her nails and biting her lip. 'Are we all right, then?' she says. 'Friends?'

I shrug. 'Of course. Not your fault your husband is quick to jump to the wrong conclusion. Or has colleagues who do.'

'I spoke to Peggy this morning. She's mortified as well.'

'So she should be.'

'I didn't interrupt anything, did I?' She makes an 'oops' face. 'Were you two...?'

I remember I'm half-dressed and reach for a cardigan that's draped over the arm of the couch. One of Aunt Mill's home-knitted creations and too warm for today. 'No. You didn't interrupt anything like that,' I say, pulling it on anyway. 'I was having a lazy day and threw this dress on when Bob turned up to make his apologies. I did not want to give him the wrong idea by sitting around in my dressing-gown.'

'You seem to have made up now, though. Getting married? That's fast work.'

'Why wait?' I say. 'If we're both sure.'

'But you've barely known each other five minutes—' She stops when she sees my expression. 'Well, sometimes it's like that, isn't it? Love at first sight.'

Bobby comes back in. Hitching up the knees of his trousers, he sits down on the couch. 'Aye,' he says. 'That's what it was. Love at first sight. For me, anyway. Who could resist such a lovely mermaid?' His tone is jocular, if somewhat forced. He's not laying his emotional life open by saying this, though he is the most emotional man I've ever known. I didn't know men could feel things that deeply. Not lovey-dovey things anyway. I thought it was only women who cried and cared—or gave the impression of caring. Barely saw a man cry before today, when Bob started sniffling. That's why I find it so unpleasant, I suppose. Disconcerting to see tears in his eyes. Against the natural order of things. Only time I saw men weeping, as far as I remember, was that night the bombs fell. They had some excuse then.

I won't marry him. Couldn't resist putting them both on the spot, that's all. I'm sickened by him, if I'm honest. His actions last night, or lack of them. Betrayal, that's what it was, and though he says he left in case he started a fight, that wasn't the only reason. He believed what Keith said, what Al added weight to with his embarrassed *ums* and *ahs*. He still does, though he may not realise it. Deep down Bobby believes what Keith said. As well he might, since it's partially true.

Of course, I wasn't doing what they imagine I was doing. Okay, Al did see me last week—that was unfortunate but I certainly wasn't doing what Keith said.

I blink when I come back to consciousness of the room. Bobby and Janice are talking about the murders.

'It's not safe for decent folk to be out,' Bobby is saying. 'How come they've not caught him yet? Surely, they should have some leads before now. How long is it since the first one?'

'Last year, I think,' Jan says. 'Before Christmas? Yes, that's right because Keith had some leave cancelled.'

I say nothing, remembering the dark days of last winter. What a year it's been. Floods and now drought. This summer is so hot, the reservoirs are drying up. The water is shrinking in the lakes and ponds. I hope—

'What do you think?' Jan says to me.

'What? Sorry, I was away with the fairies.' I put on a vapid smile to give the impression I was daydreaming about wedding dresses and honeymoons, making my eyes dewy and distant.

'Hanging,' she says. 'Should it be abolished?'

I have to admit this startles me. 'Janice! You're the one normally objecting to gruesome subjects.'

'I know. But the murders are gruesome, so why shouldn't the punishment be, too?'

'They're saying that Ruth Ellis woman'll definitely hang next month,' Bobby says. 'Though there's a campaign to stop it.'

'I know,' says Janice. 'Keith's been on about it. He thinks it should go ahead. "An eye for an eye," he says.'

'Very Old Testament,' I say. 'Didn't know Keith was particularly religious.' I give a little laugh. 'And you, Mrs Burgess, as a Catholic, should be full of Christian love and forgiveness.'

She tuts. 'You know I don't bother with all that. It was only me mam who ever went to church. Dad was never interested. Even Mam isn't exactly devout these days.'

'Well, I've always been a heathen.' I take a deep breath. 'Manda—as you can imagine—wasn't one for godliness. Aunt Mill goes to church at Easter and Christmas but that's more for show—and a bit of social interaction.'

'Times are changing,' Bobby says, as if it's a deep significant thought. 'People don't bother with church so much these days. Aye, the old ways are dying out— sometimes for the better, sometimes for the worse.' He nods at this sage pronouncement, like a wise old man.

Oh no, I'm not going to marry this idiot. I'll have to do something to get out of it. Something outrageous to frighten him off. Shouldn't be difficult.

*

Bobby hangs about trying to outwait Jan. I see him giving her the evil eye, presumably willing her to go. Jan is oblivious though, and offers to make more tea. I let her, and even find a few biscuits at the back of the cupboard for them. It amuses me to see them pitted against each other, both determined to be the one who gets me alone. What fun it is to be so much in demand. I don't care which of them wins the staring contest—makes no odds to me. I haven't yet reached the stage of wanting rid of both of them and there's nothing I need to do today, so if they want to hang around providing entertainment, let them. I've not forgiven either of them and am unlikely to do so any time soon. It's amusing to see them imagine all is well between us when it very much isn't.

The afternoon is wearing on and I know Janice is going to suggest a visit to the chip shop again soon. She can't keep away from the place, despite her middle-class pretensions. She can forget it though; I couldn't eat a thing.

Bob, of course, is hoping to get me alone and into bed to 'make up'. He can forget that as well. There'll come a point, probably within the hour, when I snap and shoo them both out but, for the moment, I'm happy to observe the dance between them, the one trying to outwit the other. They're like puppets and I'm pulling the strings. Any time I want to cut those strings, I can do so. Permanently if I want to.

Chapter Twenty-Two

We've started to plan the big day. I said I didn't want a huge wedding—don't want a wedding at all, if it comes to that—but with the size of Bobby's family, huge appears to be the order of the day. Seems he has dozens of aunts and uncles and cousins to invite, to say nothing of the odd grandparent clinging onto life in a hovel somewhere. Won't be many from my side, of course. Aunt Mill—I suppose she'll have to be invited. Janice? She'd kill to be there but she'll want Keith to be with her. I'll have to ponder about that. There's no one else, so the church is going to look ridiculous. All the Wilson lot crammed into one side and my side empty.

Still, it's what Bob wants—what his mother and that Josie want, more like. I'd go for a registry office, myself. Or elopement, if that were possible. Do people still go to Gretna Green?

I'd like a stylish dress, though. Aunt Mill can be called on to help out there. I fancy oyster satin, sleek and figure-hugging. Or should I go for a full skirt, ballerina length, with net petticoats underneath? Mmm, yes, silk taffeta in a luscious clotted cream. I saw the material in Bainbridge's. Could have it made up. Oh, I've just had a thought—who's going to give me away? Could ask Aunt Mill. I can't help but chuckle at this. Which of her dresses would she wear? The green or the brown? Maybe the funereal black would reappear. I'll have to persuade her to buy something new. Come to think of it, Aunt Mill is going to have to pay for the do afterwards, since it's the bride's family who are responsible for all that. Well, she can afford it.

I pull myself up. What am I thinking? It's not going to happen. I'm not marrying Bobby. I'm not going to become Mrs Monica Wilson, Coal Merchant's wife. I deflate. I was becoming rather enamoured of the idea. What a fool I am sometimes. On the other hand, maybe I should go ahead. Marry him. See where it takes me. The wedding day will be fun, won't it? I don't care to be the centre of attention but it's expected and I can prepare myself for it. I know I'm an emotional mess sometimes but I've nerves of steel when I need them. It'll be worth it for the laugh. Seeing them all there in their finery, done up like dog's dinners for my wedding. And all the time I'll know, secretly, it's a sham. A farce. Unless, of course, I want it to be real.

Bobby plans to ask his brother, Tom—the brainbox—to be his best man. He considered asking his friend, Will, who I've not yet met, but thinks keeping it in the family is best. He's all for family, Bobby. I might be too, if I had one. Then again, would I? After meeting his, I'm not so sure. I'm still debating whether or not to involve Janice. Bob wants his sisters to be my attendants—Angie as bridesmaid and Josie as matron of honour. Janice would be sick with jealousy at that. I might invite her purely to see her face. I haven't agreed to the sisters yet. I want Bob to believe I have other friends I could ask. Though he'll find out I haven't, soon enough. Maybe I could hire some.

Then there's the venue. Bobby—again, read his mother and Josie—suggests a church hall in Shields near where they live. Suggesting the attached church for the ceremony as well. I'm not a churchgoer and have no desire to try persuading some reluctant vicar to let me have the use of his church and his services, so I'm happy to let them do the running. Then again, Aunt Mill may have her own ideas, if she's paying. Her odd attendances at Christmas and Easter must stand her in some stead, and Aunt Mill can make anyone do anything. Forest Hall for the ceremony? It's a pleasant enough church and I used to be dragged there with her on special occasions, so in a sense it's my church too. Then again, if the Wilsons arrange it all, maybe I can get them to pay for it too. Don't want Aunt Mill's cash being wasted.

Is this all getting too ridiculous? Am I letting the idea run away with me? It's not going to happen. I can't get married. Can't give up my freedom. Yet what does that freedom amount to? Maybe I'll gain more than I give up. You daft cow, Monica, you're never going to get hitched. I hear Charlie's sarcastic voice. Give the poor lad a break and call it off now. You'll only ruin his life, like you ruin everything.

I've been remembering Charlie a lot recently. Probably because I'm now with Bobby and things are moving forward so fast. I can't help comparing the two of them. Bobby so sweet and gentle, if a little wet, and Charlie so spiteful, yet exciting.

I keep remembering that day. The day we drove up to the old gibbet at Elsdon on the wilds of the moor. It was a filthy day. Lovely when we set out—though windy—but the rain came on when we were halfway there. We'd done nothing but bicker all the way. I got sick of him deliberately aiming for sheep on the road, or swerving towards a ditch and pulling away at the last moment. I wasn't in the mood for such childish behaviour. Things hadn't been right between us for a while. He was jealous and possessive. Violent sometimes—hitting me then telling me I made him do it, because I was determined to upset and annoy him. And the things he made me do. What he said to me. The names—

cunt, stupid cunt, useless cunt, all you're good for, Cunt. His favourite word. Pet name for me.

And yes, it was exciting at first. I'd never heard that word spoken before he spoke it. I'd seen it written down, in certain books he had, and chalked on a wall once. But nobody ever said it. Charlie did though, loudly and often. Occasionally in ecstasy but usually not. Usually when he wanted to hurt me. To force me to do something I'd rather not do. He always got his way. You'll take it any way I want to give it to you, Cunt. Nothing but a whore, anyway. But I wasn't. I acted as if I was, yes, because he wanted me to—both for him and for the others. Made me dress in skirts split to the waist almost, to entice them. I won't say I didn't get a thrill from it myself, because I did. I enjoyed seeing them suffer, knowing they wouldn't be likely to tell, the way I wasn't allowed to tell all those years ago.

Charlie's knife was a heavy-bladed Bowie knife, for hunting or fishing. Beautifully balanced, so he told me—and showed me as well, how the fulcrum was at the sweet spot on the blade, near the handle. I hated it when he played knife games with me—making me put my hand on the table while he stabbed between my fingers—showing off his dexterity.

He never had to use the knife on the punters—the threat was always enough. He held it to their throats while I went through their pockets. The hauls were interesting—money, of course, but bits of jewellery sometimes as well, tie clips, cuff links, the odd signet ring, and I remember a gold religious medallion we found in a wallet, even an engagement ring once, tucked in a little waistcoat pocket. Wonder what the story behind that was. Some poor girl left without her ring. But I'm getting sentimental. What was the man doing out in Dean Street if he was planning to get engaged? She's better off without it, and him. Real diamonds it was, as well. Charlie fenced that no bother. Some of the dross we chucked in the river—the coloured metal that wasn't precious at all—but we had some good finds too. Sometimes it was fun. I'm glad all that's over though. I have Bobby now. Well, if I want him.

*

I relent and ask Jan to be my matron of honour. It means there'll be no one sitting on my side of the church when I walk down the aisle, apart from Aunt Mill—and Keith, if he insists on tagging along. Except, I keep forgetting, it won't actually come to that since I'll call it off before it gets that far. I haven't said anything to Aunt Mill yet. The Wilsons are happy to pay for everything, it seems, since it's all their family who'll be there. All I have to buy is my dress—and Jan's, of course. She's so excited about it, I'll feel sorry for her when it all comes crashing down.

I'm still in two minds about it all. I keep having these fantasies about married life with Bobby. He wants us to live by the coast—handy for him for his coal round—and he's been looking at some flats in the Dockwray Square area. It's a bit run down but it's cheap. We'll rent at first, of course, but he says if I sell my pair of flats and add the proceeds to his bit of savings—very thrifty is Bob apparently—then we can eventually buy somewhere nice. We could even take out a mortgage and get somewhere even nicer. He'll take over the business in ten or fifteen years, when his dad retires, so we'll be comfortably off, as long as people go on buying coal. And that's not going to change, is it? I wish Charlie's voice didn't keep coming into my head. I've been worried about him lately. I don't want him reappearing now everything's going so well.

We've decided on September for the wedding, so we can have a week away somewhere before the coal business gets too busy again after the summer. Bobby says he'll take me to

Scarborough for the honeymoon. He went there once and liked it, so that'll be fun.

Jan's coming over soon to discuss the dresses. She knows a good dressmaker, so I've decided to go for the cream silk taffeta. She'll wear something similar in lemon. I'll need a going away outfit as well—a little costume, maybe, and a hat, of course. I'm not much of a one for hats but these little feathery caps with the tiny veils are pretty. I saw some in Fenwick's. I'll have my hair up, I think.

Chapter Twenty-Three

When Jan arrives, we sit on the back steps to get some air. This hot weather is making everything very dry and it's likely to get hotter and dryer still. I find myself praying—if that's the word—for rain. Not on September 17th of course, since that's possibly going to be our wedding day, but before then. Lots of lovely rain, please, to make the grass grow and fill the ponds and rivers.

Jan's picked up some swatches of fabric from Bainbridge's in her lunch hour and we spend some time cooing over them. The silk really is gorgeous. She's not sure about the lemon for herself—thinks it'll make her look fat.

'I'll have to shed a couple of pounds,' she says. 'I've got some Ryvita—tastes like cardboard. Got some of those Energen Rolls as well—cotton wool flavour.' She pulls a face. 'Still, it has to be done.'

She suggests a cornflower blue for her dress, and shows me the snippet. The fabric is lovely.

'Bob can have a tie made to match,' she says, so I give in and let her have her way.

I'll have to go and tell Aunt Mill soon because the time is fast approaching when I'll have to buy the material. Unless I call it off. But I don't want to call it off. As soon as this thought comes into my mind, I know Charlie will start up in my head, haranguing me, so I get up and fetch us both a glass

of pop. Dandelion burdock for me, ice cream soda for Jan—
though without any actual ice cream, since she's 'being good'.

We're having a pleasant time making our innocent plans,
chatting as if nothing was ever wrong between us, all
betrayals forgotten, when Keith turns up.

'Jesus, is that the time already?' Jan says when I get up to
answer the door. 'Eeh, I haven't had such a good gab for
ages. I've enjoyed it.' She rinses her empty pop glass and
stands it upside down on the draining board.

When I let Keith in, the look on his face is chilling and
I shiver, despite the heat.

'What's wrong now?' Jan says when she sees him.

'Do you own a wig, Monica?' Keith says, without any
preliminaries.

I have to admit, this startles me. 'A wig?' I say. 'What
would I want a wig for?'

Janice pipes up at the same time so our voices are in
duet. 'A wig? Mon's got lovely hair, why would she wear a
wig?'

'Just wondering,' Keith says, watching me closely.

Though certainly nonplused, I keep my face straight and
my voice steady. 'Why? What have wigs got to do with
anything?'

He smiles. 'So, if I was to look through your things, I
definitely wouldn't find one?'

'Keith!' says Jan.

I look him in the eye. 'Of course not.'

'Then you wouldn't object if I had a rummage through
your drawers?' Now he's being deliberately provocative.

'Jesus, Keith, what's got into you, these days?' Jan's eyes
are wide and she's practically on fire. I'm proud of her for a

moment. Proud she's standing up to him. Pleased as well because she's on my side, despite everything.

'I would object,' I say, 'because it's an invasion of my privacy.' I hesitate. 'And I've no idea what you're on about. Maybe you'd care to explain?'

'Oh, I'm happy to explain,' he says. 'A long dark hair was found on last Friday night's victim. A long dark nylon hair. From a cheap wig.'

'Good God, what are you saying?' Jan puts her hands up to her face. 'You can't believe Mon has anything to do with... with the murder.' Her voice drops to a whisper on the last words.

Keith never takes his eyes off me and I return his gaze. He won't make me blink or turn away. I'll stare him out any day.

'Keith?' Jan jerks his arm. 'What's going on? We've been having such a lovely time. Why are you being so horrible?' She's crying now, I can hear it in her voice. Keith breaks his intense staring to look at her and I do too. Her tears are contemptible. I liked her better when she was fiery.

'It's a legitimate question,' Keith says, turning back to me, 'since you were seen down the quayside the other weekend. There's every reason to think you've been down there again, this past weekend. With a wig covering your pretty blonde locks.' He's sneering at me and I've never hated him more.

'Monica was with us the night that happened,' Jan says with a sniff. 'You can't surely have forgotten.'

'Not all night,' Keith says. 'Not in the early hours of the morning.'

'Do you seriously believe Mon would kill somebody?' Jan bats at him again. 'Seriously?'

He shrugs her off. 'Maybe not. But she may have been with the man before he was killed. May have been the distraction the killer needed.'

'I'm not listening to this,' Jan says. 'This is utterly ridiculous. We've been planning a wedding here.' She steps towards the door, then turns. 'You should go. I'll stay here with Mon. I'll make my own way home.' She holds the front room door open and gestures for Keith to leave.

'Cat got your tongue, Monica?' he says, making no move to go. 'You're keeping very quiet.'

'I have no idea what to say to you,' I say. 'Your accusations—whatever it is you're accusing me of—are crazy. You're crazy. And I'd like you to leave.'

'I really think you should go,' says Jan. 'This is getting out of hand.'

'If you've nothing to hide,' he says, ignoring her, 'you won't mind me having a look around.'

'Keith!' Jan bellows. 'Leave! Now!'

This makes him look at her again. 'I'll go when I'm bloody good and ready,' he says. 'Shut your mouth and keep out of it.'

Her face crumples and I'm almost sorry for her. No, I am sorry for her—sorry she's married to this boor. How can she stand him? She flings herself onto the couch, wailing. She's making so much racket, it's a wonder the neighbours aren't banging on the floor.

'Oh, big man,' I say. 'Big man shouting at your wife. Does that make you feel good? Eh? Superior. Nothing but a caveman.' I'd like to spit at him but I won't lower myself to his level. 'Take a look wherever you want,' I say, sweeping my arm around the room. 'Look in my *drawers*, if you want. And my cupboards. I don't possess a wig. Never have. Never likely to.'

He nods, smirks. 'So you've got rid of it already. Well, we'll find it, if it's in a bin, don't you worry.'

He won't find it because it's in the river. And this time it was an outgoing tide. It'll have been washed down to Tynemouth and out to sea, by now.

'You'll have done your week's washing, I expect,' he goes on. 'Ironed and put away, are they? Your clothes from last Friday night and Saturday morning?'

Jan sits up and shakes her head. 'What are you on about now?'

'Mind if I have a look, then?' he says, pointing to the bedroom. Without waiting for permission, he goes through and I hear him opening drawers, turning things over, in the bedroom, then the kitchen. I stay where I am. There's nothing for him to see. Not in there, anyway. My pulse is ragged now. I tell myself he won't look in the bathroom—the old scullery—where my mac is still hanging. Even if he does, he'll see nothing. It's perfectly clean and dry by now. It could have been hanging there weeks. I hear him opening the scullery door.

'What on earth is he doing?' Jan says, blowing her nose. 'I'm really sorry…'

Keith comes back into the room. 'Had rain here lately, Monica?' he says. 'It's been dry everywhere else but maybe things are different on Walker Road?'

Janice gives him a baleful look, all pouty and sulky, but says nothing more.

I raise my eyebrows. 'Meaning?' I say.

'Meaning,' he says, 'why do you need a mac in this hot weather we're having? Dryest summer for years, so why do you need a mac?'

'Because summer doesn't last forever,' I say, reasonably. 'Because it's not that long since we had floods. I also have a winter coat and boots, and jumpers come to that.'

'Not hanging up over the bath,' he says.

I shake my head. 'I always leave it hanging there. You'll see my umbrella in there as well, if you look. And my boots. It's a small flat. I keep things wherever there's space for them.'

He tries to stare me out again but I'm having none of it. 'Is all this nosing around official?' I say. 'Do your superiors know you're here? Why are you alone, if so? Why isn't there a policewoman with you, for instance? Isn't that usual when you're questioning a woman?'

'Just a friendly visit,' he says, his face hardening.

Now he's worried. He shouldn't be here poking his nose in and asking questions.

'I really would like you to go, now,' I say. 'Both of you. Sorry, Jan, but I've had enough. I need a lie down.'

'Had some late nights recently?' Keith says.

'Yes, I have. Worrying about that rubbish you came out with the other night. Can't sleep a wink, if you must know. Now get out of my home before I call the real police.'

'Oh, I am the real police, Monica,' he says, bringing his face close to mine. 'And one day, I'll find out everything.'

*

I close the front door on them and stand with my back to it. I can hear them outside, arguing. 'Wake up, Janice,' Keith says, 'she's always been a bit off. Just lately, there's been something even more off about her.'

'You've never liked her,' Jan says. 'Because she's my friend and not yours.'

'Don't be daft. I don't like her because I don't trust her. She's creepy. The way she smirks to herself and stares at you... at me, anyway. She's a weirdo.'

I'm sure he knows I'm listening. I stiffen, fists clenched.

'Why are you so suspicious of her? What's she ever done to you?'

'I've always known she was lying,' he says. 'Holding something back. Her stories have never rung true. That place she's supposed to have worked... it never existed. You know that.'

'I got the name wrong.'

'For God's sake, Janice. Wake up. She's been living a lie for years—and I'm trained to spot lies. Polis's intuition, if you like. It's like a sixth sense—you learn to spot when somebody's not telling the truth. It's obvious to me.'

They move off and I can't make out Jan's reply, though from the tone it's a denial. A denial of my creepiness, my weirdness, my dishonesty. Damn Keith. He's the one who's creepy. I wonder how long it will take him to wear her down. She's come good for the moment but he'll keep on at her until she stops sticking up for me. I push away from the door. Well, it can't be helped. Bobby's sister is about the same size, so if Jan drops out after the dress is made, that Josie can be matron of honour instead.

If the wedding goes ahead, of course.

Chapter Twenty-Four

Bobby and I go to see Aunt Mill. I meet him at Benton station and we tramp down the wooden steps hand in hand. I'm torn as regards Bob. Part of me hates him for being such a wet rag that night in the club and the other part of me is—I won't say still in love with him, because I'm not—but maybe wishing I was. Yes, that other part of me is wishing the clocks could be magically turned back so that night never happened. That he never doubted me and never left me alone in that club.

Maybe the clocks could be put even further back so none of this ever happened—but that would be asking for me to no longer be myself. Who would I be then? If there'd been no Manda, no Charlie, none of those demeaning things I had to do. Things I sometimes, as far as Charlie was concerned, enjoyed. Maybe the person I would have been wouldn't look twice at somebody like Bobby Wilson. I could have got a scholarship, gone to university, if I hadn't been so messed up at school and afterwards. I'm clever enough. I know that.

Bobby gives my hand a squeeze. 'Which way now, Miss Mermaid? Are you still with me?'

'Sorry. Daydreaming. This way.'

Aunt Mill lets us in and ushers us into the front parlour. I'm honoured, but it's Bobby who's the VIP.

'Pleasure to meet you, Robert,' she says, though she doesn't appear especially overjoyed. 'Sit yourselves down.' She's wearing her brown crepe dress today and a rather lovely garnet necklace that I don't recall seeing before. It looks odd on her to my eyes, since she's not one for flashy jewellery. Must be wearing it to impress my 'fiancé' as she referred to him when I spoke to her on the telephone.

Bobby and I sit next to each other on the dark green settee while Aunt Mill remains standing. She brings her hands together in a soft clap. 'Sherry?' she says. 'The kettle is on but I thought a small alcoholic drink might be appropriate, in the circumstances.'

Bob nods. 'Grand. Thanks.'

The decanter is on the sideboard and I don't like to think how long the sherry's been in it but I accept the tiny curved glass with good grace. When she's served us and given us an arrowroot biscuit each—can't consume strong liquor without something to counter-balance it—Aunt Mill sits down in an armchair and studies us. She nods slowly, as if she's come to some agreement with herself. 'Yes,' she says, 'you make a good-looking couple, I'll say that for you.'

I almost choke on the Bristol Cream—and not just because it's sickly sweet. I don't ever recall receiving praise from Aunt Mill before—and certainly not about my looks.

Bobby beams at me. 'Aye,' he says, gazing into my eyes. 'I think we're well matched.'

I don't know what he means by this—well matched in looks? intelligence? position in life?—but I smile and raise my glass to my lips.

'So,' Aunt Mill goes on, putting her drink down. 'Getting married, eh? No engagement first?' Her eyes flit from one to the other of us. 'You know what they say, "Marry in haste, repent at leisure."' Now that's the Aunt Mill I know!

Bobby glances at me. 'Well, we're both of age, and we're sure, so…'

I notice Aunt Mill eyeing me up and down.

'We're not getting married because we have to,' I say, smoothing a hand over my abdomen. 'We're getting married because we want to.'

'I see,' she says. 'Well, if you're sure.'

'We are.' Bobby drains his glass and places it on a little side table. 'Thanks. That was lovely.'

I sneak a sideways look at him. I very much doubt he's a keen sweet sherry drinker. I don't know whether to be impressed by his ability to carry off a blatant lie, or worried he might try it on me one day.

Aunt Mill gets to her feet. 'I'll make that tea now.' She didn't toast us with her sherry or offer any congratulations or felicitations, but that's my Aunty Millicent for you.

Bobby takes my hand while she's out of the room, clasping it in both of his. 'I think she likes me.' He winks, so I'll know it's a joke.

I nibble on the arrowroot biscuit. 'That'll be a first. She's not a people person… except on her own terms.'

When she comes back with the teapot, she summons me to help her carry the cups in. In the kitchen she says, 'He seems a nice enough lad but are you sure you're doing the right thing? You've not known him long. Shouldn't you wait a bit longer?'

'I'm quite sure. I know what I'm doing.' At that moment I am sure. I will marry Bobby Wilson, so she might as well get used to the idea.

'But a September wedding?' she says. 'Well, I suppose it'll give you a few more weeks to get to know each other.' She shakes her head. 'I still don't think it's a wise move… with your history.'

'My…?' For a moment, I imagine she's talking about Charlie. But she can't be. She never met him.

'Recent history, I mean,' she goes on. 'Your shenanigans at Tynemouth the other week. I don't suppose he knows about that.'

I pick up the tea tray. 'He does, as it happens.' I turn towards the door. 'He was the one who fished me out of the sea.' When I look over my shoulder at her, I'm gratified at the astonishment on her face. She picks up a plate of sausage rolls and follows me into the front room.

*

By the time we leave, Aunt Mill has warmed to Bobby a little. She's grilled him on his job and his prospects and seems suitably impressed. He's told her about his family and given her to believe he's from a steady background, that he's not a wastrel, and that he both can and will, take care of me and keep me in the style to which I am accustomed. Though I'm rather hoping he'll do better than that.

Aunt Mill and I had another confab in the kitchen—woman to woman—wherein the facts of life were broached, albeit in a distant roundabout manner, and I've assured her that I am *au fait* with all of that and know everything that's expected of me. And finally, she agreed to put up the cash for the dresses and flowers, though not without a discourse on the exorbitant price of silk taffeta. 'Silk!' she screeched. 'Who do you think you are, Princess Margaret?'

I know she can afford it, even if it does send her blood pressure soaring. I pointed out that Bobby's lot are paying for everything else, quite against tradition, and that she was therefore getting off lightly. In the end she agreed to the silk, through gritted teeth.

'I dare say, you'll want shoes to match,' she said, as if this was the final straw. 'And who's going to give you away?'

'You can,' I said. That shut her up. Anyway, we've agreed on it being in Shields since it's handier for the majority of guests and Aunt Mill has set herself the task of raking up a few more for our side. Seems she has a cousin in Gateshead who has a family. She tells me I met them once but I have no recollection. Don't care. She can invite whoever she likes, as long as she puts her hand in her pocket. I had intended to ask her about my father but when it came to it my courage failed me. I should ask, I suppose, but do I really want to know?

Chapter Twenty-Five

The headline, when I see it on the board outside the corner shop, is shocking.

BODY FOUND IN QUARRY
Police suspect foul play

I freeze right there in the street and look around as if someone may be observing my reaction. Taking a deep breath, I steel myself to go into the shop to buy the paper. Mrs Dack is chatting to a customer.

'Eeh, it's getting terrible. All these murders and now this. What's the world coming to?'

I glance at the pile of newspapers on the counter. As they are folded in half, I can only see the headline and part of a photograph of a car. The car?

The woman in front of me packs her bread and milk into her shopping bag. 'It's not safe to be out,' she says, 'with all these rippers and slashers roaming free. You could be murdered in your bed.'

Or in a shop queue, I think, if you don't hurry up.

She smiles at me as she turns to leave. 'Sorry, pet.'

I step past her. '*Evening Chronicle*, thanks.'

Mrs Dack sniffs and hands me one from the pile. We don't usually exchange pleasantries and today is not going to be the day we start. I put the tuppence on the counter and leave with the newspaper tucked under my arm. I am shaken and will have to wait until I'm in the flat before I read the article.

Once I'm inside, I unfold it and my doubts are dispelled. What am I saying? I had no doubts. I had hopes but I knew, as soon as I saw the board outside the shop, that those hopes were vain. There it is, in black and white. The photograph shows the Hillman being winched from the quarry, water gushing from beneath the doors. At the time the picture was taken, they wouldn't have known what was inside. I scan the paragraphs, though I can barely concentrate. Car roof seen in quarry as water levels fall. Police investigate. Body discovered inside. Believed to be that of a man.

I sink to the couch, the *Chronicle* clenched in my hands. So they've found him, then. They've found Charlie.

I read on. Unidentifiable at this stage due to length of time in water. No papers on body, nothing to indicate identity. Car number plates missing and engine number filed off. I didn't know that about the engine number. Didn't even know cars had engine numbers. Stolen, obviously. Typical of Charlie.

Missing persons lists to be scanned for possible match. Good luck with that. No one will have reported him missing. He was too erratic for anyone to realise he was permanently gone.

*

I'd been about to go for a swim and still felt a strong desire to immerse myself in water. I love swimming. Ducking my head under, submersing myself, is cleansing, renewing, like a baptism. I throw the paper down and stand up. I'm not going to hide myself away like a criminal. There's nothing on him to prove who he was and no way for anyone to trace him back to me. So there's no point in worrying.

I decide to treat myself and go to Northumberland Road next to the City Hall. I can sweat it out in the Turkish bath before I finish off with a swim in the big pool. I usually steam myself until I'm half-cooked then splash into the icy plunge pool to close my pores. It's ecstasy and I always repeat the process several times before stretching out on a lounger to recover. I say it's ecstasy, and normally it is but today is different. I cannot relax. I'm irritated by the other women in the steam room; two of them will not stop yakking on and it's all nonsense about who said what to who and what so and so did next. At least they're not discussing the body in the quarry or the 'ripper' murders, thank goodness. Still, it's so annoying I'm ready to throw something at them.

There's another woman in there as well but she's not saying much. I can see her trying to catch my eye so we can smirk at the natterers but I won't give her the satisfaction. I don't come here to socialise or interact; I come to relax and purge myself of the grime of the city. I like the way the sweat oozes out of my pores and leaves me raw and fresh and clean. I want to be clean. I do so want to be clean.

What happened with Charlie was tainting, though, and I don't know if I can ever cleanse myself of it, though it was his own fault. He was exciting, Charlie, despite his temper—well, because of it sometimes, but in the end all the green-eyed stuff, the accusations, the name calling—it all added up. And came to an end that day up on Elsdon Moor. After all the silly antics in the car, we ended up at the gibbet where a man called William Winter was hanged—in 1792 so the sign said. It's imprinted on my memory. Winter and a couple of accomplices murdered some poor old woman believing she was rich, apparently. The murderer's body was left hanging there by the side of the road within sight of the crime scene.

Left there until there was nothing left of it, as a lesson to others.

Charlie had wanted to see the spot for a while. Gave him some kind of creepy thrill, I suppose. There was a wooden head dangling where Winter's head would have been and when we got there, Charlie decided to climb up and cut it down for a souvenir. I thought that was—I don't know, gruesome? Disrespectful? Maybe I was being awkward because of the way he'd been annoying me all day. Gruesome and disrespectful never bothered me other times. Charlie said the only way to get it was for me to climb on his shoulders and hack it down, since he couldn't very well climb on mine. But it was wet and windy by then and I didn't want anything to do with it.

I refused, of course. I had my lovely blue checked skirt on and a new pair of nylons. He slapped me and threatened to drive off without me. I was furious. Then he started with the name calling—cunt, bitch, useless cow—so I agreed, simply to shut him up. Once he'd handed the knife up for me to cut the thing down—well, what did he expect? Like I said, it was his own fault.

The chattering women intrude on my thoughts and I can't stand it any longer. They've camped themselves on the beds next to me, and my thoughts and theirs are becoming entangled. I've enough to worry about without their nonsense ringing in my ears.

I head for the swimming pool and dive in from the side as I always do. I cleave through the turquoise water, swimming length after length. The pool isn't busy at this time of the afternoon and for a merciful half hour, I find peace. The physical activity banishes the intrusive thoughts of Charlie and the rhythm of the crawl soothes me. The other swimmers mind their own business and keep out of my way while I do my forty lengths. I'm a fast swimmer, a good swimmer, and I'm panting when I climb out, my heart racing, the blood vital in my veins.

Relief sweeps through me as I shower and dry off. For the moment, I've banished all the unpleasant memories. I sit in the cubicle with my eyes closed, appreciating my stillness, aware of little but the echoing sounds filtering through from the swimming pool. It's a kind of prayer, I suppose, or meditation, if you adopt a more eastern approach. I read a book about Buddhism a couple of years ago, by that Christmas Humphreys man—him who led the prosecution against Ruth Ellis. Strange how he can be a prosecutor as well as a Buddhist. I didn't understand all of it, of course, so maybe I'm missing something.

The calmness and stillness turns out to be temporary, as I realise as soon as I step back into the street. That headline is still there on the newsagents' stands, on the papers people are holding, on everyone's lips. I'm certain I can hear the buzz of conversation—Did you see—a body—a car—how awful—What's the world coming to—and on and on and on. It's in my head, I know, it's all in my head but I don't know how to stop it. It's Charlie. He's in there nagging at me as usual. Bitch. Cunt. Look what you've done now. Oh dear, Monica, how are you going to get out of this one?

I must be careful and keep control of myself. I cannot break down again, like I did at the gallery. I can't allow myself the luxury of confession. This must never be revealed. This is between us—me and Charlie. Yes, we are joined by blood, in a union that can never be sundered. This tie is stronger than any marriage. Longer lasting, because even death will not release me. We are together forever, in hell or out of it, linked eternally by my actions, even if no one else ever knows. And they must not know. They must not. Yet there's such a strong urge to tell. To shout, Yes, it was me! I did it and I'm not sorry. I'm not. I'm not sorry. But still, I do so wish I was clean.

Chapter Twenty-Six

13th July. That Ruth Ellis was hanged this morning. Be over with by now, I expect. They do it first thing, I believe. What must have gone through her head as she lay on her bunk last night, unsleeping, no doubt? And as she walked towards the scaffold. What must it be like, knowing…?

I don't blame her for what she did. Any woman would do the same to a cheating lover. Well, maybe not shoot him, that's a bit extreme. Still, you use whatever you've got to hand, don't you?

Of course, there's been such an outcry about it. People saying hanging should be abolished. Not sure I agree with that. I've given it a fair bit of thought, lately. Not sure I'd want to spend years locked up in a dreary prison, stinking with other women's smells, as I'm sure must be the case. Best get it over with. Might not feel the same when it comes to it, mind. The actual moment. God, poor woman. I shiver.

*

I'm subdued when I see Bobby later.

'What's up, pet?' he says, when we meet at our usual spot under the clock.

I remain silent. If I say 'Nothing' I'll sound petulant but I can't come up with any lie to explain my mood.

'Eh?' he says, looking into my face. 'Y'aal reet, pet?'

He knows his lapses into broad Geordie always make me smile. 'Don't mind me,' I say, at last. 'I've no idea what's wrong with me.'

'You need cheering up, young lady,' he says. 'Look, *Doctor at Sea*'s on at the Odeon. Dirk Bogarde. You like him, don't you?'

I nod and he takes my arm to escort me across the street to the cinema. It's too lovely an evening to sit in the dark watching a film but at least it will hide my face and I can allow my thoughts to roam without having to explain myself.

'Ice cream?' he says, as we go in, and I nod again. He beckons the girl over and she hands him a couple of tubs from her tray.

I don't really want it but I dig the little wooden shovel into the hard, vanilla ice cream and stare at the screen. The adverts are ending and the cartoons start. *Datta da da daaah! Datta da da daaah! It's the Woody Woodpecker song…* I could scream at the banality of it. What is wrong with me? Will this misery never cease? I've become a shivering wreck. Pull yourself together, woman! But I can't. I'm in danger of seriously falling apart. I want Bobby to wrap his arms around me and protect me and keep me from harm. And in return, I want to tell him everything. To pass the burden of knowledge on to him, so I can be light again, so I can be free and joyful. He'll stroke my hair and whisper words of comfort into my ears, his voice soft, his breath sweet on my cheek. I want to continue to love and be loved. I can't give that up. Not now. But I want to be deserving of that love. In truth, I want to be another person, altogether.

This jerks me to reality. What I'm asking is for me—the person I am—to cease to exist and another completely innocent version to take my place. It can't happen. I've got to stop being such a wet blanket, gather my forces, and get on with it. I'm me and that's that.

Bobby hears the shuddering sigh I release and turns to me with concern in his eyes. He puts his arm around me and I lean towards him in the dark. This will have to do. This will have to be comfort enough. I can ask nothing more.

*

Charlie is still in my head and the memory of that last day plays over and over, blocking out the film, despite the handsome Dirk Bogarde as Dr Simon Sparrow. The feelings surge back—my sudden hatred of Charlie, the realisation of my idiocy, as something snapped inside me. I was sick of it. Sick of the name-calling. Cunt this and cunt that. Being told I was worthless, useless, stupid, a whore, a twat, good for nothing else but to be fucked by him. When his slap stung my cheek. I was fuming. I'd had enough. But I had no plan. I went along with it because I had to stop the name-calling.

He made me clamber onto his shoulders, which took some doing. I left my shoes in the car, climbed onto the bonnet and then somehow got up, wobbling all over the place. My feet were soaking, muddy and slippery and my hair was ruined by the rain, the hair clips escaping from my French pleat. He grabbed my legs, digging his nails in through my new stockings, to keep me steady. I was tottering about and couldn't stay upright. Keep still, bitch, he said, you'll have us both over. I was sobbing, angry, demoralised. You're fucking heavy, you know. Lardy cunt. It's true I wasn't as thin then as I am now but I was never what you'd call fat. And it was his idea, anyway. A ladder tickled its way up my leg and that was the last straw. My new nylons!

I had to lower my centre of gravity or we'd have fallen over. So, when he handed me the knife, I was half crouched on his shoulders. My hair was like rats' tails, straggling over my face. I tried to brush it out of my eyes but the rain made it cling to my skin. Keep fucking still! Charlie bit me on the thigh and I cried out. He bit through my dress, so that

184

softened it, but still, it hurt. Tears of anger mixed with the drizzle. I was cold and snotty and fed up with it all. Legs like bloody tree trunks, Charlie muttered. Here, take the knife and get the fuckin' thing cut down. Be quick about it. He pricked my calf with the tip, drawing blood and sending another ladder crawling up my leg. I screeched and wanted to lash out at him. To injure him the way he so casually injured me.

I was trembling, furious, filled with hate. He was stupid to hand me the knife, but he did. As soon as the hilt was in my hands, I jabbed it towards him. Couldn't help myself hitting out at him, I was so angry. Anyone would have done the same. Maybe I only wanted to nick his ear, scare him like he scared me with his knife-play, or maybe I wanted to slash his cheek. I don't know. I wanted to jab, to stab, to prick him like he'd pricked me.

What I hit was his jugular. It was an accident. It was a tiny cut, but deep enough to be disastrous, like pricking a balloon. I didn't intend to kill him but he bled out in no time. Of course, no one would have believed that.

We fell to the ground together and I cut myself a little, nicked my hand when the knife slipped. He was gurgling and his gore spouted all over me. So, in the end, our blood mingled. What does that mean? We're blood kin now? United forever?

Chapter Twenty-Seven

I don't know how I did it. Dragged Charlie into the car. It took ages. Felt like hours and probably was, but I managed. The day was dull already, what with the rain. By the time I got him into the passenger seat, it was fully dark, the evening well advanced. We were alone up there on the bleak moor, a hundred feet or so back from the road, so out of sight. Traffic was sparse—the odd tractor, the late bus—but I froze every time headlights flared at the bend.

I don't like remembering this. Makes my guts roil. I'm not proud of it, though it was a feat of both energy and engineering. Manoeuvring him, manhandling him. He wasn't a big lad—more the wiry, nervous-energy type, but he was heavy as a dead weight. They say you develop supernatural strength under unusual circumstances, draw on reserves you never knew you had. In emergencies, times of stress. If anything was stressful, it was that experience. I was a wreck. Well, afterwards, I was. During, I was fairly calm and coordinated. It had to be done, so I did it.

I drove him a few miles to an old quarry filled with water. We'd swum there the previous summer, when we were happy. Happier, anyway. Before I tipped him and the car into the quarry, I slashed him around the face. Not done in anger, not entirely, though it was his fault I was in this predicament. No, I slashed him to make him harder to recognize in case he was found before nature took its course. By that time, there wasn't a lot of blood left in him. Most had drained into the mud up by the gibbet.

I didn't think he'd be identified easily, anyway. He had nothing on him to say who he was and even if his fingerprints were readable, he wasn't on any record. He always said he was clean, no criminal offences—none he'd been done for anyway. I believed him about that because he'd have crowed and boasted about any he did have. I doubted anyone would miss him as he lived very much under the radar. He had acquaintances not friends, and never mentioned a family. Someone must have given birth to him, I suppose, but whoever she was, she took no part in his life as far as I could tell.

Charlie didn't care for people much. They were there to be used, cheated, robbed, exploited. Saying this makes it sound like he had no good points, but that wouldn't be true. He did have good points. He was thrilling to be with and funny at times—in the early days anyway—and he was an excellent lover. I had little to compare him with, of course, but he never left me stranded. Not in that way. A great shame, what happened, a great shame. He brought it on himself, though. Can't say I loved him, though maybe I thought I did, at one time. He was so kind, those first few weeks, bringing me little presents—good soap and sweets, even when they were rationed. He had his sources, and it didn't do to enquire too closely. Don't ask, darlin', just enjoy. Now let's go dancin'. And he would whirl me off somewhere I'd never been before. Dives filled with gangsters up from London. Hidden, secret places, just this side of terrifying.

But it was all done to draw me in. That's so clear to me now. Pulled me in with his charm then turned on me. That was when the dancing stopped.

Once I'd made sure he wouldn't be identifiable, I drove the Minx onto a steeper slope and left the handbrake off. I had to push the car from behind to get it moving. Pushing and pushing until I was exhausted, legs splattered with mud and filth, skirt soaked. The rain and the mud helped in the end, though. Drawing on the last vestiges of my strength, I gave it an almighty shove and it slid smoothly down into the quarry with barely a splash. I slipped to my knees, weeping, and watched it go. It took a while to sink and I was terrified the water wasn't deep enough to cover it. At last, it went down with a sudden rush and there was nothing to see of it but bubbles on the surface. It was dawn by then, the water the same greeny-grey as the car was, and sickly looking.

I'd taken the number plates off the car before I got rid— I'm not stupid. Though I doubt if it was registered in Charlie's name. The bolts weren't too rusted, though loosening them with the single spanner Charlie owned was another Herculean task. I was determined, though, and I can achieve anything if I set my mind to it. Fortunately, I had my big straw beach bag with me, so I was able to carry the plates away in that. They went in the Tyne later.

Doing what I had to do took all night because I had to rest from time to time and when it was done, I was cold and wet and filthy. Shaking all over—my legs weak and trembly—I holed up in the woods to recover. Must have slept for a while, though God knows how. Turned out to be a lovely morning though, which was good. I washed in a stream and rinsed the mud and blood out of my skirt and blouse as much as I could. My nylons had to be thrown away because they were ruined but my shoes were fine, fortunately. I'd stashed them in the car when he made me get up on his shoulders and I'd been barefoot since then.

Once I dried off a bit in the sun—such a glorious morning—I walked the couple of miles into Elsdon to get a bus back home. I had a rolled-up raincoat in my bag so I was able to cover my frightful clothes, though I couldn't do much about my bare legs. Still jittery, I found a public lavatory where I was able to put a bit of make-up on and tidy myself up. My hand bled on and off where I'd cut it and I staunched it with a hanky—always a good idea to have one in your handbag, Aunt Mill said. A clean handkerchief and clean underwear would always see you right. It was soaked with blood by now though, so I flushed it away.

I didn't want to get the first bus because people might notice and wonder what I was doing there so early. I was surprised, therefore, to see the church clock stood at half past ten. I don't know where the time went. I kept myself away from others as much as possible and with my headscarf over my tangled hair, managed not to look too disreputable.

By that time, I was tired, starving and thirsty, but didn't dare venture into a café. As few people as possible must see me. A little local bus took me to Otterburn and I hopped on the Newcastle bus from there. I don't think anyone particularly noticed me, certainly no one remarked on anything. I still felt as if I stuck out as an obvious miscreant, though—especially huddled in a raincoat on such a lovely day. But no one ever knows, do they? What's going on in another person's head, what that person may have done, what their hands have accomplished. No one knows to this day what I did.

I slept for three days straight, afterwards. Three days, waking only for water, tea and the odd slice of toast. And the rum. I was glad of the rum then.

Chapter Twenty-Eight

BODY IN QUARRY
CLUE FOUND

This is what the headlines are shrieking today. I spotted it as soon as I got off the bus.

I checked Charlie's pockets. I swear I did. Surely, I can't have missed something. I checked the car as well. There was nothing that could identify us or lead back to me in any way. Nothing at all. He never carried anything with his name on it and neither did I. We were careful that way. So what is it the police have found?

I bought a paper in Finlay's and walked up to Northumberland Street before reading it. Standing to one side of Marks & Spencer's doorway, I scanned through it. The headline said it all, really. The article on the front page was nothing but speculation, with no mention of what the 'clue' was. No details on why it was useful to the police. Nothing but a lot of unnecessary verbiage. A small section on page two went over the known details again, in case their readers hadn't taken it in the first time, and that was it.

I tossed the paper in a bin in disgust. Maybe Jan would know something, though I doubt this is a case Burgess will have anything to do with. It's the Northumberland police who are in charge. Still, something may have filtered to him via the grapevine.

I'm meeting Jan at the dressmakers—it's the woman she knows, or who's been recommended to her. Her workshop is in a building on Ridley Place, apparently, but it's quite hard to find. I go up and down the street a couple of times before I spot the grubby doorway next to a shop, with several nameplates to one side, hers amongst them. Not well signposted at all. I hope she's better than her surroundings suggest.

A narrow flight of stairs leads almost vertically upwards and I haul myself to the top by the handrail. Just as well I'm trim. Jan's already there. She and the dressmaker are by the window scrutinising a pattern book.

'Oh, Mon, good,' Jan says, beckoning me over. 'This is the one, isn't it?'

I cross the tiny room in a couple of steps and look over her shoulder. 'Yes, that's it. I've got the pattern here. What do you think?' I don't really care what she thinks, I'm having that style anyway.

'It's lovely. This is Elsie, by the way.'

I nod to the woman. In her dusty black dress and loose updo, she exudes a certain capability. She has a pincushion attached to a band on her wrist and a tape measure around her neck.

'It's a lot of material,' she says, pursing her lips, 'with that full skirt.'

Maybe she thinks I can't afford it. 'It's all ordered up,' I say. 'Bainbridge's will drop it round to you tomorrow.'

'Along with the notions?' She peers at me as if she doesn't trust me to know what I'm doing.

'Yes—thread, zips, buttons and so on. Everything you need according to the pattern. Which, as I said, I have here.'

I produce the paper pattern—Vogue, very stylish, and not cheap.

'Let's get measuring, then.' She unwinds the tape measure from her neck.

34-24-35–that's me. Jan tries to hide her vital statistics from me but I make sure I get a look at them anyway. 36-29-38. Getting somewhat podgy around the waist, is Jan. Must be the contentment of married bliss.

'I'm on a diet,' she says, 'but I'm sure the bodice can be taken in once I lose a bit of weight.'

Or let out, I think.

Elsie fiddles about with the bits of tissue paper, holding them against us and marking larger or smaller darts and tucks as necessary. 'Since the fabric is so expensive,' she mumbles through a mouthful of pins, 'I'm going to do a dummy run with some old muslin I've got lying around.'

I moue non-committally. She can do what she likes as long as the end result is superb. If I'm going to go through with it—and I believe I am—I want to look spectacular. If I have to be on display, I want that display to be perfect.

Elsie jabs the pins back into the pincushion. 'Can you nip back on Saturday, when I've had a chance to cut and tack?'

*

Jan and I take our lives in our hands getting down the steep stairs. 'You should run up and down these stairs every day, Jan,' I say, when we burst from the doorway. 'That'd shift the avoirdupois.'

'I've still got twenty minutes,' she says, ignoring me. 'Quick bite of lunch?'

We find a café and settle down with our cups of tea. Jan has a cheese sandwich with hers; I don't bother. She very pointedly doesn't take a cake to follow, as she usually would.

I'm trying to come up with ways to sound her out about the quarry investigation, just in case Keith's mentioned anything, but can think of no opening. Wish I'd kept the paper, now, it would have provided a talking point. We natter about nothing in particular for a while, both keeping off the subject of Mister Burgess, though he seems to be looming there between us. Eventually, she succumbs.

'I've still not forgiven Keith,' she says, eyeing a plate of scones beneath a glass dome on the counter. 'He's been sleeping in the spare room.'

'Don't put your marriage on hold for me,' I say—rather nobly, if I say so myself. What I really think, of course, is that she should leave him. Why would she want to stay with a man who shouts at her like he did last week? Not like they have children to keep her there. And divorce is becoming more and more common these days. She wouldn't have any grounds for divorce, though, I don't suppose. Unless he hits her. This reminds me of Charlie and makes me uncomfortable. I let him get away with far too much. I was stupid, I know, but I was young. Anyway, he paid for it in the end, didn't he?

'He's been trying to make it up to me,' Jan says. 'Said he was sorry but that I need to keep out of police matters. Cheek! That's not being sorry.'

'No, it's not.'

'Tried to get me into a conversation about this body they found in Northumberland,' she goes on. 'I said, "Isn't that a police matter as well?" To which he was forced to agree. So that was the end of that.'

Sometimes, Jan, I think, sipping my tea, your snappy rejoinders will get you into trouble.

*

When Jan goes back to work after lunch, I wander around the shops, aimlessly at first, then I remember a little costume I saw in Binn's the other week, that could be perfect for my going away outfit. I stroll down to Market Street to have another look at it. Nipped-in waist and calf-length pencil skirt in a pale silvery grey. It's lovely but I'm leaning towards something more colourful—Bobby likes me in blue or green. I hum and harr over it so long the assistant gets annoyed with me. 'Madam can see the quality, surely?' she says. At this point, I walk out. I'll take as much time as I like deciding what to spend my money on, thank you. It's her job to serve me, not get snippy because I'm cautious making a decision.

So I'm at a loose end again. Can't face going back to the flat on such a lovely day. Glorious sunshine and a bright blue sky, though the traffic fumes in town spoil it. Noise and grit and the stink of petrol. It's a day for the coast but that won't be the same without Bobby and we're not seeing each other until tomorrow, Friday. Should have brought my book with me. I could have sat in Exhibition Park, reading by the lake. If I sit there doing nothing, I'm sure to be accosted by some sleazy character chancing his luck.

There's a dress exchange shop on Gosforth High Street that sells quality items. It's not cheap but then nothing worthwhile ever is. Can't hurt to go and have a look. I don't object to second hand if the clothes are in perfect condition. I jump on a bus and go upstairs to sit at the front. I like going up the North Road, past the Town Moor. The Hoppings are gone now, of course, though the grass is still patchy and dry where the fairground rides and trailers were. We really are desperate for rain. If only there'd been a good long shower last week, that blasted car wouldn't have shown up in the quarry. I could do without the worry of that on top of all this wedding preparation. Bobby knows there's something wrong but I've convinced him my jumpiness is to do with

Keith and his accusations. He seems to have accepted that explanation, as that's part of it anyway. Oh well, there's no sense in worrying about Charlie at the moment. Whatever they've found, it can't be anything to do with me. I wish I knew what it was though. I shiver, despite the heat. Not knowing is so disturbing. I'm so on edge, I find myself constantly jiggling my leg, tapping my feet, gritting my teeth. All very annoying.

A man flops into the seat next to me, making me nearly leap out of my skin. 'Sorry, pet,' he says, smirking at me. 'Daydreaming, were you?'

I scramble up. 'This is my stop.' It's not but I'm not sitting here with him pressed right up next to me. He swings his legs to one side to let me past. Oaf. The least could do is stand up. I have to step over his feet, with him grinning at me all the time. There are plenty of other spare seats, what's he want to park himself next to me for? Hackles well risen, I stalk down the stairs and jump off at the lights. Men! Well, some men. Maybe most men. They have no sensitivity whatsoever. Boors and bullies, the lot of them. And I was only just getting over the irritation of my dealings with that snotty shop assistant. I'm now what Aunt Mill would call 'up at high doh'—and it's not surprising.

Gosforth High Street starts at this point but the shop I want is further up. I stride along, breathing the anger out. It's this kind of rage that makes me want to hurt someone. And I've not gone more than twenty paces before I run—literally—into Peggy Hughes. She squeaks as I bowl her out of my way and the noise she produces is ridiculous. 'Mind out!' she cries, which is a cheek since she was crossing my path. She starts as she recognises me and gawps. 'Oh, it's you…' She takes a step backwards.

'What are you doing here?' I say, surprised by her unexpected presence.

'I…I…I…' she stutters. 'Work. Over there. Office.' She holds up a paper bag. 'Scones for our afternoon tea.'

She flinches as I move towards her and a sense of power overwhelms me. Stupid little creature with her stupid gangly husband. I could crush her with my bare hands. Instead, I smile. 'Fruit scones, are they?' I say, though I couldn't care less.

She gulps. 'Yes.'

'Lovely.' I touch her shoulder and she jumps back. 'What's the matter, Peggy? Look like you've seen a ghost.' I have her trapped against the metal railings beside the zebra crossing, and she squirms, casting about for a way out.

'I…I have to get back.' The bag of scones trembles in her hand.

Of course, she knows everything. How could she not? She was there that night at the club and no doubt drippy Al will have brought her up to date on the latest accusations. She acts as if she expects me to do her in here and now. And I'd be perfectly happy to make her dreams come true, if it wasn't for the shoppers wandering past, giving us disapproving looks. 'What else has he said? Your husband? I dare say he's saying the same as Keith Burgess. What have they said about me?' You never know, she might reveal things they've said in private.

'Nothing. Nothing. No, nothing.' She shakes her head and her little mousy curls flap this way and that.

'It's not true, you know. Whatever Keith and Al say, it's not true.' Well, it's not, is it? Some of it isn't anyway.

'If you say so… I don't know much about it… but…'

'But?'

'Al's very good at faces.' She's found a reserve of courage somewhere. 'He never forgets one. Never. He's known for it.'

'Well, he must have been mistaken this time.'

She presses her lips together and shakes her head again, more firmly. 'Not my Al. He's had commendations for his facial recognition. Let me past, please.'

She's like a mouse in a stand-off with a cat. I didn't think she had it in her. I'm impressed. Can't help laughing though. The size of her!

'He saw you all right,' she says. 'And that's not all. They know a lot more about you than you imagine.'

'What? What do they know about me?' I raise my arm, to keep her hemmed in.

'Al's not the only one who's seen you late at night. You must think the police are fools.' She slaps my bare arm. 'Now let me past or I'll scream.'

I step back and she scuttles away. My heart is thudding. To say I'm fuming is an understatement. I could kill.

Chapter Twenty-Nine

Bobby's coming over this evening but not for another half hour, so when there's a knock at the door, I tut because I'm not ready. I'm still smoothing on my nylons, straightening the seams and fiddling with the rubber nubs on my suspender belt. Pulling my housecoat on over my slip, I go to the door. 'I've not got my make-up on yet,' I say, as I pull it open—and stop.

It's not Bobby. It's Al.

He stands there with a serious look on his face which makes him seem more substantial than usual. Less of a long skinny drip. I hold onto the door, gaping at him. Not my finest hour.

'Are you going to let me in,' he says, 'or do you want to do this on the doorstep?'

'Do what?' I glance up and down the street, which is empty apart from a couple of people at the bus stop over the road.

'I think you know the reason I'm here.' He almost says 'ye knaa' but corrects himself in time.

It dawns on me that I do know what he's come for, and I back into the front room so he can step into the hallway. He has such enormous feet, I notice, and you can tell he's being a policeman today from the thick rubber-soled shoes he's wearing.

'Bob'll be here shortly,' I tell him—a sort of warning, I suppose.

'Good,' he says. 'He might be interested in what I've got to say.'

'And what's that?' I stand by the kitchen door, as far away from him as I can get without leaving the room. I clasp the loose reveres of my housecoat together so he can't see my black slip underneath.

'Don't try to pretend you don't know. What was all that about yesterday? Did you think Peg wouldn't tell me?'

'Tell you what?' I have absolutely no intention of making this easy for him.

'Oh howay, don't act the innocent. You threatened my wife.'

'No, I didn't.' I cast my mind back. I didn't threaten Peggy at all. I may have thought about it but I did not make any threats as far as I can remember. 'I said nothing threatening at all.'

'You cornered her and were overbearing. That's threatening behaviour.'

I spot a hairgrip on the floor and bend to pick it up. Al stands ten feet away, by the window, glowering at me. 'We were having a conversation, that's all,' I say, straightening up. 'I made no threats.'

'You blocked her in against the railings, she says, and wouldn't let her past.'

'I did let her past.'

'Aye, eventually,' he says, getting riled. 'You and me both know that your behaviour yesterday afternoon could be interpreted as threatening.'

He's becoming quite officious now but I refuse to rise to it. 'I can't imagine why. We were discussing fruit scones. We only spoke for a minute or two, because she had to get back to work.'

'Will you listen to yourself?' he says. 'Do you actually believe what you're saying? You were trying to get information out of her.'

I shake my head and huff out a laugh.

'You asked her what we'd been saying about you. D'you remember that? You were nasty with it, as well.'

I snap, pushing myself away from the doorway. I've been calm and good-humoured all this time but now it's gone too far. 'Isn't that a legitimate question?' I face him full on. The hairgrip I picked up is digging into my palm, so I toss it away. 'Or am I not allowed to know what else you've been accusing me of?'

My burst of anger seems to calm him down. He straightens his shoulders and despite myself, I'm impressed. He possesses a certain authority that was never obvious before. Presumably this is his 'on duty' demeanour.

'Anything I've said about you, Miss Brown, is the truth,' he says. 'Deny it all you like but we both know it was you I saw down Dean Street that night.'

Miss Brown? How formal he's become.

'And as Peg told you,' he goes on, 'you've been seen before. Or at least someone matching your description has been seen. Very closely matching. We couldn't put a name to you then, though.'

'You're lying.'

'No,' he says, unruffled, 'I'll leave the tall stories to you. I'm pretty sure you already know that an old tramp saw a woman matching your description, the night a man was murdered.'

'Well, if that's the case, why aren't you questioning me formally?' I bite my lip. Why on earth did I say that?

'Oh, I dare say we'll be in touch officially before long. A few details to finalise, that's all.'

A note of terror flickers through me. Wish I hadn't said that. Wish I could cancel out the last few seconds. But it'll be fine. They can't prove I was there. If they had any evidence at all, they would have talked to me before now. 'So what's this then?' I say. 'You warning me off or something?'

'An informal warning,' he says. 'This time. But if you have a go at Peg again, or anyone else for that matter, it will become official. Make sure you keep yourself under control in future.'

I shrug. 'I'm rarely out of control.'

'You know what I mean.'

The front door, which Al has neglected to close, is pushed open. 'What's all this, then?' Bobby says, taking in the tense atmosphere.

'More accusations,' I say before Al can get his version in. 'Apparently, I'm going around terrorising women now.'

Al shakes his head slowly.

'Al here—or DS Hughes, as I should probably call him—says I'm guilty of being overbearing.'

Bobby's brow creases. 'Why's that, then?' He's holding a bottle of lemonade and I can see the bubbles fizzing from the way he's swinging it by the neck.

'There was an incident yesterday,' Al starts. 'Peg, my wife, if you recall, felt threatened when—'

'Felt threatened?' I butt in. 'Felt! I'm not responsible for how she felt.'

A slight frown appears between the good officer's eyebrows now. 'I've given you a friendly warning,' he says, 'and as long as you take notice, that's the end of the matter.' He turns towards the door and Bobby steps forward to block his way.

Bob looks from one to the other of us. 'What's happened?' He's clutching the lemonade as if he's about to strangle it now.

'I'll let Miss Brown give you the details,' Al says, 'but I'd advise you to take her version with a large pinch of salt.' He lays a hand on Bobby's arm to physically move him out of the way and for a second or two there is a standoff. By now I want Al gone, damn him to hell. I certainly don't want the two of them coming to blows. Wish Bobby hadn't come so early.

'Please leave now,' I say to Al, and Bob moves to let him past.

Al opens the front door. 'Remember what I said, Miss Brown. Don't let it happen again—any of it.'

'Oh, get out!' I slam the door after him and turn back to Bob, who's still mystified. He puts the lemonade bottle on the coffee table.

'What the devil was all that about?'

I give him the brief details and sink to the couch, my arms falling slack at my sides. 'Why does everybody think I'm a monster?' I raise my eyes to him in appeal and he sits next to me, putting his arm around my shoulder.

'Nobody thinks that,' he says. 'Take no notice. I reckon it's this hot weather. It's driving everybody daft.'

'I was chatting to Peggy, that's all. I didn't realise she felt hemmed in.' I can hear the whine in my voice and it sickens me. Why should I have to make excuses?

'It's because you're so tall, pet,' he says. 'She's such a tiny thing, isn't she?'

I nod and sigh. Bobby hugs me and kisses the top of my head. We'd planned to go to the Apollo on Shields Road, to see Marylin Monroe in *The Seven Year Itch* but I've gone off the idea. Al's serious face and accusations struck me as funny at first but the annoyance of it is hitting me now. I stiffen as the anger surges through me. How dare he come to my home with his stupid accusations and insinuations.

'Here, I'll pour you some lemonade,' Bob says. 'Glasses in the kitchen?'

I nod. He knows where they are by now. I hear the *pssshtttt* as he opens the bottle. 'I'll mop it up,' he calls through.

I'd like a nip of rum in the pop but I've not bought any for a while. I could kill for a cigarette, too, oddly enough. All the old bad habits surfacing at the first hint of a disturbance. I clench my fists. All the old habits? For a moment, I wish Bobby wasn't here so I could—

'Here you are, pet.' He hands me the cool glass and I gulp it down, almost all in one go. The bubbles tickle my throat and nose and I emit a half-suppressed burp. Not very ladylike of me, but Bob smiles. 'Sign of appreciation in Arab countries,' he says. 'Still want to go out?'

I glance at the window. Beyond the greying net curtains a lovely evening is in progress. 'Yes, but maybe for a walk instead of the pictures? A nip of something somewhere to settle my nerves?'

'Aye, I was thinking the same.'

It's too early and too light for anything involving Dean Street. Too risky as well. I polish off the last of my lemonade and stand up. 'I'll finish getting dressed.' What am I thinking! I can't go down there again, ever. Far too dangerous now I've been seen. Is that a sinking feeling I detect in my gut? Well, too bad. All that part of my life is over now. It has to be. Now I've got Bobby, that has to be enough. No going back to old ways. But still…

*

Saturday morning and I'm at the dressmaker's for the fitting. Jan's late but Elsie's helping me into the muslin mock-up dress behind the screen that cuts across the corner of the room. Bit pointless us both squeezing in there as there's no one else to see. She's twitching it this way and that, mouth full of pins. It's a fairly good fit, which pleases me. A good sign that the actual dress will be perfect first time. We edge out from the corner and I hop up onto a chair so Elsie can check what depth the hem allowance needs to be.

Jan's still not arrived and it suddenly hits me why. She's been got at. Al's told Keith about the Peg incident and he's told her. My stomach turns over. Maybe she's not going to come. The flash of anger is momentary, as I hear Jan's slow steps dragging her up the stairs. She comes into the room and a shaft of dusty sunlight catches her. Blinking against the light, she looks up at me on my pedestal and gives me a curt nod. Yes. She's been told and obviously believes Keith's no doubt embellished version of the event.

'I'm done now,' Elsie says. 'You can get down.'

As I step off the chair, one of the pins in the hem catches my calf and I mutter a profanity. Elsie and Jan both stare at me open-mouthed. 'Sorry,' I say, rubbing at the scratch, though I'm not sorry at all. They want to be in my head sometimes—they'd soon get used to the bad language.

Elsie ushers Jan behind the dressing screen and they go through the performance of getting Jan's dress off and the mock-up on. Jan's still not said anything. It's very annoying. She could at least wait until she's heard my side of the story before getting huffy with me. Jan's dress needs a tiny tuck here and there and Elsie edges her into the room and moves her about as she makes minute adjustments. Jan's nails are scarlet today and look like drops of blood against the pale muslin. I can't help a little shiver at the thought but when she clambers up onto the chair for the hem measurement, I notice her toenails are also bright red and I smile. She frowns and glances down at her feet as if she thinks I'm laughing at her. When she raises her head, I beam a grin at her. I'll play the innocent when she eventually gets around to telling me what's on her mind. I'm certainly not going to let on I know, or am in any way disturbed by her manner.

Elsie pulls a pencil out of her messy chignon and jots down some notes. 'That's it, lasses,' she says, looking warily from one to the other of us. 'You can get yourselves dressed now.'

I shrug at her as I go into the corner to put my own dress back on. Jan's on her own with this one.

Outside, with Jan still not having said a word to me, I know I'll have to broach the subject. 'What's up with you, then?'

She scowls at me. 'What's up with you, more like! What was all that with you and Peggy the other day?'

'Oh, I thought the word must have got round,' I say, as we trot towards Northumberland Street. 'You and that husband of yours must have nothing else to gab about but me.' I keep it light, though I'm seething inside. Bloody Burgess and his drippy pal.

'Why were you so nasty to Peg?' Jan says. 'Peggy wouldn't harm a fly.'

'Nasty?' I stop and face her, letting the Saturday morning shoppers stream around us. 'I stopped for a chat, that's all. She happened to have her back against the railings. I didn't know she felt hemmed in. We were discussing scones, for goodness' sake. What's threatening about that?'

'All right. All right. Calm down.' Jan steps to one side to let a mother with a pushchair past. 'Should we go and have a coffee?'

We go into Fenwick's and up in the lift to the café. Jan orders the coffees. She can pay for them as well. We find a table by the window.

'Peggy was quite shaken, so Al says.' She fiddles with a napkin. 'Her work sent her home, you know, because she was crying.'

'Oh, for heaven's sake!'

'You can be a bit scary sometimes, Mon,' she says, 'and Peg's such a little thing.'

'I'm hardly going to stick a knife in her in the street in broad daylight.' I take a breath. Don't know why I said that. Wish I hadn't. Jan's shocked, I can see.

We both sit back when the waitress arrives with the coffees. Jan blows on hers. Honestly. You can take the girl out of Byker but you'll never take the Byker out of her. I stir mine slowly, tap the spoon on the side of the cup to get the drops off, and settle it in the saucer. There. That's how it should be done.

'Al says you didn't even apologise,' Jan goes on. 'You should at least have said sorry.'

'I didn't realise I'd done anything to be sorry for.' I lower my voice. 'I'll write her a note then, shall I? Even though I had no idea she would get upset by the prospect of me talking to her.' I pick up my cup then immediately set it down again. 'I did not realise chatting to me was such a terrifying experience.' Rummaging in my handbag for my hanky, I go on, 'I can't help being so tall.' Sniffing, I dab my dry eyes.

'Oh, don't get upset, Mon.' Jan pats my arm. 'I'm sure you didn't mean it. I said so to Keith. It'll be a misunderstanding, I told him.' She bites her scarlet bottom lip. 'I…I had to mention it though. I'm sorry.'

That's better. So she should be sorry, being so off with me before she's even heard my version of events. She picks up her coffee and takes a sip, leaving a big red lip print on the cup. For a moment, I'm sickened, and turn my face away. Sometimes I wish I didn't have to associate with other people at all.

Chapter Thirty

QUARRY & RIPPER MURDERS LINKED?

New evidence has come to light which suggests a link between the body in the disused quarry and the so-called 'Ripper' murders, a police spokesman has announced. The body of a man, which was discovered in a water-filled quarry near Elsdon, Northumberland just over a week ago, may be linked to the series of murders committed in locations on and around the quayside. Both the man's body and the car have proved so far to be unidentifiable but police now believe a link has been discovered between the man in the car and the recent spate of fatal attacks in Newcastle.

Engagement Ring

A diamond ring, believed to be an engagement ring, was discovered in a pocket of the jacket worn by the man.

The ring, which is a wide gold band studded with three small gems, was hidden in a secure pocket located within a larger pocket, such pockets being normally used for the protection of cash and small items. The ring was discovered last week when the man's clothes were examined by police experts but details were held back until further investigations could be made.

Local Jeweller Involved

According to police sources, the ring carries an inscription around the inside of the gold band, leading to efforts being made to locate the jeweller responsible for the engraving. A well-known local firm has now identified it as their work and have provided police with the details of the person who bought the ring and ordered the inscription. The person's name has not yet been released but it is not believed to be that of the dead man found in the quarry. Police have given no intimation of the words of the inscription.

Stolen Goods

The gold and diamond engagement ring is believed to have been stolen from the rightful owner at some time in the past few years, police sources reveal. It is suggested that this ring is one of a number of items of jewellery stolen, along with cash and other small valuables, from victims of attacks at knifepoint. These attacks took place on or around the Newcastle quayside approximately four years ago. Police now believe there may be a link between these knifepoint robberies and the series of murders which have taken place in similar locations over the last six months.

Escalation

It is understood that police are looking into the possibility that the robber or robbers who performed the knife attacks may now have escalated to murder. Victims of the earlier attacks were usually physically unharmed but evidence suggests the attackers are now killing their victims after relieving them of their valuables, instead of allowing them to make their escape as they formerly did. The attacker or attackers appear to prefer to take currency rather than jewellery or other items at the present time, presumably because of the risks involved in converting valuables into cash.

Police Appeal

Both Newcastle City Police and Northumberland County Constabulary have issued appeals for any victims of the attacks or robberies which took place in the area near the quayside in or around 1951-52 to come forward. Discretion is assured, says Detective Inspector Metcalf of City Police. 'It would be most helpful if anyone who was involved in such an incident would come forward, whether or not they believe they have information that would be useful to us. Any help the public can give us in this matter would be of great assistance at this time. The police are not interested in any other activity which may or may not be criminal. The only thing of interest to us is discovering the identity of the killer or killers. All information will be treated as confidential.'

Hillman Minx

Northumberland County Constabulary have also appealed for assistance in identifying the car—a green 1948 Hillman Minx—pulled from the quarry. They request that anyone who has any information about the car or recalls seeing one similar three or four years ago, should get in touch with either themselves or Newcastle Police. Anyone who recalls a friend or neighbour having a similar car, or any mechanic who may remember working on one, should contact DI Pattinson of NCC or call in to any police station. All information received will be treated as confidential at this stage.

I sink to my knees. He kept it. He kept the ring. He swore he'd fenced it. Showed me the money he'd got for it—a handful of fivers splayed out in a fan. How could he still have it on him? A hidden inner pocket, it says. Must have missed it when I searched him. Damn damn damn. But where did that money come from, if not from that? He lied to me. And he broke his own rule: Never hang onto anything that might put you in the frame.

Oh Charlie. Who's the idiot now?

At first, I thought he might give it to me. He acted as if he was intending to, asking me to try it on. Did it fit? Did I like it? Did it suit me? Yes, yes and yes, I answered, thrilled. Fool that I was, believing this was going to be my engagement ring. Ought to have known better by then. Did know better, but hope conquers common sense, every time. He'd never have given me something so valuable, or so incriminating. He'd never have got engaged to me—even if the ring had been from Woolworth's. I was stupid to imagine he might. Stupid to want to ever be engaged to him in the first place. Why would I want to marry a man who laughed in my face as he took the ring away? Who took pleasure in humiliating me, in my obvious disappointment? Who sneered at me because, for one moment, I thought he was a better man than he ever could be. Daft bint. As if I'd give you a fuckin diamond ring. Dream on.

Chapter Thirty-One

Bobby wants me to meet his friend, Will, who's now going to be his best man. Brother Tom has changed his mind about it and isn't keen to be on display. Pity for him. Still. I suppose it's a teenage thing. Probably got spots. We're going over to Will and his wife's house tonight for nibbles and a game of cards. They live not far from Bob, in Chirton, and I'm to stay over at the Wilson house tonight to save the faff of getting home. Am in two minds about that.

Will's a big lad, a bear of a man, actually, dark and lumbering. Same age as Bobby, apparently, though he looks older. Probably plays rugby or football or boxes—that type, anyway. Will is Bob's pal from his National Service days, now in the police force. Having to suffer an evening with another policeman is not a prospect that fills me with joy. Still, he's based in North Shields and doesn't know Keith and Al, thankfully.

'Nice to meet you at last, Monica,' he says, ushering me into the front room. He fills the hallway with his bulk and has to step well back to let us through. A faint tang of sweat comes off him—well, it is a warm night—but it marks him out as one of those excessively masculine types that I'm not at all keen on. Still, I'll give him the benefit of the doubt, for now.

The wife, Dora, also on the dark side, is as tall as me and skinny with it. She reminds me of Olive Oyl from the Popeye cartoons as she unfurls from a chair. She says hello, and for a minute or two we all stand around smiling at each other. Cigarette smoke lingers on the air and, for a second, I long to light one up.

Once Bob and I sit down, Dora puts an Alma Cogan record on the big wooden gramophone they've got. His Master's Voice, the label says, with the picture of the dog on it. She jumps up again after a minute or two of *Hernando's Hideaway* and pushes a couple of chairs back. 'Let's have a dance,' she says. Energy pulses off her, as she grabs Will's hand and they embark on an awkward two-step.

'Will it not wake the bairns up?' he says, glancing at the ceiling.

'Shut the door,' she says. 'It'll be fine.' She turns to me, as if she has to justify herself to another woman. 'They're not directly above. We'll not be too loud. Come on the pair of you, up you get.'

I glance at Bobby and he makes a face—humorously twisted but willing—then shrugs and stands up. We all have a few twirls around the room and I have to say it breaks the ice and we're soon all laughing and jolly. There's not much space but that adds to the fun as we keep bumping into each other. Will rewinds the gramophone and puts Frankie Laine on—*Jezebel*—and we bounce about to that. Then we get Guy Mitchell and Slim Whitman, but by that time we're all sweating. It's so hot. I flap my hands in front of my face in a vain effort to cool down. I'm glad of the physical movement to loosen me up. I've been so on edge lately, what with Charlie showing up unexpectedly and all that business with Peggy and Al. I'm like a raw nerve—it only takes the slightest touch to set me jangling. I hate being so jittery, so out of control.

Will pushes the casement window open wider. They have one of those late twenties' Council houses, fairly substantial and a decent size, though I prefer older places, myself—Victorian or Edwardian. Will's on the beat, Bobby told me, not on the plain clothes side like that other pair.

We have a laugh and dance for a bit longer before sitting down for a game of gin rummy—or their version of it, anyway. I'm not well up on cards but it seems like a combination of a couple of different games. We play for coppers—the monetary kind. Dora brings in a tray filled with cheese and Crawford's crackers and a bowl of pickled onions.

'Beer?' Will says, and Bobby nods gratefully. The Newcastle Brown comes out for the lads but for me and Dora it's Peardrax. Peardrax! Non-alcoholic perry, the label says. Honestly. If I have to drink perry, I'd rather have a Babycham—at least that has a bit of a kick to it. I don't need alcohol all the time, of course, but something to take the edge off would be good.

'Anything exciting going on at work?' Bobby says, while Will deals the cards.

I tense. Why is police business so fascinating to everybody?

'Some rowdiness with these teddy boys at the weekends,' Will says, a cigarette dangling from the corner of his mouth, 'but nowt too serious.' He studies his cards. 'It's this fine weather. At least when it rains it keeps them off the streets.' He chooses his card and puts it down. The backs of his hands have wiry black hairs sprouting from them.

Dora is next to go and she spends a minute perusing her hand. She's also puffing on a Player's. Maybe I could ask her for one but I told Bobby I'd given up and he's been cutting down.

'There has been some news though,' Will goes on. 'You know this body they found up at Elsdon? In the quarry?'

'Aye,' Bobby says. 'That's a way off your patch though, isn't it?'

'Oh aye, still the same force though. Anyway, there was a ring found. Did you see that in the paper?'

Bobby nods. 'I read about it, yes.'

I look down and fix my eyes on my cards.

'An engagement ring, wasn't it?' says Dora, finally making her choice and playing her card.

'Aye,' Will says. 'Well, turns out the feller it belonged to is local. Lives in Trevor Terrace.'

'No.' Bobby sits back and marvels at this as if it's the most astonishing news he's ever heard.

'Feller's no longer with the lass it was intended for, apparently.'

'Hardly surprising,' says Dora, 'considering what he was getting up to.' She blows upwards to shift a lock of short dark hair. Wreathed in smoke, it clings, recalcitrantly, to her forehead.

'The lads from Northumberland came down to see him. Hauled him in for a chat about how he came to lose it.'

Bobby looks up from rearranging his cards.

'Sounds like it was the same pair of toe-rags that robbed the bloke that came forward about the quayside murders.' Will takes a slurp of ale. 'Description fits. Wiry, dark-haired man and a tall blonde woman. Well, not much more than a lass at the time, though she'd be a couple of years older now.'

Bobby's eyes linger on me and I study my cards harder to avoid his gaze. My spine and neck twitch as though a douche of icy water has been thrown over me. I'm not the only tall blonde in the northeast, I want to shout, but don't, can't.

Bobby frowns at his hand. 'I'm knockin',' he says, folding his cards and putting them face down on the table. 'Your go, pet,' he says to me, taking a piece of orange cheddar from the plate. He reaches for a pickled onion, glances at me with a grin and draws his hand back.

My smile is weak. The cards blur and waver in front of my eyes and I shuffle them about until I see one I can get rid of. The nine of clubs.

And it's Will's turn again. 'He's been able to give a very good description of the pair,' he says, 'and the current thinking is that the body in the car is the villain's.' He looks up. 'So, we're making progress… though the lass is still a mystery. I'm knockin' as well.' He taps on the table to indicate this and Dora resumes her peering at the layout of cards.

'This hand's like a foot,' she says, but manages to put a card down anyway. 'She must be getting worried, this woman, if she's still around.'

Oh why oh why oh why? Why does the past have to force its way into the present? Why, when everything is going so well, can't it stay where it belongs? It's over. It's done with. Everything has changed—for the better. Why can't it leave me alone?

'Aye,' Will goes on. 'They got an artist to do a sketch based on the witness's description and he said it captured the pair of them to a T, apparently.' He glances at me then away again. 'Bonny enough lass, from all accounts.' He frowns. 'Makes you wonder.' He shakes his head and takes a long draught of his ale. 'I've not seen the sketches myself, but they'll be released shortly, so we'll soon see what's what. Dare say more victims will crawl out of the woodwork, once the papers get hold of it.'

My cards are slick in my damp hands and I can feel beads of perspiration on my forehead. I dab my brow with my hanky. I'm lightheaded and a fainting fit threatens. I shoot a look at Dora. 'Can I use the… er?' I say, half standing.

She hops up. 'I'll show you.' She leads me into the hallway and points me to the lavatory at the top of the stairs. 'Don't flush unless you have to,' she mouths. 'It makes an awful racket. That does wake the bairns up.'

I go up, knees trembling. You'd think I was climbing a mountain. I'm sure Hillary got up Everest faster. It's not really the lav I want, it's the sink so I can splash my face. The bathroom is right next to the smallest room, though, and I go in and lock the door. I'm shocked at the sight of myself in the mirror. My face is stiff with terror, hard and ugly. I huff out something like a laugh. Oh well, that'll stop me being recognised as a 'bonny enough lass'. I run my wrists under the cold tap. Wish I had a nip of rum. Something to calm my heartbeat. Should get myself a hip flask. Yes. Good idea.

When I've splashed and dried my face, I pat on a dab of Dora's cold cream and suck in some deep, deep breaths. The flush on my cheeks and forehead gradually subsides and I shiver. It can't be from any real chill, as the night is warm and still. Reluctance to move seizes me, locks me in position. I don't want to go back downstairs. I want to stay here, in this cramped room with the old metal bath hard against my leg and the cool china sink; with the rough old towels and the soap grubby from kids' paws. I sink to the linoleum floor, my cotton skirt rising in a puff of air around me. I'll stay here forever. Die here, maybe. Or go into suspended animation.

I start as the door handle rattles. A child's voice calls, 'Mammy? Want a dwink o' water.'

Composing myself as best I can, I stand and brush my dress smooth. When I open the door, a small girl stands there, round cheeks flushed, nightgown twisted. She steps back when she sees me. 'Firsty,' she says, insinuating a shy finger into her gap-toothed mouth.

I hesitate. Should she be drinking from the upstairs supply? Surely, she should go downstairs for water from the mains. Fresher and colder. While I ponder this, she pushes past me, stands on tiptoe and manages to get her head under the tap, her mouth a perfect circle, with a flickering little pink tongue. She slurps until she's satisfied. That can't be good for her—stagnant tank water, warm and stale. Her mother should tell her not to drink it.

A talcum-powdery, childhood smell of sunshine and jam rises from her, hot and sticky and sweet, and suddenly I'm thrown back twenty years. Up in the night, hair at all angles, skin dry and chafed, sore down there, where I'd not been sore before. The stink of bodily fluids—sweat—his, blood—mine, semen… though I didn't know those smells at the time, I soon got to know them. Was that the first time? Bewilderment and fear, and something more—a hopelessness—a sense of this is how it is now. This is how we live. A sense of abandonment, of utter crushing loneliness. Despite the cuddles and treats that were my reward. Loneliness, deep and forever—until now.

The child scampers back to her bed and I stumble down the stairs, sluggish, deadened. When I re-enter the bright, smokey living room, the game is still in progress. Life has carried on without me. They're chatting, as if they've barely noticed I was gone.

Bobby raises his head and I see he's succumbed, and lit up 'Howay, pet,' he says, puffing away. 'It's your turn again. I made your move for you last time.' He pats the chair next to him and, obediently, I sit and resume the game.

✳

219

At the Wilson house, everyone is in bed by the time we creep in. I'm to share Angie's room, sleeping in Josie's old bed, hers before she got married, that is. Bob has a little room at the front and he lets me have a look at it—single bed and a chest of drawers near the window. A couple of pairs of slacks and a sports jacket jangle on wire coat hangers on the back of the door. We have a quick kiss and cuddle but daren't do more since his parents are in the next room. My heart's not in it, in any event. I want to be alone. Need to consider things.

'You all right, pet?' Bobby says. 'You've been very quiet tonight.'

'Tired, that's all. It's the heat.'

'Well, away you go and get your beauty sleep. See you in the morning.' Another quick peck and he ushers me to the door of Angie's room. 'Night night.'

Mrs Wilson favours Winceyette sheets, which I find a bit warm for the weather, though it does wick up the sweat. Lovely in winter, I suppose. My sheets are old linen ones from Aunt Mill's bottom drawer. Glacial on a winter's night but cool and refreshing in the summer, when they're crisp with starch.

I lie awake staring at the light from outside the window reflecting on the ceiling. Angie's soft snores trickle across from her bed on the other side of the night table. It's many years since I shared a bedroom with anyone other than a lover, a man. The creaks and settlings of the house are strangely comforting. We could live here when we get married, Bobby says, while we look about for somewhere of our own. We could have this room and Angie could go into Bob's room. She won't like it, he says, but it'll only be temporary. I don't know. I wouldn't like to be in such close proximity to the rest of the family all the time. We could live in my flat, of course, but that's a bit of a trek for Bobby to get to work in the mornings. Oh, we'll work something out. If it comes to it. Will it come to it? I hope so. I do hope so.

But what if…? These sketches Will was talking about. What if…? I won't dwell on it. I won't. And yet every time I turn my mind away from it, it creeps back in by another route, until I'm maddened by the repetitive thoughts, the going over and over and over it until I want to bang my head on the wall. Why don't we have a key to turn ourselves off—a switch to flick so relief can be got and sleep brought on? The night ticks away, with me wide-eyed and haunted, until dawn and beyond, when I finally fall into a jerky comfortless slumber.

Chapter Thirty-Two

No. Nonononono. I back away. This isn't happening. No, not now. It mustn't be happening. Not now when everything is so wonderful. When I have a chance at a normal life. It's too unfair.

The police sketches are on the front page of the *Chronicle*, glaring out for all to see. Charlie's captures his customary smirk, though the face is thinner than his really was, more weaselly and mean—and mine—oh mine— Is everyone looking at me? They must be. It's so obviously me. Younger, yes, plumper in the face—I was never that plump, never—and with a tight, cruel cast to the mouth. Unlike me in many ways, but yes, unmistakably me.

I daren't even buy the paper.

She's harder faced than I am, that girl, sullen and common-looking. The hair's been given dark roots—that's all wrong—my hair's not dyed. And the eyes are too close together. She's a nasty piece of work, hardly a 'bonny enough lass'. She looks like a criminal. No. It's not right. I was never so coarse-faced. Never so brazen. He's remembered me wrong, that man, added his own hatred into the portrait, his fear perhaps, his humiliation, certainly. He's made me out to be worse than I am—the worst I can be. Couldn't admit to being robbed by a truly 'bonnie lass'. Someone with superficial attractiveness, maybe, but with a harshness at the core of her being. The sketch artist has thrown in something of his own as well, no doubt—a hint of Ruth Ellis. The female miscreant—bottle blonde, of low birth and immoral. Destined from the start to hang. That's what he's made me look like. You wouldn't want to meet me on a dark night. It would be laughable if it wasn't so terrible, so terrifying.

Charlie's got off lightly by comparison. Venial, certainly, but he's a man, he can get away with it. Cunning, dangerous—it's in his eyes—and a five o'clock shadow making him appear grubby. What an unpleasant pair we make. But it's not true. I want to scream it out. Not true! Not true to life. When we looked in the mirror, that's not how we saw ourselves. We laughed and cried and made love, and fought and spat and battled, but we didn't look like they've made us look. We did not. We weren't only that—the evil that's shown there—we were people, with normal expressions, looking ordinary, most of the time, unnoticeable. If we'd walked about the world looking like that, we'd have been arrested on suspicion of something. Being in possession of criminal physiognomy, for a start. It's an exaggeration—like an example in a book on how to spot a ne'er-do-well. It's a wonder they've not marked out the bumps on the cranium that prove us to be felons.

Yet, the likeness is near enough to be dangerous—for me. I run home to hide myself. I can't go anywhere. Can't go out again. How can I, with this face on me? I need a scarf, dark glasses. Change my hair colour, maybe, but I'd need to buy the dye first, and I'd be seen. And what about Bobby? What will he say? What will he think? Will he too see me— *me*—looking out from behind that dreadful female's features?

There's a knock at the front door and I yelp involuntarily. I won't answer. But it comes again. Sliding next to the window, I peer out. A faint breeze drifts through the gap where the sash is lowered an inch or two at the top. The postman. I crack open the door, keeping my head down.

'Can ye take this in for upstairs, pet?' he says, handing me a parcel.

I nod silently. Addressed to one of the children. Birthday present. Closing the door, I drop the package on the table, nerves jangling. How long before the knock comes—the knock that isn't the postman? The knock that changes everything? Keith, I think. He'll have seen the sketches by now. They'd have been circulated to all the police stations before they appeared in the papers. He'll know. He'll know for certain, now.

A rumbling starts up outside—an engine of some sort. Thudding, jarring. I glance out the window. Workmen digging up the road. Why? Why now? The jackhammer, or piledriver, or whatever it is, thud thud thuds, shaking the ground, rattling the glass in the window frame. My head. The heat, the smell of hot tar filtering through the cracked-open window, the grumble of a steamroller. Men laughing, shouting, as if it's a game. I slam the window closed and pull the curtains to, but it won't block them out. The racket goes on and on, all day long. Though I retire to my bedroom and close the connecting door, the noise rings in my head, the ache creeps up my neck and into my temples. But no one knocks. No one knocks and, for the moment, I am free.

Chapter Thirty-Three

It is with some trepidation that I wait for Bobby to arrive. This evening, we are intending to look over the seating plans for the wedding breakfast. Why do they call it that, I wonder? I suppose in days of yore, people got married first thing and broke their fast afterwards. Weddings weren't always made much of, according to the books I've read, anyway. A quick ceremony and that was it. Not even a white dress until Queen Victoria popularised the idea. Anyway, the meal—the tea, I suppose, that's what it'll be—tinned salmon sandwiches and trifle all round, I expect. I suggested letting everyone sit where they wanted to but Bob says some of his lot—cousins and uncles and what not—can't be trusted not to start a fight, so they have to be kept apart. They'll get up and mingle once the tea's finished, as far as I can see, so what's the point of separating them? Well, that's tonight's excuse for us meeting. We'll have a look at the list, sketch a rough plan and let his mother and sister do the rest. Makes no odds to me. Aunt Mill should be on the table with Mr and Mrs Wilson and us, but that's as far as my involvement goes. If my long-lost second cousins respond to Aunt Mill's overtures and decide to turn up, they can sit where they like. Or wherever Bobby thinks they should.

I'm rambling somewhat, I know that, trying to keep my mind away from other, darker thoughts. The police drawings. Bobby must have seen them by now but I've heard nothing from him. If he wanted to question me about it, surely he'd have come round on Monday when they were first in the paper. He'd have been round before now, that's certain. Unless he's not coming at all. Normally, I'd be furious at the thought of being stood up but I can't generate the energy for that sort of anger. Wouldn't blame him for not coming.

I twitch the curtain aside. The hole in the road has been filled in—gas main leak, it seems it was. They finished this afternoon, thank heavens. The net curtain flutters in the breeze—the hot gust of air of a bus going past, though, not a cooling zephyr. I've sluiced under my arms to get rid of the gritty grubbiness warm days bring with them, and dabbed on some of my *Soir de Paris*. Nothing will get rid of the heaviness in my abdomen though. It's not my time of the month, though it feels like it. It's the dread. The deadening, dragging, leaden lump lodged in my guts. The tightness of my solar plexus.

He's late. Is he? I glance at the clock. The pointers are on five to seven, exactly where they were the last time I looked. I pick it up and hold it to my ear. No, it's still going. Ticking away interminably. As I put it back on the mantelpiece, I see myself in the mirror. Superficially, I look fine. Somewhat pale, but that's to be expected, given I'm due to come on shortly. I'm clammy and cold though, while sweating at the same time. Maybe I've caught a summer cold.

'You're beautiful, you should know that by now.' Bobby pokes his head in the open window, catching me scrutinising myself. 'Are you going to let me in, then?'

My heart starts to beat again. Don't do that! I scream, but only in my head. Don't terrify me like that! I stumble to the door, open it and Bobby bounces in. I'm not expecting such cheeriness, such bonhomie, or the energetic affection of his hug. I was expecting—what? A dour face, seriousness, a 'we need to talk' demeanour, not this. He can't have seen the papers. He must have seen the papers. He always sees the papers. Didn't recognise me then. Can't have. Didn't see me peering out from behind that trollop's face, those chubbier than my cheeks, that crueller than my mouth, that bottle blonde, dark-rooted hair. He did me a favour, then, that man, describing me like that. He let his anger and shame cloud his judgement, colour his description. I've got away with it. Have I? Have I got away with it?

I latch onto Bobby as if he is a lifeline, clinging, clutching, folding myself into his arms.

'Here,' he says, a smile in his voice, 'what's all this about?' He holds me away from him to take a look at me. 'Tears?' he says, brushing a thumb under my eye. 'What's this all about, then?'

'Bobby,' I say, 'Bobby…'

'That's me,' he says, his smile avuncular.

'Bobby, I…,' and I say something I've never said before. 'I love you, Bobby. I love you.'

*

'I love you, too, darlin',' he says, kissing my eyes. 'Loved you from the first moment I ever saw you… all stretched out and wet on the sand, your hair spread out like seaweed.' He groans. 'Mermaid. My mermaid.'

Tangled together, we somehow make it to the bedroom.

'So pale and beautiful. Your forehead felt like marble,' he goes on, 'cold and creamy. I thought you were dead. Dead before I could know you. But you weren't. Oh, I'm so glad you weren't.' He fumbles with my blouse. 'You made me come alive. You don't know how it was… before. Before you. I had lasses, yes, course I did. Handsome lad like me?'

He breathes laughter into my ear. 'Had my pick. But no one… there was no one… till you. Till you.'

Our clothes are scattered now, and the sheets are cool on my back. Through the bedroom door I see the net curtains flip-flap at the open window. Anyone could look in. We are on display, or could be. Secret things could be seen but I don't care. I don't care. This is Bobby, the other half of me, my soulmate, my lover, my better self.

*

I didn't care before. Didn't care what I did or what happened to me. I was nothing, a nobody, a worthless piece of— What did it matter if I got caught? The deadness inside stopped me feeling, made me care little, care less—and yes, I was careless. Careless and stupid. Why did I? Why? But I did do those things and there's no changing it. No going back. Can't, however much I want to. I'm stuck with them, my own past actions. If only I'd known… if I'd known that one day— this… but I didn't, couldn't. Can't see the future. Not then, not now, though now I can sense it. It looms over me, growing closer. The end—my end—our end—is approaching. Though the days are sunny and bright, there is a darkness around them, like photographs tinted sepia at the edges, vignettes. And that darkness creeps closer every moment.

I didn't care, but I do now. Had nothing to lose, but I have now. I close my eyes. Make it go away. Please, make it go away.

I lie staring at the ceiling. A single fly, bulky, a bluebottle, buzzes around the room. Round and round, bumping into the window, making angry zizzing noises when he misses the opening yet again. You can hear the frustration as he repeatedly thumps against the glass, falls to the sill, waves angry legs in the air. Then round he goes again, until, at last,

he sails out the open window, and he's free and away, his joy
tangible in the air.

Chapter Thirty-Four

Friday evening and I'm getting ready to go out. Meeting Bobby at the usual place, planning a visit to the Oxford again. Some guest band on Bob wants to see. He likes that big band sound, whereas I'm more of a fan of crooners, myself.

I'm slipping into my court shoes, when the knock finally comes. Rat-a-tat-tat. The knock that means business. Funny how they can make it sound official, even before you know who it is. Heart in my throat, I answer the door. It's Al again but he's with an older man. Overweight, sweaty in his suit, tie loosened a notch, and top shirt button undone. Charming, I'm sure.

'DI Metcalf,' he says, brisk and purse-lipped. I raise my eyebrows and he reaches into his inside pocket for his warrant card. 'I believe you know DS Hughes.'

I say nothing, keeping them on the doorstep. Al's face is blank.

'A few words, Miss Brown?' the DI says, nodding past me. 'Inside, if you prefer.'

'I'm on my way out.' I step back to let them in.

Metcalf squeezes through the hallway with Al slipping in behind him. I don't ask them to sit down.

'I'll get to the point,' Metcalf goes on.

'Please do.' I surprise myself at how calm I am. Cool and collected. I step to the window and pull it closed. It's fortunate I'm turned away from them at that moment because what he says next sends shockwaves through me, shattering my self-possession.

'Does the name Charles Harker mean anything to you?'

I freeze momentarily but cover it by fiddling with the sneck to lock the window before turning around. 'Who?'

'Charles Edward Harker.'

I shrug. 'Never heard of him.' Mind racing, I twitch the curtains, needing something to occupy myself with.

'We have reason to believe you are—were—an associate of his.'

'Really?' I look up with a tight smile. 'Why?'

Al speaks up. 'You had a boyfriend called Charlie a few years ago. Is that right?'

Damn damn damn. Keith must have told him. And Keith will have got it from Janice. Damn the lot of them. What to do? What to say? 'I did go out with a Charlie at one time, yes. But I haven't seen him for years.' How can they have discovered his name?

'And was that Charles Edward Harker?' the DI says.

'I… I don't know. I never knew his surname. It was… a casual thing. And several years ago.'

'How long did you "go out" with him, as you put it?'

'I'm not sure. A few months?'

'I understood you were together over a year,' says Al.

'I… I doubt it. I can't remember exactly.'

The DI peers at me. 'You can't remember three or four years back? Is there something wrong with your memory? A head injury, perhaps?'

The cheek of him. Blast his eyes. 'As a matter of fact, there is.' I look him full in the face. 'It was a very unhappy time for me. Charlie… he… he drank a lot. And made me drink too. It wasn't a good relationship. I've done my best to forget it.'

'So, might this Charlie, who you're trying to forget, be Charles Harker? Might that be his name?'

What can have identified him? He carried nothing. He was so careful. And yet, he had that ring on him. What else can they have found? 'I don't know. I didn't know his full name. He was… secretive.'

Both the DI and Al stare at me, faces serious, lips pursed, brows lowered. Remind me of Laurel and Hardy. A nervous laugh bubbles up in my throat but I daren't let it out. I cough to cover it.

'You're asking us to believe you went out with this man—you were courting, in other words—for over a year, yet you never asked him what his last name was?'

'We weren't courting. It was casual. I've told you. I may well have asked him his name but he wasn't one for—' I stop. I need to ask some questions. Make out I've no idea what they're on about. 'Anyway,' I go on, 'what's this all about? Who is this person you're asking about? Why do you imagine he might be Charlie?'

'Do you know what a Hillman Minx motor vehicle looks like, Miss Brown?' The DI ignores my question.

'I… maybe. I don't know. Why?'

He produces a photograph. 'Do you recognise this vehicle?'

I glance at the photo of the car. Charlie's car. I'm shaking inside now. I'd like to sit down. Wish I'd asked them to sit now, then I could too. Can't allow my legs to give way, though. I shake my head.

'Did this Charlie, that you "went out with", have a car?'

Think. Think. Did anyone see us in it? What did I tell Jan? A horrible realisation settles in my gut. I did mention the car. Boasted to her about it, fool that I was. My boyfriend drives a—did I say what it was? Did I know what it was? Would she remember?

'Miss Brown?'

I jerk and look up. 'Sorry?'

'Did your man friend drive a car? This car, specifically?'

I can't say 'I don't know' again. It's sounding false even to me. 'He… he did have a car, yes.'

'A Hillman Minx?'

'No idea. Sorry.' I give a little laugh, girlish, foolish. 'Not a clue about cars, I'm afraid. All look the same to me.'

He sighs and reaches into his pocket for his cigarettes. Offers me one. I decline, though I'd love one, actually. But not from him. I want them gone.

'One more thing,' he says, the match flaring as he lights up. He shakes it and looks about for an ashtray. Decides to throw it into the fireplace. Stalling tactics. Does he think I'm stupid?

All the time, Al is watching me, watching me. I daren't look in the mirror to see what my face is doing, though I'm keeping it as bland as I can.

The DI goes to his inside pocket again. This time he produces the police sketch of Charlie. 'Did you see this in the paper recently?'

'Er, yes, I think so.'

'Is it the man you call Charlie, who you went out with?'

I raise my shoulders. 'No. I don't… I can't. No.'

'You're sure?' He leers at me. 'Do you have a photograph of your Charlie?'

233

'No.' And I'm quite firm with him. 'No, I don't, and he's not my Charlie. I have no idea where he is and, frankly, I don't want to know.'

'Had a row, did you? Part on bad terms?'

'He left one night and never came back. That's what he was like. Slippery. Unreliable. Always going off without saying anything. Then the last time, that was it. Never saw him again.'

'Very well. Thank you for your assistance.' He nods at Al, who's been silent throughout. 'We'll be off then.' He takes one step towards the door. 'I must say, though, you seem rather incurious as to why we're asking.'

I see Al smirk. 'Yes,' he says, 'you don't seem at all bothered that it might be your Charlie who was found in the car. In the quarry, if you recall. Deceased.'

'I don't care whether it is or not.' My teeth are gritted, jaw clenched. 'I was well rid of him, when he left. I've no interest in him now.'

'Fair enough.' DI Metcalf hauls his flab into the hallway but stops. 'Oh dear, I almost forgot.' He backs into the room again, pulling something else from his inside pocket. 'Is this, by any chance, a sketch of you?'

✳

I flop onto the couch. I'm trembling. Damn them. Damn the lot of them. They've gone now, leaving me like a wet rag. I denied it, of course, when Metcalf showed me the sketch of myself. Of her.

'Looks nothing like me,' I said.

'Oh, I don't know,' Al chipped in. 'There's a definite resemblance, I'd say.'

'I resent that. This… this woman is so common looking. How can you possibly believe…?'

Metcalf's eyes were on me the whole time. Studying me. Searching me out. 'Not to worry,' he said at last. 'Maybe we'll put you in a line up and see if our man recognises you. See if you recognise him.'

It was all I could do to stay upright.

'Well, we'll see,' he said, pushing himself through the doorframe again. 'But that's all for now. Good day to you.'

Al gave me a nod and followed him out.

And now I'm here, incapable of movement apart from the involuntary tremors. I need a drink. Water even, my mouth is so dry. Half past seven. Bobby'll be there now, under the clock, wondering what's happened to me. I can't go like this. I can smell the sour stink of my own sweat. I need to wash again, change my clothes. By the time I get there, he'll be gone. Oh God, no, he'll come here. When he realises I'm not coming, he'll come here. What'll I say? What can I say? I slump back along the couch. Ill. That's it. I'll say I'm sick. My period's due soon. Cramps. But worse. I'll say I've vomited. Didn't come on until I was getting ready. I am sick anyway. Could easily throw up. I struggle up and get myself a glass of water. Pour it down my parched throat. How long before he gets here? An hour? Maybe less. He'll know within the next ten minutes that there's something wrong.

I pull a bucket out from beneath the sink and place it next to the settee. Evidence that I'm expecting to vomit. When I catch a glimpse of myself in the mirror, I know he'll believe me. I look ill. White faced and clammy. Beads of sweat on my forehead. I close my eyes so as not to look into them. I hate lying to him but I've no choice. Anyway, what's one more fib amongst all the others?

Chapter Thirty-Five

He believes me. How bad does that make me feel? I don't want to be this person. I've given up being her. Why do I have to be pushed back into that role? I've moved on. Yes, I know. I know I've done bad things but that's all over now. I won't be doing them again. No. Not even pretending just for thrills. I won't go down there again.

If only. If only I could take it all back. Make it not have happened. I'm rehabilitated. Isn't that what legal punishment is for? Partly, at least, it's to rehabilitate the criminals. Well, I've already done that. I've rehabilitated myself. But that won't be enough for them. Keith and Al and that awful Inspector Metcalf. It won't be enough. They'll want their pound of flesh.

Bobby stirs beside me. He's so handsome when he's asleep. Awake too, of course, but sleeping gives him an extra softness, a vulnerability that inspires protective love. I do love him. I know that now and I don't want to lose him. That's what makes this so hard. If I had nothing to lose, I wouldn't care what they did to me. But it's different now. The redemptive power of love. Hah! Much good it will do me.

He half opens his eyes, sees me watching him. 'Mornin', Miss Mermaid' he says, all sleepy and mumbly. 'Feeling better?'

I nod. 'Morning, my love.'

His eyes open fully at this. 'Am I? Am I your love?'

'You know you are.'

'No other lass has ever said that to me.'

'What? That she loves you?'

'Not like that, no. They've said the words, sort of, but not those words.' He yawns.

'You're still half asleep. You're not making sense.' I kiss his nose.

'Most lasses don't so much say it, as make it known. In other ways. They cling to you. Follow you about. Hint at marriage.' He sits up and runs his fingers through his tousled fair hair. 'Mind you, most lads don't say it either. Scared of seeming soft. Run a mile before they'd say it. Those three little words.'

'I've never said it before.' I look away. 'And I doubt I'll say it again—to anyone else, that is.'

'Glad to hear it.' He wraps his arms around me and pulls me down beside him into the warmth of the bed. 'Now then, where were we?'

*

It wasn't a headline story this time but in a few paragraphs at the bottom of the front page. A family member has come forward, it said, having recognised the police sketch and the car. A family member? He wasn't a complete loner after all, then, Charlie. Even he had relatives, however much he tried to ignore them. So that's how they found out about him, discovered his name.

It doesn't specify who the family member is—someone who suspected his involvement in criminal activities, presumably. I put the paper aside and drink my tea. Bobby picked up the *Chronicle* at the corner shop earlier, when he went out for milk and bacon. We're having a lazy day, since it's overcast and there's nothing we need to go out for. May go back to bed. I want to pull the covers over my head and hide from the world. Wouldn't it be lovely to go into a sort of suspended animation? Alive, but not needing to deal with the world and daily life. To be curled up warm with Bobby forever and ever. If only.

I'm surprised no one has commented on the sketch of me—of her. I thought that would be the end of everything, once people saw that, but no one's mentioned it. Not Bobby, or Aunt Mill, not even a dirty look from Mrs Dack at the shop. Jan's probably been got at by Keith but she's not said anything. No, it seems I've changed enough not to be recognised in that chubby girl—which wasn't an accurate portrayal of me anyway. That's something, I suppose.

We're lazing about, Bobby stretched out on the couch, me curled up at one end with his feet on my lap, when the knock comes again. That dreaded rat-a-tat-tat, loud and officious.

'Who the devil…?' Bobby sits up with a jerk.

My heart quails. No, not while Bobby's here, please. I grip his feet, his socks slightly damp against my trembling hands. 'Let's not answer it. Let's creep into the bedroom, so they can't see us.'

'Who on earth is it?' He strains towards the door, as if he can see through it if he tries hard enough.

'It'll be the door-to-door brush man. The Indian. Sells tea towels and dish mops, you know.' I'm whispering but my there's a shakiness to my voice.

'With a knock like that? Cheeky beggar.'

The knock comes again and the letterbox rattles. 'Miss Brown?'

Metcalf. I close my eyes. Make it go away, please.

'Who's that?' Bobby points to the window. 'That's that Al, feller, isn't it?'

And yes, there he is peering through the net curtains. He taps on the grubby glass. 'Monica?'

At the same time, Metcalf shouts through the letterbox again. 'Miss Brown? Open up. We know you're in there.'

Bobby leaps up. 'Bloody cheek.'

I shrink back against the arm of the couch. What I want to do is hide behind it.

Bobby yanks the door open. 'What's all the racket about?'

'And you are?' says Metcalf.

'Robert Wilson,' supplies Al. 'Miss Brown's intended, I believe.'

Metcalf barrels Bobby out of the way and comes into the room. Al follows, returning Bobby's glare with a somewhat sheepish look. I'm frozen to the couch. I won't move. I never want to move again.

'We'd like you to accompany us to the station, Monica,' Al says, 'if you don't mind.'

'Whether you mind or not, I'm afraid,' says Metcalf.

'The station? The police station?' Bobby looks from one to the other of them. 'What's this about? What's going on?'

'Monica?' Al's doing his best to be conciliatory. 'Best if you come with us. No fuss, eh?'

I can do nothing but stare at him.

'If you'd like to put your shoes on?' His voice is gentle and calm, as if he's encouraging a shy child, or coaxing a timid animal out of a hiding place.

'Will one of you tell us what's going on?' Bobby roars. 'She's going nowhere until you do.'

Metcalf turns to him. 'A few more questions, that's all. And a line up. We've got our witness coming in this afternoon.'

'Witness? Witness to what?' Bob appeals to me. 'More questions? What do you mean?'

I gather all my courage and stand up, knees spongey and unsteady. 'I answered some questions yesterday,' I tell Bobby, 'about a former acquaintance of mine. Sorry, I forgot to mention it.'

'Forgot?' says Metcalf. 'Tch tch, your memory really is shocking, isn't it?'

Bobby starts towards him, fists clenched, and I put my hand on his arm to stop him. 'It's fine. I'll go. It'll be fine.'

'Did you say a line up?' Bob says. 'A line up? What for?'

'We'll explain the situation to Miss Brown at the station,' Metcalf says. 'Come on. Chop chop. Sooner we're gone, sooner you're back. That's assuming...' He widens his eyes but lets the sentence hang.

Al fills in the dots. 'If what you've been saying all along is true, you have nothing to worry about.' He bites his lip and shoots me a sad glance, which I take to mean he's not at all convinced I'll be coming back any time soon.

Chapter Thirty-Six

The police station is dismal. Institutional sludge greens and dirty creams. Like a hospital, only worse. They show me into an interview room.

'This is an informal chat,' Metcalf says, 'so you won't need a legal representative.'

Just as well, I think, since I've no idea who that would be.

'You've not been arrested and you are, theoretically, free to go whenever you want to, but I strongly advise you don't avail yourself of that privilege just yet.' He slaps a buff file on the desk and sits down with a grunt. The wooden chair groans under him. Al sits next to him and I'm opposite, with a short expanse of scarred table between us.

'So, Miss Brown.' Metcalf purses his lips and studies me.

I meet his gaze. He's not going to intimidate me that easily. After my initial wobble, I've got a hold of myself. I can still be steely when I need to be. I'm nobody's pushover. I amuse myself imagining what I'll do to him, if I ever get the chance.

'We know you frequent the bottom of Dean Street, Side, and under the bridges, Dog Leap Stairs and so on. You've been seen in that area more than once.' He flips open the folder and glances down at it. 'A derelict gave a fairly accurate account of a woman answering your description, another witness has described a young female of your general height and appearance—as you might have been a few years back.' He looks up as I give a short laugh and raises his eyebrows. 'And, if that's not enough for you, DS Hughes here, saw you on the night of…' He checks his notes. 'Twenty-ninth to Thirtieth of May when you were presumably plying your trade in the general area under discussion.'

I smile and shake my head. 'I ply no trade, Inspector Metcalf. You are very much mistaken, if you think that.'

'Then what were you doing down there in the early hours?' He makes a steeple of his hands, tapping his fingers together. 'If not that, what, pray tell.'

I say nothing. That's for him to find out.

'There's nothing open down there,' Al says. 'Nothing going on at that time of night. Nothing a woman would be interested in, anyway.' They both consider me, and I, boldly, consider them back.

Metcalf gets out his Players. 'Smoke?' This time I take the proffered cigarette and he lights us both up. He smirks at Al. 'Young Hughes, here, doesn't partake. No vices, eh?'

Al nods sideways. 'Squeaky clean, me, man.'

Metcalf pushes a flimsy tin ashtray into the middle of the table and makes a show of smoothing the glowing tip of his tab, though there's been no time for any ash to form. I draw in deeply and let a stream of smoke out, aiming it past one side of his face. He sits back. For a moment, I'm in a Jimmy Cagney film, all shadows and haze and gangsters' molls. In films though, the femmes fatales always flirt with the private eye, or make sassy comments to the police, and they're heavily made up and wearing provocative clothes. I'm without make-up and in my loose 'at home' dress—an ancient blue checked gingham number—and my hair's in a plait. I couldn't look more of an innocent if I tried. Maybe I should have refused the cigarette, to maintain the illusion.

'Let's run through what we know,' the DI says, flicking through the file. 'The quayside, or near as damn it—where we've already established you've been seen—was the locus, some years ago, of a series of crimes. Several—possibly numerous, for all we know—men were held up at knifepoint and robbed. From information received, we know that a man and a young woman perpetrated these attacks. As you know, witnesses have given us descriptions of them.' He looks up.

Witnesses, he said. Plural. I hold his gaze and he goes on, our eyes locked.

'The man, it has been suggested, is one Charles Edward Harker. The police sketch of Harker was recognised by a family member. A car that was pulled from a flooded quarry was also identified as belonging to Charles Edward Harker and we have reason to believe that it was Harker's body that was in the car when it was found.' He looks at the file again and turns a page. 'The sketch of the young woman, described by the same witness who described Harker—while admittedly not looking much like you as you are now—is of a girl of similar colouring to you, and from what the witnesses have said, of similar height.'

He sits back and raises his eyebrows. I shrug, and say nothing. 'All very circumstantial, I know,' he goes on, 'but…' and here he slaps the file and raises his forefinger, 'but… you, on your own admission, once had an association of some duration with a man called Charlie. Do you see where I'm going with this?'

'I'm getting the picture.' I maintain my icy calm. 'But I'm afraid the picture that is forming is erroneous.'

'Erroneous?' he says. 'Hmm. That's a shame. We thought it was developing rather nicely, didn't we?' He turns to Al for confirmation.

Al nods. 'We did, aye.'

I flick ash into the ashtray. 'Then you'll have to think again.'

'There is more,' Metcalf goes on. 'We have reason to believe Charles, or Charlie, Harker—the man in the car, you recall—was murdered. And we have further reason to believe that the woman—this young girl, now grown up a bit.' He swivels the sketch around so I can see it. 'May now be involved in a series of similar robberies in similar locations to the earlier ones. With whom, we are as yet unclear.' He looks at me enquiringly. 'Any ideas?'

I shrug again. 'Why should I know?'

'Maybe you noticed something going on,' Al says, 'when you were wandering around down there for reasons of your own. Did you, Monica? Did you see anything untoward?'

I return his gaze, my face like stone, hard, unmoving. 'No.'

'Of course,' says Metcalf, 'this time around, the attacks were much worse. This time around, the victims are unable to come forward as witnesses. This time around, the victims were dispatched. Murdered. But you saw nothing of this?'

'No. I didn't see anything.'

'So, you do admit you were down there?' Al says.

'I admit nothing.'

'*A propos* of that,' Metcalf says, 'I mentioned the line-up, didn't I?'

I go cold at these words, and for a moment am unable to reply. I give a slight, shrugging nod.

'Well, I think our man should be here by now. Go and check, Hughes, there's a good lad.'

Al leaves the room. As I grind my cigarette into the ashtray, DI Metcalf starts to whistle.

*

They escort me through into another windowless room and Metcalf disappears, leaving Al in charge. Several women stand on a low platform. To say I'm shocked is an understatement. Most of them look nothing like me. They are shorter, darker, fatter, and even those who are of a similar colouring or height, are ugly or hard-faced. Maybe that's a good thing. I will appear an innocent next to this lot, in my homespun dress and Heidi plait.

Al gets us all to line up and puts me somewhere in the middle. I don't want to be right in the centre. It's too obvious—when in doubt, choose the middle way. He's trying to make me stand out, I'm sure of it. But where would be better? The beginning or the end of the line? Anyway, I don't know which direction the witness will appear from, as there are doors on both sides of the room.

My legs are trembling. I want to sink to the floor. Pull yourself together! Be strong. Any sign of fear will give me away. I glance right and left. The women on either side of me are calm. Well, why shouldn't they be? They aren't suspects. One rather coarse female at the end is chewing gum. Another looks drunk.

The door to the right opens and Metcalf ushers the witness in. A clamminess crawls across my brow and I feel the blood drain from my face. I must look grey. Queasiness threatens to overwhelm me, and I have to force myself to remain upright, not to sway, not to give myself away. Please don't let him recognise me. Please.

Metcalf gives the man instructions. 'Take your time. Have a good look at each one.' He sweeps his eyes along the line and I swear his glance lingers on me. 'Point her out, if you see her. No hurry.'

We've been told to look straight ahead but I can't stop myself sliding my eyes towards the man. No. I mustn't. Mustn't show any interest, or nervousness. I must act like the others—as if I couldn't care less—but I'm cold with terror.

The man steps in front of the first woman. I'm aware of him from the corner of my eye. Musn't look. Mustn't look. It seems to take forever. A slow progress towards me. A sideways shuffle, pause, shuffle. Minutes go by, or maybe hours. Time has gone awry. The strip lights flicker and the windowless room grows stuffy. The walls and ceiling are not fixed in place. The floor rises towards me occasionally.

When he reaches the woman next to me, I am aware of the bulk of him. His suit, a hint of sage green tie. I hear him breathing unevenly, get a whiff of sweat. He's nervous too. After an age, he steps in front of me. I stare straight ahead, look right through him, avoiding his eyes. I don't recognise him. Why would I? They all look the same. Or at least, they all blend into one another, afterwards.

I smell his breath now, as well as his sweat. Slight halitosis—that baked bean smell—mixed with tobacco. Must have had a calming fag outside before his ordeal. He's terrified. Terrified of me, presumably. Of coming face to face with me again. Hysteria tickles my throat, demanding I laugh. I swallow. Clamp it down. If I shouted 'Boo!' at him now, he'd soil himself. But much as I'd love to, I daren't.

He studies my face, my body, taking a good look up and down. Has a nervous tic in one eye and his fingers twitch by his sides. At last he moves on, though he glances back at me. Can't quite make up his mind. The girl to my left sniffs loudly, insolently, and he jerks backwards. Coward.

When it's over, the women disperse, two or three, including the sniffer, are escorted back to their cells. Most have come in off the street and are let out to go about their business. The one with the hardest face turns out to be a policewoman. Shares a laugh with Al, before she goes on her way. And there's only me left. He didn't pick me out. Came back to have another look at me, but he looked twice at the other blondes as well. He had no idea. I heard him muttering to Metcalf, probably saying, 'Sorry.'

So the finger has not been pointed. I survive another day.

*

On my way out, I see Keith Burgess lurking by the front desk. He steps in front of me. 'You might have got away with it this time, Monica, but we've got other things up our sleeves.' He sneers at me. 'We've got other witnesses and more will come forward. One of them will pick you out. Only a matter of time.'

I ignore him and try to move past. He grabs my arm. 'It's over. Give yourself up. Save us all a lot of time.'

'Let me pass.' I see the desk sergeant glance up.

Keith steps aside. 'Only a matter of time, Monica.'

I brush past him, confused emotions seething.

Chapter Thirty-Seven

'They can't think it's you. That drawing in the paper. They can't think that's you. Can they?' Bobby shakes his head. 'It's funny—Tom said—he said it looked like you.'

Tom. The brainbox. I knew he didn't like me.

'Gave him a clip round the ear and told him not to be so cheeky.' He appeals to me, puzzlement in his eyes. 'It's not you. I said so. I told him. Of course, it's not you.'

He wants me to tell him he's right. That it isn't so. That of course it isn't me. He wants me to reassure him. For me to laugh and say, no, they've got it wrong, they're mistaken. I can see from the beseeching expression in his eyes that he longs for me to say that. He wants to pull the words out of me. If I say that, everything will be all right again. He'll believe me. He wants to believe me. He trusts me to tell him the truth. How can a man in love accept that the woman he's fallen for is a nasty little criminal? He'd accept what I say, whatever I say, rather than that. In face of incontrovertible evidence, he'd believe me, if only I'd tell him it isn't so.

And because he trusts me, because he'll believe me, I find myself unable to say the words he longs to hear. Better to disappoint him now, than at some future time, when he'll find out the truth anyway, and know I've lied as well as done other things. And I'll have lied to *him*, to him personally— and that would be the worst crime of all.

*

'I don't believe it. I don't believe it! No. That's ridiculous.' He slams his palm against the wall. 'You couldn't have done something like that. What are they saying? That you and this man, this accomplice, robbed people? At knifepoint? No. No no no.' He's shaking his head and his fair quiff flies about his forehead. 'You couldn't have. Not you. Tell me it's not true.' He grabs my hands. 'Monica, pet, tell me it not true.'

But I can't. I want to. I wish with all my heart that I could say the words he wants to hear; that all this would go away. But it's gone too far. There's a subtle change in the atmosphere and I realise that, no, he won't believe me now, anyway. Not really. He may want to. He may say he does, but it'll always be there, between us. The doubt.

He sinks to the couch. 'So… everything they said, Keith, Al, all that… it was true?'

'Not all of it,' I say. 'I was never on the game. That was a ploy to reel them in. It never got that far. Either when I did it with Charlie, or when I did it by myself.'

'Oh well, that's a relief.' He looks up at me with scorn in his eyes. 'Not a prozzie then, that's something. Just a… what? A robber? A horrible little knife-wielding robber?' He pauses. Shivers as though it's winter. 'Not when you did it with Charlie,' he repeats my words, 'or when you did it by yourself…' He closes his eyes. Shakes his head. 'By yourself? You kept on doing it by yourself? When this Charlie was gone? So, you mean…?' Tears roll down his face. His dear, darling face, swimming with them.

'You mean… let me get this right… these latest robberies? No. No.' He rubs his hands across his wet cheeks and his expression hardens. 'That's not what you're saying, is it? That you didn't just rob them, you… killed… No. You couldn't have.' His voice breaks. 'How many…? Oh God…'

'I wish it had been different.'

'And this Charlie? What happened to him?' He's sneering now, sneering so he won't break down completely. 'How did he end up in that quarry? That was you as well? Finish him off, did you? What, no further use to you?'

'It wasn't like that. He hurt me. Made me do things…'

'You could have walked away! Told him to get lost. Gone to the police…'

I shake my head, arms hanging by my sides. What's the use? What's the point? There are no excuses. Not any longer. 'I'm sorry, Bobby. I'm so sorry. If I'd known…' I reach down and cup his face in my hands. 'If I'd known the world contained someone like you. That I could be loved by someone like you.'

He leaps up and pulls me to him, his movements rough. He loves me but no longer cares if he hurts me. Wants to hurt me. His fingers dig into my upper arms and his kisses are violent. He bites me, chews my lips, kisses me savagely. When he drags me to the bedroom, I go willingly. I'd go anywhere with him willingly. He rips my dress open at the front, the faded gingham tearing like paper.

The sex is hard, thudding, unlike anything we've ever done together before. He pounds me, claws me, squeezes my face, digs his nails into my cheeks. He wants to damage me, kill me even, to stop me being who I am. I yelp when he bites my nipples, bites my earlobes, all gentleness gone. Nip-nip-nipping at me, as if he could tear away the part of me that is evil, the part that did those things. No dewy-eyed tenderness now, but a vicious assault which I accept as my due.

I respond to his feverish anger with caresses. Stroke his hair, his brow, the nape of his neck. 'I love you, Bobby. I love you.'

He groans, grits his teeth. 'I fucking love you too, you, you…' He can't say the word—bitch, or cunt, or whatever insult is on his lips. Can't say it. I may have turned him temporarily into a monster, but it's not who he is at heart. 'How could you do that, when I love you? How could you?' His hands tighten around my throat, shaking me, shaking me, squeezing tighter, his fingers finding my trachea.

'Do it,' I whisper.

He climaxes, cries out and collapses onto me, spent in all sorts of ways. Our sweat and tears and sexual fluids mingle. We are a soup of exhausted passion. 'How could you do those things, when I love you?'

Ah but Bobby, I did it before I loved you. I did it before I knew what love was.

*

We lie side by side, hearts thudding as one. Anger radiates from him. Rage, disappointment, despair. His eyes are open, staring at the ceiling. How can I heal this distress?

'Give yourself up,' Bobby says, at last. 'It'll be better for you.' He hitches himself up, lights two cigarettes and hands me one.

'Better? Better how? I'll still hang.'

'No,' he says. 'No. The mood of the country is against hanging now—for women, anyway. After the outcry over Ruth Ellis? They won't do that again.'

'Oh, I think they will.' I take a draw on my cigarette.

"They'll understand. When they hear what you went through as a child. They'll fall over themselves to be compassionate. Whether you deserve it or not.' His voice is flat, dispassionate.

'I can't see that being the case. But even if they don't hang me. There'll still be prison. I don't want that. I value my privacy. You must know me by now, Miss Anti-social.' I blow out a long stream of smoke and manage to create a smoke-ring, unintentionally. It hovers near the ceiling and we both gaze at it. 'I'd hate prison. Crammed in with other women—thieves and swindlers and baby murderers. No, I don't want that. I'd rather hang.'

'Then you've nothing to lose by giving yourself up.'

I shrug. 'Maybe.'

'We could go now. I'll come with you.'

He must still love me. He does still love me.

'I know what I did was dreadful.' I shake my head. 'But to me, it was about cleaning up the streets, putting the frighteners on men who were only looking for one thing. It's a service I performed.'

'A service? A *service?*'

'And I'm truly repentant, really, I am.' I spread my hands. Ash drops onto the eiderdown. 'But why do I have to face it now? The punishment?'

'You've no option.' He sucks smoke deeply into his lungs and holds it there.

'But if I've really changed and wish I hadn't done the things I've done… regret the evil I've been party to. If I honestly truly believed I was doing some kind of good…'

He turns his head to look at me. 'Some kind of good?' Disbelief slows his words. Sarcasm coarsens them. 'Some kind of good?'

'Bobby… please… I thought I was preventing further harm. Those men may have been abusing women and girls, maybe even boys… physically or emotionally, I don't know.'

'That's just it! You knew nothing about them. The men—they were strangers—poor sods who happened to be in the wrong place at the wrong time.'

'I know. I know. But I believed—truly, with all my being—that I was saving other women, girls, from the sort of torture I went through. Immediate physical torture… and mental torture that would have lasted their whole lives. Can't I be forgiven for that?'

I ignore the expression of disgust on his face and press on. 'I'm an entirely different person now. Would punishing the woman I am now wipe out the crimes of that girl—the girl I used to be? Would locking me up prevent future crimes? No, it won't, because I've already abandoned that way of life.'

He's staring at me in amazement but I go on. 'Will hanging me bring back those I have killed? No—and I'm sorry about that. Honestly, I truly am sorry. If hanging me could change the past, I would gladly give myself up and accept everything that's coming.' I reach for his hand but he jerks it away. 'Wouldn't it be better to let me live—freely— and do my best to bring goodness and love into the world? Wouldn't that balance out the harm I've caused? Oh, I know it'll need to be a prodigious amount of goodness and love, probably more than I can manage in a lifetime, but shouldn't I be at least allowed to try?'

He sits up fully and so do I. I'm bleeding now, the rough sex has brought me on. Tears roll down my cheeks—yet what right have I to tears? Who am I weeping for? Not for those I have harmed. Not for their families, their friends. No. I weep for myself. At least I can be honest about that. I am sorry for them—my victims. I truly am. If I'd known then what I know now, I would never have done those things. Could never have done them. I truly did not realise men had finer feelings. All I ever saw was lust and want in them, and a willingness to hurt in order to satisfy that want. I only ever saw them weep when they were hurt themselves. They never wept for me. Until Bobby. Bobby alone has wept hot tears for me, and for that I am truly, truly sorry.

'Can't the transformative power of love wipe out the crimes I've committed?' I ask, and it's a genuine question. 'I'm no Christian, Bobby, you know that. I'm probably a pagan at heart—a heathen, a sinner, some would say. But love isn't only the prerogative of Christians, is it? It's for everyone. I see that now. It's for everyone, even me.'

'You're barmy,' he says, as if it's only now dawning on him. 'You're a bloody mad woman.'

Chapter Thirty-Eight

When he's gone, the door slammed behind him, I slide down the wall, hunched into a foetal ball in the angle of the skirting board and crumbling lino. That's it, then. Over. All over now. Nothing matters any more. Why couldn't he keep on loving me? Why couldn't he accept that I'm not the woman—that awful creature—that I used to be? As long as I was with him, I was a different person. If he ever loved me, he should have kept on loving me, and forgotten about her.

Night falls, darkness creeps across the room and still I crouch, a dead thing, dead in all but reality. Well, that can be rectified. If I could be bothered. The lamp outside comes on and the light outlines the furniture. Tawdry, like my life.

They'll come soon. They have to. Has Bobby spoken to them? Told them what I said? Maybe not but even so, there can be no more secrets. If not today, then it'll be tomorrow. Sometime soon. A spark stirs in me. Before they come, I can do one more thing. What does it matter now, anyway? One more won't matter. No point in denying myself, as there's nothing left to gain. With Bobby gone, I can be her again.

I creak upwards, joints stiff. Wash my face. Comb my hair. Find sanitary products. Then I dress. Dark clothes. Split skirt. Low-cut blouse. And tucked up into the sleeve of my mac, the needle. Aunt Mill's knitting needle, honed to a fine steel point.

I go to the phone box outside Mrs Dack's. 'Janice?' I say, when she answers. 'Is Keith there?'

*

Here I am again, on the late bus to town, trundling along with all the sleepy people. No wig tonight and no headscarf. I don't care who sees me, who recognises me. If I'm going to go out, I'll go out with a bang. Ensure prison isn't an option. There's a change of plan tonight, though, and I get off at the Cathedral, walk along to Black Gate and go down Dog Leap Stairs.

I said I'd meet him at the bottom of Dean Street—the usual place—where it curves into Side. But I won't be there. I'll be halfway up the stairs, watching, just in case there's any funny business. I must maintain the element of surprise.

'Come alone,' I told him—Keith, of course. 'If I'm giving myself up, I may as well hand myself in to you. Then you can get the credit. You can even say you caught me at it. I don't mind. Whatever's best for you, really.'

He said nothing but I could hear the query in his silence.

'It's over,' I said. 'I know that now. No hard feelings?'

'Right,' he said, and I could picture the thoughts going through his mind.

Of course, he won't trust me. Of course, he'll bring back-up. I'm not stupid. As long as I can get him alone for a moment, that's all I need. So I'll wait, halfway up the stairs and get him to come up to me. That way, I'll know no one is with him. They may be lurking around the corner, out of sight, but they won't be near enough to help.

Shhh! There he is. Mooching along, stopping to glance over his shoulder now and then. A light mist swirls at the junction under the High Level Bridge. He stands still, casting about for me, wondering which direction I'll appear from. Making sure his pals are well-concealed too, no doubt.

256

The waiting is delicious. My guts loosen but I'm empty. Hollow. The tremor of anticipation is electric. I'm flat against the sweating wall, watching him, waiting for the perfect moment to make my move. He paces from the left to the right corner of Side. At the bottom of the steps, he sticks his hands in his pockets and peers into the murk. I hurl the stone towards him, making him skip out of the way as it hurtles past him. Now he sees me. His fists clench and he glares up at me. I beckon. After a glance right and left, he puts a foot on the bottom step.

'Come down,' he calls.

I shake my head. If he wants me, he's going to have to come up. He senses it's a trap— of course he does—but what can he do? If he shouts for his colleagues, I'll run. He must know that.

More swift left-right glances. He has to come and get me, or be labelled a coward. I know how he's thinking, just as he knows how I'm thinking. He won't be beaten by me. His arrogance will see to that. And here he comes, cautious at first, one step, two step, then a decision to startle me by speeding up.

He comes at a run now. Look how fit he is. Al that tennis. All those sessions in the police gym. I stand in the centre of the stone step, calm, unmoving. I'm not startled. I'm perfectly composed, except for the trill of excitement prickling up my spine. Energy shoots from my fingertips, my palms tingle. The needle is up my sleeve, all I have to do—

And he's upon me. Fast.

Chapter Thirty-Nine

But I'm faster.

The needle hits bone, deflecting it from the passage to his brain. It slides in along his jaw up under the skin beside his ear. His scream is bloodcurdling, damn him. Usually, they don't have time to scream, or even feel any pain because it goes in and up into the brain, I give it a quick stir and there's an end to it.

No such luck this time. The others were taken by surprise, you see, whereas Keith wasn't. Knew what to expect. Lost my advantage.

He clutches at me and we teeter together. My heel slips over the tread, jerking us off balance, and away we go, tumbling together down the damp mossy steps. Pain. My head hurts. My knees. My back. But he's come off worse.

Screeching and moaning and wailing, he struggles to his knees, blood running through his hands where he's clutching at the needle. The fall must have pushed it further in. If he pulls it out, he's done for, but he probably knows that. He won't bleed out if he leaves it where it is and gets to hospital in time. So he'll live. Might have a scar, but he'll survive. His screams ring across the deserted street. I pause. I could yank it out myself—but the others are coming. Shouting, breaking cover.

Kicking off my stilettos, I run. Along Side, Queen Street, up Akenside Hill, heart going ninety to the dozen. I risk a glance back. See a huddle around Keith, then one breaks free. Comes after me.

On again. Up the hill, past All Saints at the top and up the steps, two at a time, to Pilgrim Street. I peel off the plastic mac along the way. Run down to the bottom of Pilgrim Street and onto the Tyne Bridge, footsteps pounding behind me. Far enough away. I'm fast, fleet-footed, light. My pursuer is heavy, breathless, lumbering. Some plod panting in pursuit. He's earth; I'm air. I can fly.

The bridge soars above, curving across the night sky. The triple lamps shine dimly through the light mist drifting in with the tide. White curling fingers wreath around the stanchions, like steam rising from the river.

A foghorn sounds, way down at Wallsend, mournful and fitting—a ship coming in on the neap. I clamber onto the parapet, hanging onto a lamppost, the cool roughness of the painted metal against my skin. The smell of the river, rising, sulphurous. My stockings are ripped, feet cut and bloody. Didn't notice it, whatever it was I stood on, glass probably. I stand upright, knees trembling, hands gripping the post. The blood makes my feet slip and slide. I'm cold, shivery, shaking—no not cold, shaking in fear. I admit it. I don't want to fall before I'm ready.

He comes onto the bridge, my pursuer. They. They come onto the bridge. Three of them. Two in uniform. Flatfoots, thudding the pavement, their footfall echoing up into the superstructure, making the sleeping pigeons coo, disturbing their rest. Little traffic passes, but a car stops on the opposite carriageway. Some late night gawper wanting a tale to tell when he gets home. Ready-made excuse, perhaps. They're walking now, the three of them, Al and two constables, slowing as they draw near. Further off, there's another one. That DI Metcalf, from the look of it. Visibly puffing, out of condition. Lumbering, slow, none of them as swift as me.

My toes curl over the edge of the parapet as I stretch an arm out to ward them off. 'Don't come any closer.'

Al holds the PCs back. 'Miss Brown. Monica. Please come down.'

I shake my head. What's the point? I may as well jump. Better that than hanging. Or years inside. Year after stinking, cloistered year. If I thought he'd wait—Bobby—but he won't. How can he? It's over. I've lost him. It's all over now. I turn away to face the river. The ship appears at the bend, lit up, looking gay and festive against the grey of the night. The foghorn sounds again. My call to action. This is it. My audience awaits.

'Monica.' Al again. 'Don't do it.'

I smile over my shoulder. 'Stay back, or I will.' One torn foot lifts and reaches into nothingness. 'I will.'

The DI is with them now, and three other cars have stopped to watch, headlights illuminating the iron girders of the bridge, making the rivets stand out in high relief. The PCs are attempting to move them off but failing. Everyone is having such a good time. A bit of excitement, adventures to relate. The ship is nearer, ready to dock at the Malmo wharf. Men on board, back lit, readying ropes and gangplanks. The butter boat maybe, or some tug over from Sweden or Norway. Merchant sailors, ready to roll off and mosey around the quayside for whatever they can find. Which won't be much tonight, what with the police presence down there. Girls will have knocked off and gone home. Or elsewhere.

I look down at the water, black and oily, choppy and disturbed, rippling ahead of the ship, reflecting the twinkling lights of the bridge. 'Bye bye, Bobby,' I whisper. 'Bye bye, my love.' My voice wavers and I haul in the deepest breath I've ever taken. Maybe my last. 'I'm so sorry. Bye bye, my darling.' And I let go of the lamppost, teeter for a moment, neither earth nor air.

Al shouts, 'No!' but it's too late.

I can fly.

Note from the Author

Thank you for reading
Dog Leap Stairs

I hope you enjoyed it.

If you did like *Dog Leap Stairs* and you want to help readers find this and my other books, please write a short review on the website where you bought it.

Your help in spreading the word is much appreciated. Reviews make a huge difference in helping new readers find books and it only needs to be one line.

Thanks again.

☺ ♥Barbara Scott Emmett♥ ☺

Why not try books by other Pentalpha Publishing authors?
pentalphapublishing.weebly.com/

Also from Pentalpha Publishing Edinburgh:

Don't Look Down

by Barbara Scott Emmett.

Holiday Mystery with a hint of Romance

Set against the backdrop of the snowy medieval town of Nuremberg, this novel moves at a hectic pace. At times gritty and dark, it is also an entertaining account of an ordinary woman's attempts to outwit the bad guys and rescue her friend.

On a Christmas break in Germany, Lauren Keane finds herself having to investigate the disappearance of her best friend, Katti. Katti can be unreliable - but she knew Lauren was coming to visit. Surely, she wouldn't just take off without telling anyone?

With the help of Wolf – Katti's brother and Lauren's ex – Lauren uncovers a web of corruption and obsession involving kidnap, sex-trafficking and murder. No one, it seems, is quite who they claim to be.

This escapist ride will sweep you up and keep you turning the pages as you hurtle towards the climax high on an icy hillside.

Available as paperback or ebook:
https://www.amazon.co.uk/dp/B08M88KS1W

About the Author

Barbara Scott Emmett did the overland hippie trail to India, visited families in their homes in Turkey, Iran, Afghanistan, Nepal and India. She went over the Khyber Pass in an ancient truck, driven by two men - one on the steering wheel and the other on the brakes.

She's spent time in a mud hut in Pokhara with banana trees in the garden, stayed in a hotel in Kabul which partly collapsed during the night (nobody noticed), and travelled all over Australia — at one time living in a place called Fairyland. *The Land Beyond Goodbye* was inspired by her time in the Northern Territory.

She worked on *The Man with the Horn* while staying in a chalet in Germany and a gypsy caravan in Cathar country in France. *Don't Look Down* was inspired by many visits to friends in Nuremberg, and *Delirium: The Rimbaud Delusion* came out of her love for Symbolist poet Rimbaud, and visits to Charleville in France.

She visited Russia and the Ukraine when they were part of the Soviet Union, got stuck in Baghdad for three days when the was a war on, and got married at Graceland - but not by an Elvis impersonator.

She survived winters in a draughty caravan in Scotland, spent many years in London and Edinburgh, and is now back in her home town of Newcastle upon Tyne. *Dog Leap Stairs* is her homage to the Toon.

Also by Barbara Scott Emmett

The Land Beyond Goodbye – *General Fiction*
Don't Look Down – *Mystery*
Delirium: The Rimbaud Delusion – *LitFic*
The Man with the Horn – *LitFic*
Drowning – *Short Stories*
Wasps & Scorpions – *Pomes*

Also from Pentalpha Publishing Edinburgh

The Bumble's End
The Long Drop Goodbye
The Bumble on Beale Street
(The Bumble Books by Jimmy Bain) – *Comedy Crime*

Garlands & Shadows – *Fiction*
The Girl in the Paperweight – *Fiction*
The Warbeck Trilogy – *Historical Fiction*
And other books by Karen MacLeod

Pentalpha Publishing Edinburgh
pentalphapublishing.weebly.com